A WOMAN WORTHY OF *CONAN* . . .

In a world where other women accept what they are given, Red Sonja gets what she wants. And woe to the man who thinks that her sleek body and mane of flame-red hair could be his for the taking—for her sword-arm is as strong as her will, and Red Sonja belongs to no man. She roams a barbaric world, a free woman with a sword for hire, in search of gold and adventure. She travels light; a good horse and her sword are enough, and the companions she meets along the way soon learn to keep their distance. And in the course of time, it is only natural that legends should grow up around her name, and that men should speak of her in hushed voices around their campfires . . .

The Red Sonja Series by
David C. Smith and Richard L. Tierney

RED SONJA #1: THE RING OF IKRIBU
RED SONJA #2: DEMON LIGHT
RED SONJA #3: WHEN HELL LAUGHS
RED SONJA #4: ENDITHOR'S DAUGHTER
RED SONJA #5: AGAINST THE PRINCE OF HELL
RED SONJA #6: STAR OF DOOM

THE RING OF IKRIBU

DAVID C. SMITH & RICHARD L. TIERNEY

ACE FANTASY BOOKS
NEW YORK

RED SONJA #1: THE RING OF IKRIBU

An Ace Fantasy Book / published by arrangement with
the Estate of Robert E. Howard

PRINTING HISTORY
Ace original / December 1981
Second printing / November 1982
Third printing / April 1983

Cover art by Boris Vallejo

For information address: Ace Fantasy Books,
200 Madison Avenue, New York, N.Y. 10016

ISBN: 0-441-71163-4

Ace Fantasy Books are published by The Berkley Publishing Group,
200 Madison Avenue, New York, New York 10016
PRINTED IN THE UNITED STATES OF AMERICA

INTRODUCTION

THE CREATION OF RED SONJA

An Introduction by ROY THOMAS

Many and varied are the heroic-fantasy creations which, over the years, have begun their lives in prose and cold hard type, only to be adapted later into comic-books and comic-strips—those strange, hybrid popular art-forms that combine words and pictures in a way unique to the last century. Edgar Rice Burroughs' Tarzan comes instantly to mind—along with Arthur Conan Doyle's Sherlock Holmes, Lester Dent's Doc Savage, and most especially Robert E.Howard's Conan the Cimmerian.

In a more recent reversal of the trend, an increasing number of comicbook and comic-strip creations are finding themselves transformed into the stuff of paper-back novels, often with astonishing fidelity to the originals. When we come to Red Sonja, fierce swordswoman from majestic Hyrkania, the story is a complex one.

As the proud midwife who presided over this unique birth, I hope you'll allow me a few paragraphs to explain:

Since the middle 1960s, I've been a writer and editor for Marvel Comics. From 1965 until rather recently, I busied myself scripting the adventures of such modern-day superheroes as I had known in my 1940s youth, adjusting them with some relish to the style developed by Stan Lee in connection with artists Jack Kirby and Steve

Ditko in the early sixties. *The Incredible Hulk—Spider-Man—The Avengers—Dr. Strange—Fantastic Four*—at one time or another I wrote them all.

By decade's end, however, I was growing a bit restive and looking for something new, something where I'd be able to stretch the limits of the Marvel style just a bit.

Thanks in part to the mountains of mail that poured into our Madison Avenue offices every weekday, many possibilities presented themselves for my adaptation of outside literary sources into the Marvel mainstream.

Enter Robert E. Howard, Conan the Cimmerian, and —*Red Sonja, She-Devil with a Sword!*

Among many other fantasy creations which our never-reticent readers told us they'd like to see in comics form was one Conan the Barbarian, primary concept of the late Robert E. Howard.

A Texas fantasist and contributor to the legendary *Weird Tales* pulp magazine in the late 20s and early 30s —Robert E. Howard killed himself in 1936. Before his death, however, he had virtually invented the subgenre we now call "sword-and-sorcery" fiction, taking elements from past masters of fantasy such as William Morris and Lord Dunsany and merging them with the supernatural horror of Lovecraft, the adventure-pulp works of Talbot Munday and Rafael Sabatini and even Edgar Rice Burroughs. REH (as his devotees call him) was both an eclectic and an *original.*

For years Howard's prose languished in moldering pulp magazines, except for one largely unsuccessful hardback publication in the 1950s. Then, in the middle and late 1960s, under the editorship and guidance of L. Sprague de Camp and with much diligent work and research by Glenn Lord, two of the Texan's most notable creations began to appear in a series of paperbacks. Conan and King Kull made their neo-debut on the heels of a mild Edgar Rice Burroughs boom and a more notable enthusiasm for the works of J.R.R. Tolkien.

Marvel was not interested in such things at the time. Still the torrent of letters kept pouring in, asking us to adapt current heroes into comics: Tarzan, John Carter of Mars, Tolkien's hobbits, Doc Savage—and Conan the Cimmerian!

Finally, starting in the summer of 1970, we did. *Conan The Barbarian,* after a slow start, grew to become something of a comicbook phenomenon. I've scripted some 4000 pages of Conan titles to Date, with the end nowhere in sight.

Once we got started, the Conan comics series cried out for interesting *supporting characters*—extras who could pop in and out of the series from time to time, for continuity's sake.

There were minor characters galore in both the original stories and the comics, but they had an alarming tendency to get killed off—leaving Conan free and unhampered to wander off to new exploits, new supporting characters, next month. Not much continuity there.

And as for the *women*—!

Occasionally, Howard had invented a truly rounded female character for us to bring into the comic and adorn those fabulous, blood-drenched stories which were the author's major interest. But mostly his ladies seemed to exist only to be rescued by the bronzed barbarian—the latter-day equivalent of Sleeping Beauty or Snow White, with Prince Charming doing double duty in a way Walt Disney would never have approved of.

There were, of course, a few notable exceptions.

The earliest of these more fully-realized women was *Bêlit*—the Shemitish she-pirate and self-styled "Queen of the Black Coast," in REH's story by that name. Supposedly, Conan cavorted with her and her black corsairs for two or three years. However, Howard obviously had little interest in his dark-haired heroine, covering most of Conan's sojourn with her in a couple of paragraphs, then skipping from their meeting to Bêlit's death in a single, memorable story which gives her hardly any character at all. (What there is isn't very likable; she allows some of her own corsairs to be killed in a death-trap, making sure only that she and Conan aren't hurt.)

The second such sword-wielding lass, and the last in Howard's fantasy tales, is *Valeria of the Red Brotherhood,* another female pirate whom Conan meets a decade or so after Bêlit, in the excellent story "Red Nails."

Valeria is a much better-realized character than Bêlit, though she travels in the space of a single suspense-laden novelette from an independent swordswoman to a helpless, naked captive writhing on the bloodstained altars of time-lost Xuchotl (to be rescued by Conan, natch). At the end of "Red Nails," Valeria and Conan wander off northward together, vowing to become partners in piracy. And she seems to have given in to the Cimmerian's masculine charms, as well, after earlier suggesting she'd run him through if he came within clutching distance of her.

Howard was not entirely against the idea of women adventurers with blade in hand. For instance, later research by Glenn Lord (now literary agent for the REH estate) uncovered various complete and semi-complete tales of one "Dark Agnes," set two or three centuries ago—but these are mock-historical stories, not "sword-and-sorcery."

And, finally, there was—*Red Sonja of Rogatine.*

I first learned of this minor, one-story creation of Howard's in an article printed in the Hugo-winning fanzine *Amra,* which is devoted largely to things Howardish, around the time I began developing the Conan comicbook.

I had been casting about already for a female equivalent of Conan—not an absolute *doppleganger,* mind you, but a character similar in skills and attitudes in certain ways, yet with a somewhat different point of view.

Already I knew that she must have red hair (because Bêlit was black-haired, Valeria was blonde, and brunettes are a drachma a dozen).

Already I knew that she should be from a more civilized land than backward Cimmeria, and not really a barbarian like Conan and Kull; one savage lurching about among ancient, decadent civilizations was already enough, thank you.

The aforementioned *Amra* article (written by one Allan Howard, presumably of no relationship to REH, and reprinted in a limited-edition book) dealt with several Crusader stories by Howard which had been published in such historical-adventure pulp magazines of the 1930's as *Magic Carpet* and *Oriental Stories*. Of special interest to me was a tale called "The Shadow of the Vulture," set during the siege of Vienna by the Turks in the sixteenth century. The hero of the hour, officially, was a blustering, hard-drinking German knight named von Kalmbach, one of REH's many Conanesque heroes. To quote Howard expert Fred Blosser in an article on the subject, the Russian-born hellcat Red Sonya of Rogatine "is described as a tall redhead who carries a saber, a dagger, and two pistols; she is kept busy throughout most of the tale saving von Kalmbach from assorted close scrapes." (Hmmmm, I thought at once . . . a woman after my own heart.) The article even suggested, with prophetic validity, that had Conan met her, "she might have been a bit too much for him."

Intrigued with the possibilities of yanking Red Sonya of Rogatine from the sixteenth century and plunking her down, with changes, into the Hyborian Age inhabited by Conan, I swiftly adapted "The Shadow of the Vulture" as the 23rd issue of the magazine, with the aid of artist Barry Smith, turning von Kalmbach into Conan and Red Sonya into—*Red Sonja*.

Why the change of a single letter, from "y" to "j"? Why "Red Sonja" in the comics, and not "Red Sonya"?

Originally, the alteration occurred to me merely because the "j" looked more exotic. However, as time went by and Red Sonja became more popular, I realized that, despite my love for "Shadow of the Vulture," Marvel's Red Sonja was not completely, totally Howard's Red Sonya.

Already by the second story featuring her ("The Song of Red Sonja," in *Conan* #24, which won the comicbook industry's own Academy Award for1972), I had begun to see certain divergences from the original, such as (I like to think) Howard himself might have done if he'd decided to bring his red-tressed she-devil into the Hyborian Age.

For one thing, from my favorite modern work of literature, William Butler Yeats' Cuchulain play "On Baile's Strand," I took the vow which Yeats indirectly attributes to the Celtic warrior-queen Aoife: "He said a while ago that he heard Aoife boast that she'd never but the one lover, and he the only man that had overcome her in battle."

That may sound vaguely like rape today, but in Red Sonja's life, I made that vow of chastity a conscious, willed thing. It is Sonja who sets the standard, and who will mate with the man who can best her with sword or axe. No rape here, just a set of standards strange to our modern eye.

There was also, of course, a touch of Joan of Arc in Sonja's stormy origin—but Joan of Arc was a leader, not a hand-to-hand fighter.

Others may point to C.L. Moore's fantasy creation Jirel of Joiry. But excellent as the Jirel stories are, Moore herself seems to have been influenced both by Joan of Arc and by Howard. (She was a great fan of Conan, who probably also influenced her SF hero Northwest Smith.)

In the past couple of years I have found myself having to explain to various souls, who've been paging furiously through the Conan paperbacks, that they'll not find

Red Sonja there. Now at last, thanks to all the earlier-mentioned authors and historical figures, but ultimately to Robert E. Howard, we have not only Conan the Cimmerian, but also *Red Sonja of Hykania.* And she is quite deserving, I think, of a series of books all her own!

Until now, she has existed mainly in some two dozen issues of her own bimonthly comicbook and in irregularly-spaced issues of Conan's titles, and most recently in the daily-and-Sunday "Conan the Barbarian" comic-strip which artist Ernie Chan and I churn out lovingly for newspapers from sea to shining sea. But now, she has come full circle at last—back to the prose format which birthed her.

Back to the medium in which her namesake and partial prototype, Red Sonya of Rogatine, first held forth some four decades ago, in the pages of *Magic Carpet.*

David C. Smith and Richard L. Tierney, already familiar to Howard buffs for their well-done pastiches of REH heroes such as Bran Mak Morn, Black Vulmea the pirate, and others, have put together an exciting story, dealing with a period a year or so (at least) in the future of the comicbook Sonja.

Thanks to both of them—and to Glenn Lord and agent Kirby McCauley and Ace Books, both for making me Advisory Editor of this series, and for letting me tell, once and for all, the story of the creation of Red Sonja.

I only wish Robert E. Howard were still around to read Smith and Tierney's Hyborian-Age tale from sorcerous start to sword-slashing finish.

I think he'd approve.

—Roy Thomas

Prologue

The sorcerer sat upon his high throne, elbows on knees, chin resting on his upraised fingers. In deep, shadowy sockets his eyes burned and flickered like particles of lightning half-obscured by lowering storm clouds. He was dressed, as always, in a stark black robe of antique cut and poised in his simple, austere way that nevertheless immediately drew attention to himself. Near him stood braziers of burning incense. On the walls flamed thick torches and on low tables small oil lamps burned. Yet the tower chamber seemed dark, its air thick with the odor of sorcery—the odors of gummy tars, incenses, and moldering books.

The black-robed wizard said nothing; yet the man before him, standing alone and feeling unprotected, seemed to sense within that heavy silence all the resonant fury of an impending storm. The yellow, flaming eyes spoke louder than any words might have done.

Then, the silence was broken.

"You have failed me." The sorcerer's sibilant, whispering voice, controlled and even patient, was yet vibrant with malignancy. That voice did not echo; it seemed to travel no further than the shadows beyond the wavering torchglows.

"You have failed me, Duke Pelides," the wizard continued. "For all your boastings and great-sounding promises, you have accomplished nothing in the three months you have served me."

Duke Pelides could not answer that charge. But a proud rage welled up in him, a feeling of angry frustration that this corpse-called-sorcerer should presume to malign his honor.

"Where is that which I hired you to seek out?" the sorcerer went on relentlessly. "Why have you not found it, as you promised to do?"

Pelides colored. His heavy warrior's hands fisting at his sides, his fury mounting, he stepped forward to defy the wizard and his shadows. "And what of you, Asroth?" he charged heatedly. "During these three months your much-vaunted sorcery has not shown you the Ring's whereabouts, save for a vague indication that it may be here in the southern part of the Kothian nation. Ha! Do you know how many leagues of land that encompasses—how many cities, towns, villages, and castles I might have to search?"

"*Silence!*" The word broke from Asroth's lips like the clangor of an iron gong. He rose up from his throne and stood tall in his black robe atop the dais, glaring down at Pelides with fury and scorn. His wizened features, his thin hands and neck, his gaunt features all belied the true power within him—sorcerous power, centuries old. But despite his inhuman age, Asroth was not one to long brook frustration without seeing to it that someone suffered a penalty—and now he was ready to punish.

"I have given you enough time, Pelides—more than enough. My gold was not paid you merely that your troops might go randomly looting and whoring about the land. Had you kept them more closely to their assigned quest, they might have succeeded by now. You have taken advantage of me enough, Pelides. I shall no longer put up with your incompetence."

Pelides's anger was suddenly replaced by a feeling of alarm, of dangerous forces stirring against him.

"But—perhaps the Ring does not even exist!" he cried

out. "Surely, if it did, other sorcerers would have discovered it ere now."

"The Ring exists, fool—make no mistake about it. The Ring is more real than you or I—than all this swarming race of worms that calls itself mankind. It has outlived Acheron and even the kingdoms of Atlantis. It is more ancient than this onyx throne, older than this fortress, antique beyond even the dreams of these very mountains! Sorcerers long before me have owned it, only to lose it because its secrets were beyond their wisdom and the will of its dark spirit greater than their own. Did you think, Pelides, that you, an ordinary mortal, might find it by merely galloping about the countryside letting your men plunder, occasionally threatening an old hag or a scholar of antiquity? Yes, Pelides, I know your methods, if such they can be called—I have watched you from afar!"

Pelides blanched. Fear gripped him, then shame, and finally anger took hold of him again. Asroth sneered.

"You failed your overlord in Corinthia," said the wizard. "Since then, you've failed to find a place for yourself as an honorable soldier. And now you have failed me. Corinthia may banish you, and the soldiers of other lands refuse you service in their armies—but now you have failed *me,* Duke Pelides. And I demand a more exacting service than crowns and armies."

Pelides's right hand instinctively reached for the pommel of his sword.

Asroth laughed—a soulless laugh, frighteningly diabolical and powerful, the laugh of a giant confronting a flea. "Your sword is strengthless as water in this room, Duke Pelides. Draw it and see."

Pelides hungered to try his blade against the taunting sorcerer, yet feared that should he do so Asroth would instantly strike him down with magic, perhaps even slay him in some manner that would damn him eternally. No—Pelides did not wish to goad the sorcerer. He dared not. He wished to live for now, perhaps to return one day and finish this quarrel on more even terms.

Asroth chuckled harshly and turned away from Pelides, sitting down again on his throne of black onyx. Pelides did not move.

"What a coward you are," Asroth hissed at him. "I wonder that you were able to bear the armor and arms of Corinthia at all."

Pelides clenched his teeth. "You're trying to bait me, Asroth," he growled.

"Am I? How petty of me. But I am surely too old and wise for that."

Pelides drew in a deep breath. He sensed a subsidence of the tension. The crisis seemed to have passed, the confrontation—the battle of wills—ended.

"Since you no longer need my services, Asroth, I will be gone."

Quickly, Pelides turned on his heel and went to the heavy door of the chamber.

Asroth asked him: "Are you not going to ask gold of me?"

Pelides turned, eyes narrowing.

"Or are you too frightened, Duke Pelides? Are you afraid that if you asked for the balance of the payment for your services, I might grow wrathful and blast you to Hell? Is that your fear, Pelides?"

Instantly, shame engulfed Pelides. He tensed, pride and anger battling with fear, as he struggled to decide whether he should go on through the door or stand his ground against Asroth with a naked sword.

"What a child you are, Pelides," said Asroth, his voice a gloating whisper. "What a child you are—a child who deserves to be punished."

Pelides froze, watching the wizard carefully. Asroth barely lifted one hand, slightly motioned with one finger. But in that moment the flames in the incense braziers seemed to die down, and for the space of a heartbeat the chamber floor rocked unsteadily. Pelides stood firm, though a feeling of sickness plunged through his bowels.

Then the feeling passed, and Pelides was barely aware that anything had occurred at all. And yet—

"What have you done? Asroth—what have you done?"

The sorcerer was no longer gloating or smiling; the effulgent glow was in his yellow eyes once more, hateful and burning.

Pelides jumped forward in a cold sweat, ready to plead, ready to kill.

"What have you *done,* sorcerer?"

Asroth sucked in a breath of the incense-laden air, slowly, as if savoring it, then said: "Look into the mirror, disobedient one. Look—and see what your treachery and failure have earned you."

"What have you done?" Pelides stumbled around the room, his feet unable in his anxiety to find sure footing on the flags. He looked one way, then another, and his vision seemed to blur. Strange scents seemed to flow into his nostrils; there was something distorted about his hearing; his mouth was dry and raspy, his vision alternately blurring and sharpening—

Then he caught his reflection in a burnished silver mirror. From there, halfway across the chamber, another Pelides stared at him—a Pelides grown unutterably hideous. A Pelides with a man's body in Corinthian armor, but with a face grown monstrous—a face *inhuman . . .*

"What have you done to me? Asroth!"

Asroth sneered, watching him, eyes burning, hands tensed on the arms of the throne.

"What have you—?"

Pelides choked. He turned away from his reflection and his thick hands grabbed for his sword. Steel shivered and whined as it was ripped free from scabbard —and Pelides, wailing with horror, ran headlong to rend and kill.

Even Asroth was unprepared for the speed of that attack. The sorcerer had time only to mutter a protective curse and throw up one thin arm in self-defense. Pelides's straight sword bit into the wizard's forearm, rang against the bone—and Asroth snarled, spat, and drew his arm away.

There was no blood. The bone had not even snapped. All that showed of Pelides's attack was a short slice in the sleeve of the wizard's black robe.

"Fool!" Asroth gripped Pelides's sword blade in his other hand and twisted it. The sword, as if suddenly become a pliant vine, turned in the sorcerer's grasp and was quickly rendered into a worthless coil of steel.

Pelides fell back, cowed, all rage and reason blasted from him. He backed to the door, mind still swimming, as Astroth stood upon his stepped dais bobbing in his vision—until the jolt of bumping into the portal reawakened some of his awareness. Instantly, he threw down his useless sword, hauled open the heavy door, and bellowed for his soldiers.

Asroth stood where he was. He knew of the six guards that Pelides had brought with him for protection. Now they came rushing into the chamber, half a dozen armed and armored rogues, quick on their feet and eager to slay.

Not one of them noticed Pelides' transformation in the dimness of the chamber, so used were they to hearing his voice and blindly obeying his orders.

Asroth laughed. "Beware the incense smoke, fools!" he shouted at them. "It will devour you!"

The six warriors had hardly raced halfway across the flags before the thick smoke from the braziers halted them. To their minds, the gray and bluish strings of mists seemed to take on the shapes of hideous phantoms. The first man shrieked as a writhing viper, twice as long as himself, trailed from a tripod and sank its fangs into his breast. He sworded it, but his steel only sliced through it effortlessly as if it were mere air. A second and third soldier battled a reaching, huge-taloned paw that covered and clenched about their heads and suffocated them where they stood. Two others valiantly confronted a massive demon's head, but the hungering maw of the monster quickly swallowed them up whole before they could fight. The last man went down as swift-growing flowers enveloped him, their poisonous, needle-toothed petals sucking life and breath from his every pore.

Within a moment it was over. Pelides, aghast, stood backed against the jamb of the open door, staring at the six stout warriors who had fallen instantly—the moment they had reached the coiling mists from the incenses braziers. Each face was frozen in a horrible grimace of agonized death, muscles stretched to the limits of endurance in fearful reaction to what they thought had attacked them. Yet there was not a trace of a wound on any of their bodies. Pelides trembled in a cold sweat, forgetting for the moment his own sufferings.

Asroth held up a hand. "Pelides, get you hence. You cannot bring more soldiers against me. Your pitiful army will abandon you before the day is out. No one will look upon you and abide the horror of your aspect, for you are more hideous than the foulest imaginings of mankind. Begon—or I will slay you slowly and dip your soul again and again into the bowels of Hell!"

Pelides reeled out the door, but as he did so he raised his fist at Asroth and howled out, half mad with hatred: "I'll *find* the Ring, sorcerer—I swear I will!"

Asroth did not move or answer.

"I'll *find* it!" Pelides's voice broke in a wail of torment and he staggered away down the hall, cursing and sobbing.

Asroth stood dark and solitary upon his dais amidst the incense smoke, his shadow falling like a blot across the corpses stretched on the stone flags. He raised his hands silently; the room grew darker, and from the deepest shadows crept squat, ink-black shapes like hunched dwarves, with pointed ears and green-glowing eyes. Soundlessly, they laid hold of the dead bodies and bore them away to some indeterminate region within the shadows.

The torches flared and the illumination in the room

swelled to the level of its former dimness. Nowhere could there be seen a trace of bodies or black dwarves.

Now Asroth stepped from his dais and walked to the silver mirror. Staring intently into it, he whispered balefully: "The Ring. Show me the Ring. Where is the *Ring?*"

It was no use. The ancient minions of Ikribu had hidden it too well, covered it too carefully with years and years of protective spells. And Asroth, only recently reawakened from a centuried sleep, had not yet regained enough of his sorcerous power to force aside that mystic shield.

"Show me the *Ring!*"

He gripped the sides of the mirror with his talonlike fingers. His eyes burned even more fiercely than when he had slain Pelides' soldiers. His entire frame shivered in one willful, tremendous act of concentration as he attempted one more time to burst through the ancient spell hiding the Ring of Ikribu.

"Show—me—the—Ring!"

And suddenly—though his vision swam with the effort, though his legs trembled and his thin limbs knotted and his veins bulged as if they were about to burst—Asroth's mighty concentration gained him one fleeting vision. From the misty, polished recesses of the ancient mirror there emerged, hazy and uncertain and gray, the unstable image of a city—a walled city, lying dark on a low, green plain.

Asroth strove to concentrate harder, but already the vision had faded. It was gone. It *had* been a city. Yes, a city—and Asroth had recognized it.

He relaxed, slumped against a table, nearly swooning from his recent effort, then slowly made his way back over the naked stone floor to his throne. He knew that city, it was only days distant from his fortress.

Soon he would have the Ring.

Chapter 1

The Quest

Outside the tavern the wild night stormed. The rain had continued for three days, and tonight had become a downpour. Immense gray clouds crowded the black skies; lightning danced and flashed, brightening the shadowed lands where moon and starlight could not. The many small rivers of the southern fields of Koth were swelling and threatening to flood, while on the few muddy roads that crisscrossed the terrain wagons had bogged down; horses and their tenders were wading ankle deep in the mud.

But inside the lonely tavern situated along a high road somewhere between town and field, men and women drank and caroused and cursed the storm. The place was filled with travelers who had accumulated over the past three days. But though they were crowded, they were for the most part happy wayfarers, for Izak the hostel keeper always made sure to have plenty of reserves of food and drink the year round. And so tonight, while the world outside drowned in a springtime flood, the motley crew in Isak's place were noisily festive.

Amid the lively press, battle-scarred mercenaries from various lands rubbed elbow and flank with mailed Kothian soldiers. Only a scattering of civilians were present: a pair of merchants, an unfortunate noblewoman and her maids who were forced to share the table with several unkempt and too-friendly young wenches. All present were being subjected to the lugubrious whinings of a lute-strumming rhapsodist in rags, a young Nemedian unable to find board and room in any lord's castle—and small wonder, given that the dogs at the fireside, baying for scraps, came across more tunefully than he.

One man bellowed gruffly for more beer; another called to a serving wench to come and avail herself of his lap; while yet a third yelled at the strumming Nemedian, obscenely but good-naturedly instructing him where he might more advantageously place his lute.

"And when you've done that, here's a copper—go cure your voice with a tankard of ale!" The rogue glanced over the crowd, grinned loutishly, then turned to a tall young man standing against the great fireplace. "Hey—you, too, lad—drink up and put some cheer into that sour face of yours."

The young man, Allas, ignored the comment. He was handsome, and rather well-dressed in fine mail, a satin tunic, and embroidered cloak. Up till now he had been fighting a losing battle for the attention of the crowd. Having arrived only a short time ago, his hair and clothing were still damp, but even such a rain as the one outside had not been able to cool the ardor of his speech. For Allas was asking for recruits; asking these warm, cozy, comfortably drunken men—soldiers for the most part—to hoist sword rather than cup and fight in the dwindling ranks of his usurped Lord Olin.

"Allas!" someone else called out to him. "We've listened patiently and you've had your say. Now, take the good advice you've been given—calm down and join us at the ale jack. No man here intends to enlist for a fight on a night like this!"

"Are you all cowards, then?" Allas retorted; he hoped for an angry response to that, but got only derisive hoots. "What—do you think Lord Olin can't pay for the use of your swords? You men are soldiers; are you all so wealthy that you can refuse employment because of a night's bad weather?"

"You're only working yourself into an ill temper, Allas. Sit down and drink up!"

The youth gestured with impatience. "You disgust me—sitting here swilling like hogs when you could be earning gold and treasure. Not two days distant Lord Olin is waiting in his camp, ready to buy swords to replenish his ranks. Will you not aid him in his attempt to regain his lands, to oust the foul sorcerer who has despoiled his city?"

"Sorcerer, you say?" called a lean-faced warrior from a far corner. "Young man, are you asking us to heft steel against sorcery?"

More faces turned in the youth's direction and the rowdy turmoil of the tavern lessened somewhat. Allas sighed heavily and lifted his hands, gratified that for the first time tonight he was gaining some unity of attention.

"Aye, it's true, I'll admit it," he said. "Wait—hear me out. A wizard has in truth captured Lord Olin's—!"

But his voice was drowned in a rising clamor of hoots, catcalls, and ugly demands that he either take his place tableside or outside in the rain. Allas fumed.

"I'm offering you *gold!*" he stormed. "Are you so afraid at the mere mention of—?"

But it was no use. Allas angrily grabbed a brew from one of the full platters being carried by a scurrying serving wench, feeling a need to cool his dry throat.

"That'll be a copper, lad," called Izak from behind the bar.

Allas dug into his purse and irritably threw the coin across the counter.

The bellows and cheers and arguments clamored again, louder than ever. Under pain of death, the Nemedian lutist had at last ceased his attempts at song and had taken up the leg of a fowl at a table; the plump serving wench accepted her invitation to the lap of a rogue, who bounced her till she spilled a tankard of beer down her front, whereupon he offered to dry her.

Allas finished his brew, continuing to stand. He was warm and dry now, his throat refreshed, but though the glow of the ale had somewhat diminished his disgust and irritation, he was still far from relaxed. Finally, he set down his cup and with renewed energy, took up his cause once more.

"Men—men! Won't even *one* of you join my Lord Olin in his need? The way is not far, and there is rich reward—"

His voice was drowned out yet again, this time by the sudden opening of the tavern door. Wind and rain blew in with fierce abruptness, dampening and chilling the room. Voices cried out harshly, demanding that the intruder get quickly inside and shut out the storm. The newcomer, dressed from top to toe in a dripping gray cloak, slammed shut the door and stomped water from wet boots.

"Come in, come in, I beg you," cried the portly Izak from behind his bar. "Take a seat by the fire, I'll bring you ale. Will you have some beef or fowl?"

Half the faces in the tavern had turned in the direction of the newcomer, to measure him up and decide if he were worthy to join their bawdy company. "A bit thin, perhaps," remarked a sharp-nosed fellow; "Aye, but carries himself like a soldier," opined his fat companion around a mouthful of pheasant.

But to Izak's offer the stranger answered: "Aye. Beef and ale, and bring it quickly."

It was no soldier's voice.

Now the gray cloak came off in a bold arc, spraying water droplets, and beneath it was revealed—a woman. She was tall and fair-skinned with a head of long, tousled, flame-red hair—and she was armored. A long-sword swung in the scabbard at her side, a knife at her hip. She wore a brief vest and skirt of silvery scale-mail that covered her breasts and hung from her waist, but left her limbs and midriff bare—good armor, but too little of it for practicality and evidently worn less for protection than as a symbol of her untamed spirit.

The raucous noises in the tavern dropped and faded to silence.

The flame-haired woman of armor and sword draped her cloak on one arm, took the stairs down into the tavern, and pushed through the press to an empty chair near the fireside. All eyes followed her. And as she sat down, Allas immediately took up his theme again, taking advantage of the surprised silence:

"Again I implore you . . ."

But the eyes staring in his direction were not looking at him, but rather at the newcomer, who now stretched her limbs before the crackling flames of Izak's stone hearth.

"Are you men cowards?" Allas railed. "Surely you must—"

Izak came by and shook his head stiffly at Allas.

"Enough," he muttered warningly. "Don't try them further." The good hostel keeper then turned to his latest guest and set a steaming plate of beef and a cool cup of ale before her, taking his time to admire her splendid figure. She suddenly looked up at him with piercing sapphire eyes.

"How much?"

"Uh—five Kothian minars, in all. Have you traveled far?"

"A week on the road, the last three days of it in this rainy hell. Thanks for your fire, I'm chilled to the bone! Have you any rooms left?"

"Alas, no." Izak's gaze continued to linger. "But there are the stables . . ."

"The stables, then. Is there someone to tend to my mount? It's as tired as I, and it stumbled in a rut."

"Not hurt, I hope."

"Not seriously, but it needs rest and fodder."

"My son will tend to it. Izak!" he called, and a youth appeared from a back room. "Tend to the horse outside."

"It's a dappled roan," said the woman.

"The dappled roan. Quickly, quickly!"

Izak the younger cursed under his breath, pulled on a cloak, and headed out into the storm.

"Is there anything else, then?"

"This is fine. But you can bring more ale."

"Surely," said Izak. With a puckish grin and squinting eyes, he made his way back to the counter, and when he returned he remarked, very thoughtfully: "That was —uh—five minars, in all."

The red-haired woman grinned sidewise and produced it from her pouch.

The noise in the tavern had commenced again. But now the irrepressible Allas, despite the recent warning of the innkeeper, renewed his pleading.

"Soldiers, again I implore you! My Lord Olin will pay you gold—and, moreover, he will lead you to untold treasure. What more can I offer?"

The red-haired woman, who was spearing a slice of meat with her dagger, paused and looked up at Allas. "What are you talking about, boy?"

Instantly, Allas turned to her and explained. "My Lord Olin is fighting to regain his kingdom of Suthad. His army is sorely depleted, and he has sent me and others to recruit as many swords as we can. The rogues in this house"—Allas raised his voice—"are braggarts and windbags, it seems, but not at all the soldiers they claim to be."

"I'll prove that false, if you'd like—with or without steel!" growled one of the guests, but Allas ignored him.

"How did it come about," said the red-haired woman, "that your Lord Olin lost his city? Are there wars in southern Koth? I had not heard—"

"Tell her about the sorcerer, Allas!" rasped a harsh voice from the other side of the room. "That'll win her over."

Rough laughter followed the soldier's interruption. But the woman did not seem overly concerned.

"Sorcery?"

"Aye, lady." Allas swallowed tensely. "As I was about to explain, a wizard named Asroth has taken Suthad. In spite of a stout defense, Lord Olin and what remains of his army were forced to abandon the city. That was but eight days past. And now we need troops—"

"You need mercenaries—aye. Good luck, then. These seem a loutish lot." Her eyes sparkled as if at a jest.

Allas took hope. "I see that you carry a sword by you," he said. "Are you a soldier, then?"

"I have fought as one. Tell me, Allas—do you find it unseemly for a woman to live by the sword as these rogues do?"

"Did I imply so? If I did, pardon me. Anyone who straps on the sword and wears it openly will soon be tested to prove their mettle. I trust you've proven it if you've come this far with that blade on your hip. My Lord Olin asked me to recruit soldiers—and if you're a soldier, no matter the cut of your figure, then I ask you to fight in a just cause."

The woman grinned anew, appreciating Allas's frankness. She bit into another chunk of hot beef and savored it as she ruminated over the young man's petition.

"May I ask your name?" said Allas. "I must admit, I *am* just a bit surprised to find so comely a woman in rough swordsman's garb."

"Sonja," she replied, washing down the good beef with a deep draught of ale. She smiled thoughtfully. "Red Sonja, late of Hyrkania, where steel grows like wheat and the women are a match for the men."

"Will you join my Lord Olin's army, Red Sonja?"

Sonja pondered the matter, and Allas waited nervously for her response, hoping that if he could gain just this flame-haired woman for a recruit others might be shamed into following her example.

"Your lord is paying in good gold?"

"Aye, fairly and generously. He has gold with him,

and the city treasury awaits him in the palace when Suthad is recaptured."

"Has he a strong crew?"

"In numbers, far less right now than he needs. But if you mean in courage, then I think every man we own is worth thrice in mettle any in this room.

Sonja smiled again; young Allas would not cease his attempts to shame these rogues into action.

"Yet I must remind you frankly," he went on, "that we fight against a strange sorcery. Our army was routed by demon soldiers of the wizard's conjuring."

Sonja shrugged and swallowed the last of her ale, then told Allas: "A foe can always be met, no matter what his weapon." She slammed down her cup, called for more.

"Then you'll join us?"

"For gold—aye, Allas. I've heard that Olin's an honest enough ruler, and my purse is low."

Allas had heard what he wanted; he had his recruit! Instantly, he turned and faced the crowd.

"*Hie,* you dogs!" he bawled out heartily. "I've gained a sword for Olin's company. You rogues ought to be shamed for cravens to hear it. Red Sonja of Hyrkania will join Lord Olin in his fight! Now, what others here will stand and show courage?"

Allas paused, fired with enthusiasm and rather proud of himself. He glimpsed Sonja smiling again, as at a private joke. Yet no one else rushed forward eager to lend his sword. Allas scowled at the disinterested or grinning faces before him.

"You cloddish dolts! What's *wrong* with you?"

A few nearby bravos chuckled and cheered. Then the plump serving wench rose from her soldier's lap and swaggered through the press, head poised defiantly, hands on broad hips. When she reached Sonja's table she thrust back her shoulders provocatively and parted her lips in a deliberate smirk.

"Well, look here!" she called to her friends across the room. "Is this a man or a woman with whom Allas has begun his army? I thought 'twas a man, for I see a man's sword, but here's also a bosom to make Ishtar's maidens blush—"

Sonja colored and tensed. "Hold on here, girl—!"

"—and though she's dressed in armor, I think the armor's poorly joined—"

"Wench, you'd do better to serve more and sip less—"

"—poorly joined—as is the sword to the sex!"

Sonja stood up, face nearly as red in anger as her hair. "My *sword's* my armor, tavern scum," she rejoined hotly, "and I'll wager it's faster and sharper than your tongue!"

The soldiers cheered, hoping now to watch a cat fight.

"Do you hear her?" laughed the buxom wench shrilly, turning about to face her audience, hands still on hips. "Our red-hair can't tell the difference between—"

She got no further, for in that instant Sonja's patience snapped and she planted her muddy boot vigorously on the broadest part of the serving wench's bottom. The girl shrieked and went tumbling, head over heels, across the tavern floor amid the dirt and mud and spilled ale.

Instantly the hall erupted into activity as dozens of sturdies rose up to applaud and whistle and cheer for more. Sonja growled a curse at them, but then shared a grin with Allas as she turned back to her table. Izak, behind the counter, howled to the crowd to calm themselves, fearful that his carefully tended tavern might be ruined in a melee.

But only one man showed real anger—the wench's boyfriend, who had gained his feet with the rest, and who now smashed his empty drinking cup to the boards and roared, "You can't treat her like that, slut!"

Sonja eyed the man narrowly; he was obviously half drunk. The tavern grew silent as the crowd quieted in anticipation.

"Get up!" the man roared to the sobbing, cursing wench. He grabbed her by her long hair and yanked her, whining, to her feet. "Get up and move back. I'll show you how we treat women who think they're *men!*"

He stomped across the tavern toward Sonja, hand moving for his sword. There was a wild scurry as the crowd pressed out of the way, knocking over chairs, spilling cups, and shoving aside tables to make room for swordplay. Sonja stood her ground calmly.

"Soldier," she said quietly, "my quarrel's not with you. Let's settle it peacefully. Don't draw that sword."

"Scared, eh?" The man roared with laughter. "I see *you're* wearing a sword. You'd better know how to use it!"

"No need for that," Sonja told him, still calm but resting her fingers on her sword's pommel. "Take a seat and have another cup. We will talk it over and not spill blood—"

"Bare steel, bitch!" howled the man, whipping out his blade.

Allas bent close to Sonja. "He's drunk, or he wouldn't mean it. Stand back—I'll take him."

Sonja shoved Allas away, at the same time drawing her own blade. "Stand back yourself, lad. I'll show you the temper of the steel Olin's hired."

"Ha—she gets it out of the sheath!" laughed the soldier coarsely. "Now, can you play with it, lass? Or is it too heavy for you?"

He moved closer, carelessly, seeming more amused now than wrathful, and poked his sword at Sonja contemptuously.

Like striking lightning, Sonja parried his blade, whipped it aside, hacked it down to the floor—then ripped open the fellow's tunic—Three strokes in one motion.

Gasps went up from the collected rogues in the hall.

The drunken soldier snarled, swayed and caught his balance, then howled savagely: "So you *can* handle it, can you? Then I'm done playing games with you!"

"Tarim's blood!" Sonja swore at him, her anger finally showing. "Put up that sword and—"

Too late—the inspired hero was angry, ready to kill for shame and drunken honor. He moved in quickly, steel lancing in for a disemboweling thrust.

Sonja darted to one side, parried and feinted, matching two strokes for every one of her adversary's. This only served to anger the man further; his blood was up, his face gleamed with sweat, and he seemed to be sobering quickly. Suddenly he charged, and Sonja, a sword-length away in the cramped tavern, defended herself in earnest.

Steel clashed as the combatants circled. Voices called out excitedly from the crowd but Sonja ignored them; she could not afford any distractions. Damn this drunken dog! Must she kill him over such a trifle as a few curses? She would avoid it if possible . . . .

His next move changed her mind. She was backed against a table when the man grabbed a chair and flung it at her. Ducking, she missed her chance to parry his next lunge and only her supple quickness saved her from having her side sliced open. Just in time she caught the next swing of his blade on her own. But now the rogue, frenzied with shame that a woman might best him at swords, rushed in with a mighty roar and swung at her head.

Sonja cursed and parried with all her strength. This was in earnest now, and she'd had enough—the fighting instinct had taken hold of her.

Suddenly the drunk found himself forced back by a whirlwind rush of strokes that he could barely fend off. He cursed furiously as Sonja backed him up to a wall. Steel sparked. She slapped his sword point to the floor. For an instant she held him there, his sword locked beneath hers.

"Mitra!" she swore. "Are you done now, you drunken pig? Give it up!"

She stared into his glaring eyes; his face was gaunt and haunted, his hair and moustache dripping with sweat, his forehead and cheeks glossy. He bared his teeth in a strained grimace, then panted:

"I—give it up—woman . . . ."

Sonja relaxed, stepped back quickly, and watched the man for any hint of treachery. Cheers and whistles went up from the crowd. Sonja waited, then turned to move back to her table—And the rogue's sword slashed at her back.

Sonja whirled and thrust her point into the soldier's chest, pulled back, then into the belly and into the throat and back—within a heartbeat. The rogue's sword clattered on the wooden boards; he coughed once, bubblingly; then slowly he bent and crumpled to the floor; his body, sliding down the wall, left a smeared bloody stain.

"Gods!" Allas breathed hoarsely, his the only voice in the room. "You're as good a swordsman as I!"

Sonja fought back a hysterical laugh. She let the remark go by as, breathing hard, she faced the crowd in the tavern, eyeing every face and looking for challengers.

There was none. The rogues who had watched the fight showed no inclination to mock the flame-haired woman for carrying a sword on her hip. Some few even applauded.

Slowly Sonja returned to her seat, lifted her ale cup, and finding it empty, cursed and called to Izak for more. The taverner instantly obeyed her request, then backed off. He did not linger as before, and if he momentarily had had it in mind to ask her to make good any damages, he apparently had reconsidered it.

Allas, regaining his composure, turned once again to his audience, intending to make as much as he could of the fact that this Red Sonja of Hyrkania was a member of Lord Olin's mercenary army. But before he could speak a huge man strode forward, stout but muscled, sporting a thick blond beard and looking more like a village patriarch then a master of steel. He beamed a cheery smile as he faced Sonja with a disarming sparkle in his eyes.

"That was a fine display, soldier!" he said, laughing gustily. "By Mitra, I never thought I'd live to see a woman fight as well as a man! I'm proud of you."

"Oh?" Sonja eyed him carefully. "I trust you didn't lose a friend to my fine swordplay."

"What? That swine? I don't know him. But you've shamed me, Red Sonja of Hyrkania, into taking up sword beside you. I was heading for Argos with no mind for local wars, but now I think it'd be a deal more pleasurable to fight alongside such a sword as yours."

"I'm flattered," Sonja replied, not sounding at all flattered by the bearish rogue's advance. She swallowed the last of her ale.

Allas gripped the man's arm with enthusiasm. "Do you mean you're joining up with Olin?"

"Hell, why not? My name's Som, and I fight with two swords. Will that kill the devils and sorcerers for you?"

"Aye!" Allas turned to the crowd and cried out: "Now, who else will join? Come ahead—step forward!"

But he found it was no longer necessary to plead. The sight of battle seemed to have swayed a sort of balance, seemed to have been just the thing to coax these ruffians into Olin's mercenary ranks. Allas gained two dozen swords that night—most of the men who had been in the tavern during the three-day rain.

He thanked Sonja a thousand times. And after the last man had called out his name and Allas had written it down and rolled up his thin parchment, the youth tore open his purse and threw the last of his coppers across the counter to Izak.

"Buy her ale!" he cried out, laughing. "Buy her all the ale she wants!" Then he turned to where Sonja sat at the table, the center of the gathered ring of freshly hired mercenaries. "By Mitra," he swore, his excitement getting the better of him, "you're beautiful!"

Sonja nodded to him in silent thanks and tilted her cup, unconcerned about his comments on her beauty and swordsmanship, and wondering a bit as to why fate had used her to coax these brawling louts into fighting Olin's war.

* * *

The rainstorm had stopped by morning.

One by one the mercenaries, after squaring their accounts with Izak and the tavern wenches, left the inn and made their way to the stables to tend their horses. Mists yet clung in the air and the low fields beyond the sloppy road were drenched, swampy pools. But early sunlight lit the air, and the trees and grasses were dewed with streamers of brilliant droplets that shone like gems. Birds chirruped from the sparse woods, and Izak's dogs frolicked and splashed in the yard. The mercenaries, mounting up, yawned and stretched, then trotted over to form a staggered line before the hostel.

Allas and Sonja were the last to mount. They thanked Izak for his patience and generosity, but the taverner seemed less eager to listen to their small talk than to see them ride at last from his premises.

Allas took the lead of his assorted crew and Sonja paced her horse beside his; behind, the ruffians they had gathered were jesting and laughing and sharing reminiscences of the various table wenches in good Izak's employ. The mists cleared away and the sun beat down more strongly as they made their way along the muddy road.

As they topped a hill Allas stole a final glance back toward the tavern. He saw two small figures behind the building carrying something between them that appeared heavy and awkward, and guessed it to be the corpse of the drunkard Red Sonja had slain the night before.

Allas looked over at her. The swordswoman had not put on her gray cloak this morning, but had tucked it behind her saddle, and now rode in only her silvery mail. The bright morning sun glinted brightly on the scales and made her smooth, tanned flesh seem to glow with vibrant health. Allas watched her. Her long, touseled hair, now more brightly orange-red in the daylight than it had seemed last night under the dim torch glow, fell wildly down her shoulders and back. She held her head high, eyes watching levelly ahead, her total attitude one of composed vigilance. She held her mount's reins easily but firmly in gloved hands as they rode over the crest and down the gentle slope.

Sonja sensed Allas looking at her. She faced him, regarded him without a smile, but her eyes seemed to say that she accepted him in an open spirit of honest companionship.

"They're burying that rogue you slew last night," he commented tonelessly.

Sonja shrugged. "He made an error," she replied in the same even tone of voice. "He misjudged me. Too many have done that in the past, and no doubt it will happen again." She looked at Allas and the corners of her mouth rose in the faintest trace of a smile. Then she looked again to the treacherous road and leaned her horse away from a rut. And so the company continued east under the new day, riding to war.

Chapter 2

Wings of Death

"But—who are you?" Allas asked Sonja.

The company had stopped, late in the afternoon, in a cool glen where there was shade for the soldiers and water for the horses. The mercenaries were all gathered together informally, sitting on rocks or leaning against trees, opening some of the provisions they had purchased at the tavern. Sonja was standing by her horse as it drank from a small brook; she had examined its leg and had satisfied herself that its hurt was no more than superficial. Allas stood beside her, chewing on a piece of brown bread.

He was fascinated with her; that much had become apparent to Sonja during the ride, for Allas's eyes often rested on her, and often he seemed to be studying her with a perplexed or curious wonder.

"I take it you've never met a swordswoman before," she remarked, amused at the thought.

"No, I've met some. But none as handy as you with the blade. You handle yourself better than most of these rogues, I think. Where did you learn such skill?"

Sonja rubbed her horse down, combed its mane with her hand and finally faced Allas, cautiously. She did not like to speak much of herself, or share much of her past, or contemplate too greatly who or what she was. She *knew* who she was, knew where she had come from and where she had been, and much of her past was best left sleeping.

"My father was a farmer in Hyrkania," she told Allas. "Before that, he'd served as a soldier. He taught my brothers swordplay as soon as they were able to walk, and I paid attention to him. I practiced on my own. In my wanderings, I've had opportunity to learn quickly."

She turned, leading her horse up the bank toward the deep shade.

"And are your brothers as adept as you?"

"They're dead," Sonja told Allas grimly. "They died years ago."

"Oh." Allas immediately felt guilty for inquiring, and presumed no more. He sat down beside Sonja as she perched on a large stone and unwrapped some of her brown bread and pheasant.

Munching hungrily, she asked Allas: "And what about yourself?"

He shrugged, as if it were not much of a tale to tell. "I was born in Suthad," he answered. "I was serving on patrol when this came up."

"Tell me of this wizard who's taken your city."

"His name is Asroth. I know nothing more than that. He appeared ten days ago on the horizon with thousands of ghosts at his command."

"Ghosts?"

"Aye—they swept over the city as if it had no defenses." Allas trembled as he spoke, remembering the unreal vision of it, like a nightmare come to life, something wildly unimaginable happening before there was time to think, as a sudden tidal wave descending upon a desert city. "We had no chance," he continued. "Armies we have held at bay before. Soldiers can be fought. But our defense was useless. *Useless!* We locked the gates and mounted the walls and stood six deep. These ghosts —phantoms—came through the walls! They poured through the bricks of the walls as if they were shadows!"

He was speaking eagerly now, alarmed at his own remembrance. The cool sunlight of the shady grove, the bright twinkling sunlight that broke through the thick foliage overhead, seemed less real now to young Allas than did his memory. But he calmed himself, not wanting the other soldiers to overhear.

"If they should learn what we're up against," he confided to Sonja in a low voice, "they might not want to fight."

"Perhaps. But if we're fighting ghosts," Sonja said evenly, "then how did you and Olin and your men survive the attack at all?"

"They may not have been proper ghosts," said Allas, thinking with difficulty for a right word. "They were creatures of some unreal substance that could be cut with swords, but—they walked through walls as if there had been nothing there, and when we struck one down, three more took its place. Yet they must have been partly material, for many of us were slain with wounds—though many more, especially among the civilians, died without a mark on them. What could they have been? Was Asroth conjuring them from the air?"

"Maybe," said Sonja, wrapping up the remainder of her food, "you were not fighting phantoms at all, but your own men. If Asroth had cast such a spell, you might have thought every soldier around you to be your enemy."

Allas brightened with incredulous insight. "Can such a thing be? And did the others, then, die of sheer fright?"

Sonja pursed her lips. "I've fought stranger sorcery. A Khorajan poet once told me: 'A magician's strength is in illusions of fear; if he can make his enemies reveal their souls to him, then half his magic is accomplished.' "

Allas shook his head. "I have never heard that. What does it mean? Surely you're not saying that there isn't any sorcery?"

Sonja stood up and shook her head. "No. No—there is sorcery, never doubt it. But, like our weapons, young Allas, sorcery is a two-edged sword and where one edge might cut your foe, the other might cut yourself. Hadn't we better be moving on?"

"Yes, you're right. Yes." Thoughtfully Allas rose. Red Sonja, it seemed, was more perplexing a woman than he had earlier considered. "Yes. We'll have to camp tonight, but we can make it to Lord Olin's encampment by tomorrow, I think."

He led the way back to the glen where the mercenaries sat, and called for them to mount up.

The day remained sunny, with no hint of any further rainstorms. Allas and his company made brisk time and the mercenaries showed no hint of the concern or fear they had shown the evening before in the tavern. They seemed to enjoy each other's comradeship, different as they were, and the warrior from the East jested with the warrior from the West while the soldier of the North good-naturedly claimed greater prowess than his cousin of the South. They were a roguish crew, and like most of their kind, quick to anger and as quick to forget, save in matters of earnest pride.

The warmth and pleasantness of the day did not abandon the evening. As the rim of the sun dropped below the far horizon Allas bade his company dismount and make camp on a high knoll that had suitably dried during the day. His soldiers first tended to their mounts with concern and care, as experienced travelers do, then quickly built fires and this time roasted their meals.

Sonja sat by herself at her fire, declining the company of the others—not out of animosity, but because she preferred solitude to pointless banter and empty professions of great comradeship. But as she sat contemplating the first stars of dusk, a mercenary approached her fire. It was Som, the bearish ruffian who had applauded her the night before.

"I see you've finished one wineskin, Red Sonja. Care to share the last of mine? Or will you stick me for a drunkard?"

Sonja chuckled and motioned him toward the fire. "My temper, like my sword, Som, is scabbarded for the time. But I do tend more to myself than most."

Som sat down with a sigh and a grunt. "Aye, aye," he nodded, settling his bulk and proffering his wineskin. "It's easier to trust oneself more than most others. Drink."

Sonja sipped some of the wine and handed the skin back, wiping her lips. "That's good," she remarked with some surprise. "Who would have thought that rattrap held such good drink on its premises?"

Som flashed a white-toothed grin. "I pass through there three or four times a year, and so Izak often shares his better stock with me. It's the best companion to have along on a long, hot ride."

With a mock flourish Sonja saluted him, then knelt to throw another branch on her fire.

"I still marvel at your swordsmanship," Som told her. "Quite a display. You carved him well. I admire a man whose steel is tempered with wit and judgement—man or woman, as the case may be."

"I've no patience with rascals who expect the world to excuse them where they make no allowances for themselves."

Som nodded. "Which is why each one must look out for himself." Som laughed sharply, struck by a sudden thought. "I pity most the fool who would force his attentions on you."

"I've made a vow," said Sonja in a low voice, guardedly, while looking into the flames. "I've pledged that no man is man enough until he bests me at swordplay."

"An honest challenge."

But Sonja did not hear Som's remark. She continued staring into the fire, as if seeing something there—perhaps a ghost or a vision.

Som finished his skin and heaved his bulk to his feet. "And I wish you well, Red Sonja."

She looked up at him. "Aye—and yourself."

"Till the morrow, then," said Som, and walked off to his own campfire.

Sonja turned back to hers. Memories came to her. Solitude settled upon her. Nearby, the horses snorted and men coughed, yawned and growled—hard men, sharing curses and settling down for slumber.

From his fire, Allas called to Sonja: "We'll reach Suthad by midday tomorrow."

"Till morning then, Allas."

"Aye." And he settled himself down for a deserved rest.

But Sonja was nervous; Allas's questions that afternoon, and now Som's remarks, had brought remembrances to her. The flames of her campfire were like the flames of Time, devouring all that was thrust into them —greedily, remorselessly, consuming them forever.

Flames. Like Time.

She remembered her father—a retired mercenary, his left leg butchered in his final campaign and replaced with one of wood. That wooden leg, clomping hollowly on the floor of the family's home, had seemed to beat a rhythm into the young Sonja's heart—or had marked time like the clacking of water clocks. Her father—and the family.

Her brothers, younger than Sonja herself. At that time she had seen less than twenty harvests, she was oldest, and her father had not allowed her to join the boys' mock swordplay. Her mother had disapproved even for the boys. Yet old Ivor, no longer able to ride to war himself, enjoyed coaching his sons in the rudiments of soldiery. "They'll make fine warriors," he'd mutter pleasantly, watching them go to with wooden short swords and hide shields. "They're Hyrkanian, aren't they?" He'd laugh. "They have my blood in them, don't they?"

Sonja, too, had her father's blood in her. She was tall and clean-limbed, strong, eager for approval, jealous of her brothers. On nights, discontent with household duties, she would sneak outside to a favorite haunt of her own, a tumbled ruin of some ancient structure in the woods, and there she would practice, alone, with only the winds and trees and stars to watch her. Alone, and unable then even to wield her father's war sword.

But they had been happy. A warm family, a good family—until Death had come. Until fire had come. Until only she of all of them had remained alive—alive, but wounded in body and mutilated in spirit.

The flames reminded her of that day when the mercenaries had appeared, the day her father, ax in hand and sweating from chopping firewood for the cool autumn nights, had seen them coming and bade the family take cover indoors. The mercenaries had approached, five of them plus the one in command . . . the one in command . . . the one with the hideous face, a laughing, square skull of a face that grinned constantly with the expression of a demented goblin, arrogant beyond the devils in his strength and mein.

"Ho, Ivor! So you've become a *farmer* now? But you haven't forgotten *me?*" The face . . .

"No, old comrade." Her father's broad back shiny and muscled, contrasted against the dark sheen and muscles of the mercenary's mount. "No, I could hardly forget my former second-in-command." His muscles tensing, the ax in his hand twitching, because he knew the ways of mercenaries. Was this vengeance for some long-ago indiscretion in her father's youth, some wildness he had selfishly enjoyed in his younger days?

"I am now first in command, Ivor. *First!*" The eyes of the face callously and casually looking beyond Ivor, searching through the windows of the cottage as if to see what booty was to be had. "Will you join us, old *comrade,* for the winter campaign in Khitai?"

"I would, old *comrade,* had I not lost a leg in my final campaign."

The amused smirk. The insolence in the eyes, the grinning teeth. "Sounds like a poor excuse to me, Ivor. Or—

a *cowardly* one." The eyes searching through the windows of the cottage, then turning back to her father, suddenly going hard. "Kill him."

It had happened so quickly. Too quickly. Her father on the ground, a hurled spear through his chest. Her brothers, rushing frenzied from the house with what weapons their young muscles could handle.

"No! *No!* My *sons! My sons!*"

Her mother beheaded quickly to still her screamed protests.

Boots stomping into the house . . .

"What's this? A *girl*—trying to lift a *sword?*"

It was soulless, the memory, and so brief that time had stopped for Sonja. Still, it came back to her so vividly and with so much reality that she wished again for a vengeance that had been denied, or compromised, years ago.

Beaten. "Be *still,* you little hellion!" Five of them, five men, striking her, laughing, laughing.

And then the *face.* "Would you *kill* her, fools? I think the wench can offer us *better* sport.

Bruised—dragged about—with the sight of her father and mother and brothers, slain and bloodied. With the sounds and smells of Death still ripe in her brain—savaged, raped.

Raped.

"You might find yourself loving it, wench!"

Pain—searing, tearing pain—the walls of the house that had held so much love transfigured into a blurred chaos of mists and tears and shadows. And the *face*—through all of it, the face. *Hideous* . . .

Sonja shook herself back to the present and stood up. The fire was dying low. Around her, the company had nodded off to sleep. She was sweating; her brain was on fire; old hatreds still had the power to inflame her anew. She kicked dirt onto the fire, looked up at the bright stars, heard Allas groan as he rolled over in his sleep.

"But—who *are* you?" Allas had asked.

Her campfire was out, the gray funnel of smoke pulling sluggishly upward and dissipating above the trees. Sonja wrapped herself in her hooded cloak, sighed deeply, and lay down beside the dying coals. She heard her mount nicker and wished it a good rest. She forced herself to relax and forget. The past was dead.

With one hand on her sword pommel—her father's sword—Red Sonja stretched out, closed her eyes, and sought the sleep that would bring tomorrow's dawn the faster.

Olin's camp held three thousand strong—a rather small army. Yet Suthad was a small city. Sonja wondered how many had died fighting phantoms. It appeared to her that the remnants of Olin's original force were clustered around the large commanders' tents pitched on a steeply sloping hillock; while about this core there sprawled, as spokes on a wheel, mercenary regiments of varying size. The turrentine rainstorm appeared to have taken its toll, for groups of soldiers were yet hoisting fallen tents and covers upright, and ditches were being dug to drain away collected pools of water that might spread disease.

Allas hailed a superior as he led his small force into the campground. The officer waved back a salute and spoke to a man next to him, who took off immediately on horseback, no doubt to alert Lord Olin that new arrivals were come. Far to the east, very distant, Sonja detected another group of horsemen approaching at a leisurely pace—more recruits, no doubt.

Toiling soldiers hailed Allas as he led the way toward the tents sitting farther up the hill. A few mercenaries, milling about here and there, paused in their work to survey the newcomers, shielded their eyes and stared momentarily, then bawled out hearty curses when they recognized old comrades or rivals among the lot from Izak's tavern.

By the time Allas reached Lord Olin's tent, only he and Sonja and Som remained of their company, the others having wandered off, in ones and twos, to accept the welcomes of their fighting brothers.

"How many did you raise, Allas?" asked Lord Olin, after he had greeted the young soldier. "I saw but a handful when you entered the camp."

"Aye." Allas' tone was apologetic. "Twenty-six men, my lord."

Olin eyed Sonja. "And a woman."

"And—a woman."

Olin smiled. "Welcome, swordswoman. What is your name?"

"Red Sonja, of Hyrkania."

Lord Olin nodded in approval. "Hyrkania—a nation of warriors."

He was, Sonja judged, a powerful man. She had earlier held reservations regarding the sort of warrior prince who could flee his own land while leaving an enemy in possession, but Lord Olin now left no doubt in her mind that he was a strong, capable man, a born leader, and the equal of anyone on the field. He was tall and heavily muscled, the brawn of his arms and chest revealed beneath the cut of his tunic and light armor. A full-bodied mustache and beard, well trimmed, added to the regalness of his dark-skinned and handsome face. His eyes, deep and black, were somber but intelligent—and (it suddenly seemed to Sonja) burning with fires reflecting the same sort of private turmoil that must sometimes burn in her own eyes.

She felt an immediate affinity for this man, she who was obliged to be a quick and accurate judge of strangers or suffer the consequences. She had developed a sensitive instinct concerning human worth and integrity; the moment a person entered a room, if Sonja could feel in him a kindred spirit, she was often able to see below the surface and recognize the core of the other's being and know whether he was scoundrel or hero, worthy or unworthy, to be trusted or to be held at a distance. So it was with Sonja upon seeing Lord Olin eye-to-eye for the first time.

Instantly she seemed to recognize him; instantly she seemed to respect him and empathize with his plight. Instantly he awoke startling chords within her—feelings that till now she might have denied existed.

Olin offered her his hand. "Welcome, welcome."

And Sonja took it and shook it firmly, grasped it as if she were Olin's equal, and somehow knew in that moment that the greatest commanders see themselves as no better than the newest of their followers.

"And who is this?" Olin asked.

"I am Som, Lord Olin."

"By Mitra, Som, I'd say you're more like three men than one!"

The commander shook Som's hand, then turned to his young recruiter once more. "I know you've gathered me a good crew, Allas, but would there were more of them. I'd hoped for greater numbers."

"I know it, my lord. The storm nearly drowned me, and when I reached safety in a tavern I tried my best to recruit all the soldiers present. The twenty-six I brought with me were all that I could manage—and even, then, Lord Olin, I might not have done this well had it not been for Red Sonja."

Olin was looking beyond Allas, noting how a group of men were going about their work; but he was listening nonetheless, and now he faced Sonja and asked Allas what he meant by that.

Proudly Allas related how Sonja had slain the drunkard who had challenged her in the tavern. "You should have seen her, my lord—she but toyed with the great rogue, holding him back effortlessly, and finally stabbed him not once, but thrice in such a skilled display as hardly any man in this camp could hope to equal!"

"I am intrigued," said Olin. "May I ask where you learned to use your blade so well?"

"My lord, I told you I was born in Hyrkania," Sonja replied with a smile, as if that were answer enough.

Olin laughed, but did not pursue the matter. "Allas," he said, "I am going to wait one more day, to see if the other recruiters I sent out return with any worthies. But I dare not delay longer than that. Mitra only knows what Asroth is doing to Suthad while we dally." He sighed, and clasped his hands behind his back. "It is the torment of all Hells, waiting here and not knowing. . . ." Then he brightened and pointed down the slope. "Here comes your young lady, Allas."

Allas turned and saw a young woman dressed as roughly as any man in the camp come running up the hill, waving to him and calling his name. "Tias!" he called back, and nodded for her to hasten. Then he bade Olin excuse him, and hurried down to meet her.

"His lady?" Sonja asked with some surprise.

"When we were forced from Suthad," Olin explained, pain and regret evident in his voice, "some few of the women and wives of my soldiers made it through the gates at the last moment. Tias was one of them. By and large, these women are working as hard as the men here in our camp. Some have learned the rudiments of weaponry."

Sonja studied the slim, dark-haired girl on Allas's arm. She, no doubt, was unused to rough work and war, for she seemed hardly more than a mere slip of a child.

"Allas has told you both of what awaits us in Suthad, has he not?" said Olin.

Sonja and Som nodded. "He told us what he knew," Sonja explained. "The phantoms riding through the walls and slaying the people. But why, Lord Olin, is this sorcerer so intent upon your city?"

"I do not know." Olin's brow contracted in puzzlement, his fists clenched at his sides. "I do not *know!* That day dawned as bright and normal as any day before it. And then, instantly, it was fouled by that—disease—that sorcerer. And I do not know why."

Sonja looked at him; his face was lined and tense with worry.

Allas and Tias returned to the group, hand-in-hand.

"What have you been doing, Tias?" Olin spoke to her

as if she were a younger daughter.

"Helping the men with that rain ditch," she said, pointing down the slope. "We're hauling away—" Her eyes fell on Sonja.

And Sonja read the girl's sudden fears in her expression.

Allas gripped Tias's hand the stronger and proffered an introduction. "This is Red Sonja of Hyrkania."

Tias lifted an eyebrow. Red Sonja of Hyrkania, vibrant and confident, stood a head taller than did she, and was garbed in leather and armor as rough as her manful manner. Tias felt intimidated, no less by Sonja herself than by the obvious tone of respect in Allas's voice.

Tias looked away. Her dark hair blew into her face and she stubbornly cleared it away, though the wind continued to play with it. "Come, Allas," she said quietly. "There's something I want to show you."

Allas didn't understand, but he glanced at Olin and Olin nodded, gave him leave to depart, and thanked him for recruiting as best he could.

As they walked away, Tias leaned on Allas and talked to him, hoping she was concealing her jealousy but fearing in her heart that Sonja might be a rival for his affections.

"It's growing chilly," Som declared after Allas and Tias had departed. He eyed thc skies.

"Aye," Olin grumbled. Winds were rising from the north and blowing in huge invisible waves from across the farther fields, rippling over the grassland like waters on a dry sea. "If we see any more rain, we'll be drowned out. I wonder if Asroth has sent these storms."

He looked around his camp and noted the horsemen approaching from the east. "More recruits," he sighed. Then he pointed to a large tent beyond his own. "Sonja and Som, in there is food and drink, such as we have, if you wish it. I know your ride has been long and strenuous."

Som shrugged and pressed his hands together, flexing his muscles. "I'll help those dogs down there with their hauling."

Sonja asked Olin: "How far is it to Suthad?"

"A day's ride and a half. You cannot see the city from here—it lies north of us, there, beyond that fringe of woodland on the far horizon."

The sky was darkening beyond the woodland Olin indicated.

Sonja was about to ask him another question, when behind her the door of a tent flapped open and a man dressed in armor and a dark cloak stepped forth. Olin looked behind him and nodded a greeting. Sonja and Som turned.

The newcomer was tall and rugged in appearance, and his head was entirely encased in a heavy ebony casque. His features were wholly hidden; only a hint of his white eyes showed through two eye slits in the front. A raised ridge like a false nose was open at the bottom to allow for breathing, and a horizontal slit provided an expressionless mouth. Otherwise, the mask was a blank mockery of the human countenance.

The soldier in the Ebun helm bowed stiffly, paused to study the two beside Lord Olin, then strode off down the slope toward the mess tent.

Sonja looked to Olin, perplexed and astonished. "And who is *that* Lord Olin?"

"His name is Pelides—Duke Pelides. He was born Corinthian, but from what he's told me his land has disowned him. He has been a mercenary officer and a robber and a battle chief, but he became involved with the sorcerer Asroth several months ago and for some reason Asroth damned him. Pelides claims that Asroth so disfigured his face that for anyone to look upon it would mean madness or death."

Som sneered in disbelief, but Sonja looked behind her again. Pelides had disappeared into the tent.

"He was *allied* with Asroth?" she asked Olin. "And you allow him here?"

"He came to Suthad just one day before—the attack. He tried to warn me that Asroth meant to harm my city. Aye, he appeared before my throne a self-proclaimed outcast and outlaw, a strange man in a mask, and bade me to prepare for war. I thought him mad and threatened to imprison him—yet, on the following day his prediction came to pass.

"His ambition is my own, Red Sonja—to gain vengeance against the sorcerer, Asroth, and slay him. I therefore trust him in my camp. I feel he is not double-dealing me. His own immense hatred against Asroth blots out anything else in his mind."

"A fanatic is not to be trusted."

"I agree. But so far, Duke Pelides has given me no cause to doubt him and he's provided valuable information."

Sonja felt uncertain. A chill wind suddenly blew up, stronger than before, and she shivered; heavy black clouds were rolling in majestically from the north, rolling in too quickly, more quickly than was natural.

Olin followed her gaze. "As I feared," he muttered, and spat on the ground. "More storm. I am certain that Asroth is sending us foul weather—the storms have come from the north for the past four days."

But Sonja felt she sensed something else in the air besides the increasing chill and gusting winds. Something. . .

She tapped Olin on the shoulder and pointed. "Look there—are those part of the storm clouds? They *can't* be!"

Olin searched the sky.

"There, Olin—beyond . . ."

Olin saw. Against the storm clouds, and half-hidden against their towering mass, were other dark things in the sky—small dots moving too independently to be associated with the clouds. Fluttering, swooping bits of black outrushing the rushing storm . . .

"They are *not* clouds," Olin said, staring transfixed, blinking to clear his vision and trying to decide *what* they were. But they came from the north . . . .

Suddenly Olin turned and cried out sharply to a man farther up the hill: "Sound an alarm! Prepare!"

A strident horn blast followed his command. Instantly all the soldiers in the wide field below paused at their labors, laid down hoe and pole and buckets of earth and water, and looked to Olin, then to the northern skies.

The small things against the clouds had grown larger and were keeping pace with the storm clouds. Sunlight was swept from the far fields as the sky darkened and seemed to draw over itself a coverlet; in the last brightness before the unnatural dusk swallowed Olin's camp, the flying things became distinct, and sunlight glinted from them haphazardly as they soared far off and high above the land.

"They are men," Olin whispered, tensing for war. "Flying men with swords." Then, to his trumpeter in a huge bellow: "To arms! Asroth sends us more sorcery!"

Chapter 3

Men of Vengeance

There were thousands upon thousands of them, dropping from the skies as a rain of death—bronze-armored, sword-wielding, floating and flapping and swooping down in wide, low arcs, their black wings glinting like greased leather. They rode the wind that went before the rushing storm clouds, whirled along with the dark shadows that blackened the day above them.

There was no rain, no lightning, no ominous thunder. Only fierce winds heralded their coming, and they themselves were the storm. They descended in waves, flapping, shrieking, armor clanking and weapons glittering; Olin's soldiers were blown back by the sheer impetus of the swarming attack.

Olin shouted: "*Kill them!*" and threw himself into the tempest. Many of his men followed his example, yelling war cries.

Sonja stood her ground and drew her blade, the weight of it feeling good and trusty in her hand. Som, beside her, growled and watched warily as the things dropped continuously from the heavens, the boiling dark clouds vomiting them down in endless processions, descending more swiftly than true rain. They were not quite flying, it was now apparent, but half-gliding swiftly, borne on the winds.

It was also apparent that they were not quite human,

but grotesque, nightmare-spawned mockeries of angels: their vast black wings, like the leathery folds of flying lizards, were grafted to gibbering, drooling homunculi; necromantic man-bats with feral, bloody eyes; sharpened, needle-like teeth; and blotched, gray and black skin which shone with the noxious rainbow phosphorescence of rotting meat.

A dozen swooped down at Lord Olin, their swords and axes aimed for him, and the wind of their wings nearly threw him off balance. Olin crouched low as steel clove the air above him, then rose up and leaped as the winged men sped past, managing to carve one of them from throat to belly.

The marauder shrieked madly; the sword flew from its fist. For an instant it streaked on by the sheer impetus of its glide. Then its great black wings crumpled like papery ashes and it tumbled head over heels to the earth, bronze armor flashing in a blur. A mist rose up with the dirt and mud—the wings had disappeared.

Sonja and Som crouched tensely as the airborne legion swept over the hillside. The knot that had just passed Olin was now rushing for them. Sonja ducked; a blue flash of steel whipped past her side and she rose up on braced legs, swinging, and caught one of the things on its armor. More oncoming blades streaked for her. She dove to the ground, rolled, caught sight of a swooping belly, thrust up—

The winged creature screeched as Sonja's sword ripped into its side. The spray of blood momentarily blinded her. She ducked instinctively and fell to her knees as a black shadow swooped over her; wind bit at her scalp, and a short lock of her scarlet hair flew from her and floated to the ground.

Som bellowed with glee; the rush was upon him and he leapt to meet it, longsword whirling in a wide arc. An ax aimed at his neck veered and flew past him, still clutched by its owner's severed hand, and the head of another winged man exploded in a splatter of blood as

Som's sword finished its swing. Behind swooped another black flier and Som, having had no time to recover, grabbed the creature's harness with his left hand; he was torn back, his heels plowing up twin furrows, but his great bulk hauled the creature out of the air and they fell together in a heap. The great wings beat frantically about him, stirring up a suffocating blast of wind, and Som found himself looking into the thing's snarling, almost-human face. It howled in fury, its eyes burning an inhuman red, and then its white teeth lunged for Som's throat—but in that instant Som's blade found its mark and the hate-contorted face sailed from its shoulders.

Som grabbed the thing's sword as its head bounded down the slope, cursing to see its wings crumple and turn to dark mist. He rose and wildly brandished a blade in each hand, carving blurs in the air, then roared a battle challenge as two more of the things swept toward him.

Sonja, temporarily foeless, glanced down the hillside and saw that the creatures were all over the field now, still descending in an endless swarm from the moiling dark clouds—multitudes of them appearing as pinpoints of blackness far above the earth, growing larger as they swooped down to fall in packs upon the milling crowds of soldiers crowded on the hill and fieldland. The shrill cries of man-bats and mercenaries alike rent the air; the hammering clatter of steel on steel arose thunderously on all sides. The men jumped and slashed at their airborne foes, weapons flashing as wings covered them; winged warriors and soldiers went down in heaps, struggling in the mud and the damp grass.

Then Sonja saw Allas standing near the base of the hill, Tias cowering at his feet—and seven winged creatures swooping at them, their swords protruding beneath them like long fangs. Sonja cursed; she jumped, ran, slid down the hillside, saw she could not make it in time, grabbed a large stone and hurled it. One of the winged attackers shrieked and was knocked awry, flapping uselessly. But then the others were upon Allas.

The young warrior threw himself forward, sword up, and caught one of the loathesome things. Its guts spilled as it continued its glide, doubled up, a crimson trail dribbling in its wake. A second and third sword darted toward Tias; Allas whipped back and hacked the arm off one of the creatures, parried the thrust of the other. Tias huddled on the ground and screamed, unharmed. Sonja yelled, ran for Allas—but already the unholy things had swept past. Allas gained his feet, grinning, blood-spattered, sword trembling in his gloved fist.

"How many—*are* there—Sonja?" he panted.

She shook her head, looked to the skies. "They're thinning out, I think—"

"*Look out,* Sonja!"

Instantly she dropped to her knees as a sword slashed the air above her. Then she was up, swinging steel, and her blade met resistance. There was a thud and a howl.

Sonja yelled a Hyrkanian war cry and ran as a legion of the horrors dropped suddenly around her and Allas. Moving quickly, she provided an uncertain target for the winged nightmares, who seemed slower in their reactions than humans. Swords and axes whipped about her; instinctively she jumped and crouched in all directions, skipping and ducking this way and that, intermittently glancing up and striking when the wind of a wing or the glint of armor warned her to do so. It was madness, fighting such enemies; though they seemed sluggish in movement and had little control over their flight, their swift air speed was to their advantage, such that a quick upward glance to determine one's next attacker could bring a sword through the eyes.

But as Sonja backed up the hill, sword swiftly slashing in all directions while black shadows swooped and sped on, she was able to occasionally glimpse the battle on the field below. The ranks of the man-bat, were definitely thinning out, and it was obvious now that when they had glided entirely across the field and come to earth, wings flapping uselessly, they were easily overcome. They seemed not even to have the strength to stand. All their ability apparently lay in their first long descent, in the power and speed of streaking down from the high air to skirt just above the heads of the warriors, to kill an unseeing enemy. Sonja was astonished at how unskilled the horrors were; when their speed slackened, they could only flap laboriously in the air, struggling to stay aloft, whereupon any soldier could hack them to bits or carry them down.

Yet though the numbers of the winged men were now obviously thinning, Olin's men were kept hacking and leaping desperately, while black flapping shadows still covered knots of men. Soldiers were hauled into the air even as their swords struck mightily against the armor of their soaring enemies.

By now, at last, many of the troops had taken up their bows, and as the long swarm of winged men swept down from the leaden skies, Olin's stout archers drew bowstrings and loosed shafts. Unhuman howls of death resounded in midair as batlike figures collided high above the fields or plummeted, black mists trailing behind them, into trees or upon the sward or into stagnant puddles.

But still the winged things that remained continued to lift hapless soldiers into the air. Even while those men dealt death wounds to their foes they were carried high and dropped, thrashing and screaming, to crash on the corpse-littered field or into pockets of other warriors crushing their own comrades.

Yet the crisis of the battle was now past. Sonja, cutting at whatever winged foes approached her, fought her way up the rise of the hillock. A final batlike monster sped down at her, mouth gaping and steel swinging; she jumped and rolled, cut, and felt her steel bite solidly into flesh and bone. The thing was carried shrieking on the winds down the slope, rolling into a crowd of six mercenaries who chopped it to smoking bits.

Sonja heard an outcry behind her. It was Som, bellowing in blood-lusting glee as a winged thing swooped at him and his blade ripped it open from throat to belly. It hissed hugely as its blade went flying and it tumbled on through the air. Then Sonja saw Duke Pelides, his iron helmet and rich cloak all blood-spattered, leap into another thing's path with upraised blade to slash open its side. It shrilled wildly, red spray gushing from its wound, wings flapping uselessly and already misting as it was carried in its descent to Sonja. And Sonja, marveling at the tenacity of the thing, jumped at it and clove it from shoulder to spine. The broken grotesque continued its drop, trailing gore, till it hit the ground and rolled down the slope, leaving a wide red smear behind it on the grass.

The battle was ended.

Olin stood panting with dripping sword at his side, surveying the damage. Som was slicing off the head of a wounded but yammering monster. Suddenly a last nightmare attacker shrieked through the air, its sword aimed straight at Som. Som saw and crouched, skewering the head he had just lopped off, then turned and hurled it, like a stone from a sling, straight into the face of the oncoming creature. The skulls crunched together resoundingly and the thing tumbled down to earth, its sword falling free, its head twisted at an impossible angle. Som laughed hugely.

"That's the last of them, by Mitra!" he bellowed.

Olin raised his sword in salute, then glanced into the clearing sky. There were no more points of winged blackness up there. Silently he tromped over the grass, overstepping fallen corpses in bronze armor. Sonja saw Pelides moving to meet him, and Som also, laughing heartily as he came, kicking at demon bodies in his path. His harness was splashed with gore and the two swords he carried might have been hammered from frozen blood. Sonja walked to join them.

All across the field the survivors of Olin's camp were lifting their dripping blades and loudly proclaiming their victory. The dark clouds swept on by, boiling, receding; and daylight brightened the grasses and trees. Dark mist rose, swirling, everywhere, stirred fitfully in the new, clean breezes—a mist composed of thousands and thousands of black inhuman wings, dissolving. And as those dark mists lifted, everywhere lay corpses in bronze armor—a sea of blurred gold in the fresh sunlight, as if some god from on high had spilled a tub at his metal shop.

Sonja, breathing hard, stared down thoughtfully at a pile of carved, armored dead.

Pelides was saying: "There can be no doubt, Olin."

Olin nodded. Sonja looked from one to the other as Som came up beside her.

"No doubt of what?" she asked, swinging her blade to free it of blood. "No doubt of Asroth's sorcery?"

Olin's gray eyes pierced hers. "Aye," he said grimly. His voice trembled; not from fear, but from a sickness which seemed to spasm from his great heart. "They came from the north—directly where Suthad lies. And they are not entirely unhuman."

Sonja had already recognized that fact; but now a strange idea came to her. "Do you mean—that they were once *men?"*

Pelides nodded slightly. Olin, pointing his dripping sword to a stained, bronze cuirass, brought her attention to an embossed emblem. *"All these men were members of my palace guard, Sonja.* They were—protecting the palace, and were trapped behind when my men and I were forced to flee."

"Then Asroth—?"

"Metamorphosed them," Pelides finished for her, his voice sepulchral from within his hollow mask. "And by illusion caused them to appear greater in numbers than they actually were. Necrumancy, Hyrkanian . . ."

Sonja stared at the corpses, understanding, as Olin

walked away in horrified disgust.

More mercenaries arrived just before sunset, as Olin's troops were removing the last of the bronze-armored cadavers from the borders of the camp. Olin welcomed these men, and thanked his recruiters for gaining so many swords. He explained to them what had occurred this afternoon and then, as evening slowly fell and the men in the field built fires for their suppers, Olin called his commanders and recruiters to him, to explain to them that on the morrow they would march for Suthad, to make war against Asroth.

And while Olin and his leaders held conference on the height of the hillock, his soldiers and mercenaries down below roasted meat and sipped from skins of wine and jugs of beer, holding their own council. The mercenaries were of a mind to quit the campaign; they had learned this afternoon what it meant to fight sorcery, and many of them no longer had the inclination to go to war against weird armies and weird winds. Lord Olin's regular troops sneered at them and reminded them how one man had been able to slay four or five of the winged men on the average; they also had recognized those creatures as Olin's palace guard,transformed, and bruited it about that Asroth's sorcery actually relied more on inducing fear than in its actual power. What had they to fear from rainstorms and a few winged zombies? If Asroth's sorcery was all that strong, why did he not sunder the earth beneath their camp or slay them wholesale where they sat, eating their meals? The newcomers to the ranks —those several hundred horsemen who had arrived late in the afternoon—were uneasy but undecided. They asked questions and heard answers and tales about the battle that had been done.

"I'll have no more of it," grunted one large fellow. "I've sold my sword to many campaigns, but I don't want to die with a sorcerer's curse on me."

"Then you're a coward," a man of Olin's charged

him. "If your sword's worth hiring, why can't it fight sorcery as well as flash? You didn't run from the battle today. No, it's only your fearful thinking that is unmanning you. But now, with our numbers and the knowledge that we've defeated his first attack, we can go on and *destroy* that sorcerer!"

The new recruits were still of two minds. Some, fresh to battle and innocent of sorcerous war, were eager for the fight; others, taking to heart the alarmist views of the still-bloody mercenaries, felt the contagion of fear about fighting sorcery on its own terms.

Lord Olin had no such doubts to quell his steadfastness. As campfires sparked and glowed about him and the stars came out behind the vanished sun, he faced his commanders and detailed for them what might await at Suthad, a day and a half distant. Twenty men were there, hardened veterans all, captains and generals, as well as Duke Pelides in his iron casque. Sonja, curious to hear what might transpire, was there also, standing at the outer fringe of the group, and Olin made no objection to her presence.

"Asroth will be awaiting us," he told his men. "He has already sent sorcery against us. But we defeated his attack, we defied his mockery, and now we have even more men than before! Our swords out there number five thousand strong. We have valiant, ardent soldiers of our own badge and we have seasoned, expert mercenaries who will fight alongside us for gold. And the women among us heave learned to use broadsword and ax."

A few eyes turned to Red Sonja, but she ignored them.

"We *will* defeat Asroth, I am certain of it. We all left families and friends behind in Suthad; I have seen my own sister slain by the foulest magic, and I know many of you have seen the same defilement befall your own loved ones. Astroth has sorcery and surprise on his side; we now have steel, and the desire for just vengeance.

Mitra aiding us; we will send Asroth back down to the festering Hell from whence he came!"

The officers applauded and voiced their approval. Olin was succeeding in rousing them to a fighting mood, reminding them of their mutual anger and outrage and lust for revenge. But Sonja, standing just outside the circle of gathered commanders, glanced at Duke Pelides from time to time; she sensed no firestorm of emotions in him, no charged energy of determination to fight with Olin for a common good. He stood apart, leaning against a tree, arms crossed almost indolently on his breast. His iron mask glowed redly in the firelight, and Sonja wondered what secret passion burned in his breast.

As Olin continued to talk, Sonja walked over to Pelides and stood beside him. He nodded to her but did not change his leisurely stance against the oak. Sonja bent near to him and whispered, conspiratorially: "What do you think, Pelides? Can they do it?"

He answered with a shrug of his broad shoulders, then said: "I do not think Olin is underestimating Asroth. But he knows he must work his men into the fighting lust."

"Can sheer numbers of swords outdo the sorcerer?"

"It is possible, Hyrkanian. Possible."

Sonja felt somewhat irritated by his noncommittal responses. "You'd like to slay the sorcerer with your own hands, wouldn't you, Pelides?"

She watched him, watched the slits in his midnight mask, caught the shifting liquid whiteness of his eyes deep within the shadows interior.

"Aye," he said, his voice hollow and resonant and metallic. "I will."

"And what harm did Asroth do to you, Pelides?"

"Did not Olin tell you?"

"Why do you wear that mask, Pelides?"

He turned and faced her. The ebony of his mask, pitted and hard, glowed strangely with the colors of the campfires, and the reflection of that glow ruddied Sonja's own features. "Were I not to wear this helm, Hyrkanian, the sight of my naked face would blast your soul to a ruin." He said it plainly, almost in an offhand manner, and that tone of understatement added a weight to his words.

"Asroth cursed you?"

"Aye. But I know how to destroy him."

Sonja waited. Was Pelides telling her the truth? Why did she feel this instinctive mistrust for him?

"How will you destroy him, Pelides?"

The man remained silent, as if he had not heard her.

"Pelides, why did Asroth attack Suthad in the first place?" She could not see his eyes.

"Olin knows where I stand, Hyrkanian," he said, the timber of his voice rising. "It is not your business to question. Yours is a hired sword—you were not recruited as commander, Red Sonja."

With that, Pelides repositioned himself against the oak, and by his stance, immediately seemed to erect a wall around himself.

Sonja walked away slowly, uncertain, feeling that she trusted Pelides even less than before. She wondered if Pelides had been wholly honest with Olin, and whether, were it within the scheme of things, might sacrifice Olin and all his troops in order to slay Asroth with his own hands.

Olin's council had broken up and his commanders were now making their way down the hillock to join their companies in the field below. Sonja saw Olin beckon to her.

"Come, Red Sonja, I'd have you share a cup with me, if you will. My throat's dry from speechmaking."

Sonja accepted and followed him inside his tent, where he poured two cups of wine and handed one to her. She studied the man. Tall, rugged and handsome he was—and, it suddenly seemed to her, with the weight of an unnatural doom, an unfair destiny on his shoulders.

"Did your speech do any good?" she asked him.

Olin sighed. "Those are my own men. They'll follow me. They have a vested interest in seeing Suthad returned to them. But they're also—afraid? Perhaps not afraid, but wary. Evil looms before them like a tunnel, like a wall of blackness, and they're uncertain . . . ." Olin set aside his cup. "It is five times more worry, making war against one sorcerer, than it is to make war against a nation of men."

Sonja sipped her wine and walked to the door of the tent, stood there a moment as if musing privately, then glanced out. She wanted to speak her mind to Olin, tell him that she did not trust Pelides. She waited, watching, till she had drunk half her cup, then she turned and eyed Olin squarely.

And she saw him watching her, saw his gaze openly lingering on her in an appreciative manner—the gaze of a man enjoying the sight of an attractive woman. Their eyes met and he smiled slightly, a smile of understanding that was somewhat mingled with a sad tiredness.

Sonja understood too. She sipped her wine.

"What is outside the door?" Olin asked as he moved to refill his goblet.

"Pelides, Lord Olin."

"Oh. Is he nearby?"

"No—but I do not trust him."

"Ah-hh!" Olin lifted his cup and eyed Sonja again, then sat down in a chair. His pose was automatically that of a ruler at his ease. "And why do you not trust Pelides, Sonja?"

"Do you trust him?"

Olin shrugged, sipped his wine. "I trust him as long as I can keep my eyes on him, Sonja. Does that ease your mind? We both know that he is a driven man."

"Olin, did he ever tell you why Asroth attacked Suthad?"

"No. Do you think he knows?"

"If he spent time with the sorcerer—"

Olin waved a hand at her. "Pelides is a proud man. He may know more than he says, but I think that his silence is due mainly to his pride. He has been grievously wounded and he is not so willing to share things now."

"You make excuses for him. But how long have you known him?"

Olin sighed tolerantly. "I have my own opinion of him, Sonja. I trust no one to extremes; no leader of men can do such a thing. But I do not think Pelides is a dastard or an evil man."

"I think he could commit dangerous acts, if allowed."

Olin shrugged. "Perhaps. In any case, I doubt that Pelides's stay with my army will be more than very temporary. He wants to get his revenge on Asroth. As soon as we reenter Suthad, I'm sure that Pelides will feel that my army and I are of little further use to him. And *that,* too, is as far as I trust him."

"Have you ever seen his face?"

"No," said Olin. "No doubt he is vain of his looks." And he smiled.

Sonja smiled back, and accepted Olin's offer of another cup.

"Pelides is but one of my worries," Olin confided, pouring the wine and handing it to her. "I don't understand why he fills your thoughts so much."

"My instincts seldom betray me, Olin. I sense something strange about him."

"No doubt. No doubt." He watched Sonja as she tilted her head and drank the wine, admiring the cut of her features, admiring the way she held herself, with all the confident pride of any officer of his ranks. "No doubt . . ." he repeated, moving again for his chair. He sat, and was about to continue, when a guard entered the tent and bowed low, saluting.

"What is it?"

"The mercenaries, sir. A number of their leaders ask for an audience."

Olin frowned. "Very well." He shot a glance at Sonja

as his guard exited. "I feared this—the fools."

He rose and went out, Sonja following him. Beyond the campfires of Olin's commanders stood the leaders of a number of the mercenary crews—four of them, large men, sporting a motley assortment of armor and weapons. Olin stepped past his guards and moved to the front of those commanders and attendants who had collected before his tent.

"What is all this?"

"Lord Olin," said one of the mercenary chiefs, "our men have decided they want no more of fighting for you. We're pulling out."

Olin did not deign to respond—he held the chieftain's eyes with a stern and steady gaze, forcing the rogue to bluster, "We want no more of fighting against magicians and sorcery, Lord Olin. It's as simple as that."

Olin stared at their rough and bearded faces that gleamed with sweat in the light of the campfires. "You all agreed to fight for me when you signed up. You knew the terms of service. I agreed to pay you when we reached—"

"Aye, and that's the other thing," spoke up another of the mercenaries. "We want to be paid for our day's fighting."

Lord Olin stiffened and stood tall, his dark eyes blazing with anger. "You'll be paid when we reach Suthad—and you'll fight in this army as you signed on to do!"

"You can't order us around!" howled a third of the brutish chieftains. "We agreed to fight for you—for gold. Now we're not going to fight anymore, but for what fighting we've done, we want our rightful pay. We know you have gold in that tent!"

Olin's lips curled back and a deep growl sounded from his throat. For the first time, Sonja saw him furious—not with battle lust but ready to slay nonetheless, out of honest anger.

"You *dogs!*" he roared. "For breaking your word,

you don't even deserve your lives—but *those* I'll give you, for this day's fighting, and consider yourselves lucky. No gold for traitors!"

One of the chiefs stepped forward; Olin's guards moved close to him, hemming in their commander.

"We've fought, and we want our pay!" he growled angrily.

"I'll pay you in steel!" Olin shot back, stepping ahead. The muscles of his back bunched, the thews on his arms swelled with tension as he confronted the mercenary. "You'll be paid in gold if you march with me to Suthad. Or if you want payment in death, then stand against me—now!"

The mercenary glared in fury but said nothing.

"Very well," said Olin. "Then you have a third alternative. You may ride out of camp now with your craven skins still intact. How many cowardly swine do you command?"

The mercenary's features contorted with anger but he backed down, muttering: "Five hundred . . ."

"Then take your five hundred and ride to Hell!"

But another of the rogues stepped ahead, hand lifting to his sword pommel. "*Gold* is what we—"

Olin faced him, a grim smile on his lips. "*Draw* that sword, if you dare!"

The mercenary paused.

"Draw it! My face will be the last you'll ever look upon. Draw that sword and be paid in steel, damn you!"

The mercenary relinquished his grip on the sword.

"Then get out of here," Olin hissed. "Take your dogs and go. Or if you've a mind to fight for your loot, then face the true fighting men down there!" He threw out a hand in a gesture that encompassed the valley below his tents, where thousands of campfires glowed like animal eyes in the night. "Begone!"

They went. Angry and sullen, they backed down the slope, not daring to turn their backs on Olin, thinking him to be of the same character as they. Then they were gone, and within a few moments there came the thunder of riot down below, as their troops howled for their premature rewards.

Olin called to his trumpeter: "Sound the ready!"

Immediately the harsh blare rang out, and immediately Olin's soldiers sprang to the alert; the sounds of thousands of swords and thousands of boots drifted up the hill. And the mercenaries, suddenly thinking better of their intentions, ceased their tumult and began to mount up. In a short time they were gone from the camp and were skulking away in the darkness.

Olin waited as the last thunder of their hoofbeats receded into the distance, waited until his camp had returned to calmness again. Then he turned again to make for his tent.

"The newer recruits are still with us," Pelides commented to him in a muffled tone, "but they have been made restive by these doings."

"Aye," Olin agreed. "I feared as much. No doubt more of the hearties will turn tail when they get a taste of real fighting. What cravens serve me!"

He turned and went inside.

Sonja stood where she was. She watched Pelides as he walked away, presumably to retire also for the night. Gradually the tenseness in the camp subsided, and Sonja began to consider where she might sleep. Her mount was tethered farther down the slope, under the protection of a tall tree surrounded by a thicket, and she herself preferred the safety of sleeping among trees when they were available.

Walking away from the area of Olin's tents and those of his commanders, she felt the fresh calm of the night overtake her. It was a pleasant night. A slight breeze sighed, while nightbirds called and crickets chirped. Down in the valley men were grouped in loose knots about their fires, the sounds of their conversation and lusty singing lifting up to the clear stars overhead. Sonja paused and remarked those stars, sensing their solitude and distance, feeling the vast immensity of the skies as an almost tangible thing. And as she watched the sky and the fire-dotted field below, her glance fell to the south. Far out upon the open plains, so distant that they were nearly lost on the hazy horizon, she spotted more yellow lights. Campfires.

Mercenaries—?

"Sonja."

She turned, alert, catlike, to meet Allas. Tias was on his arm.

Allas grinned at Sonja as he walked up to her. "A pleasant night, Sonja, is it not?"

"Aye."

"And what think you of the desertion?"

Sonja did not reply but pointed to the south. "Look there, Allas. Do you see those lights?"

He automatically put his hand to his forehead, as if shielding his eyes from a noonday glare. "Aye," he said slowly. "Campfires."

"Who could they be?"

"The mercenaries, probably. Or a caravan of travelers."

That answer did not satisfy Sonja. "No. No, for some reason I—"

But she was cut short by the sound of someone else approaching. Sonja turned, and saw Pelides's mask, like a black hole in the starlight, perched eerily atop his dark-cloaked form.

"Do you enjoy the night?" he asked hollowly. "Or are we plotting strategies?" He seemed to laugh; the sound rang grotesquely from within his helmet.

"Look there, Pelides," said Allas. "There are lights on the southern horizon."

Pelides seemed barely to glance in their direction. "What does it matter?" he said shortly.

"Sonja thinks it important."

"And what does Sonja think they are?" Pelides asked Allas.

Sonja looked at Pelides, but did not answer. Slowly Pelides moved off, continuing his walk.

Allas looked after him and shook his head. "A strange man," he whispered. "Would that I could see beneath that mask. How terrible can it be? A mask cannot truly hide anything, save a face."

"Aye," Sonja replied, thinking that Allas had a good way with words. "Aye, Allas. And I think that that is all he will hide from us. Just his face. The rest will come out."

She looked again to the south, then bade Allas and Tias good-night and walked towards the thicket where her horse and a night's rest awaited her.

Chapter 4

In Suthad

Olin's army moved out the next day at dawn—four and a half thousand men, counting both soldiers and mercenaries—heading north for Suthad. The morning was bright and clear, as calm and refreshing as yesterday's morning had been before storm clouds and sorcery had swept down on the fields.

The troops proceeded in tight ranks with Olin's commanders at the lead of their men, and the mercenary chiefs—those that had not deserted—riding at the head of their rough companies. Som, with two swords now hanging from his belt, cantered beside Allas and Tias. Duke Pelides rode at the head of the line, to the left of Lord Olin; Sonja, at Olin's request, rode on his right.

Som grinned. "I think our leader has taken a liking to Sonja," he muttered.

Tias looked at him, concern in her eyes. She brushed back a wayward strand of her dark hair and glanced at Allas. He had heard. He looked over to Som questioningly, then broke into a grin himself.

"Aye," he said. "And who could blame him? She's as good a soldier as he, probably, and pleasing to look on as well."

Som pursed his lips, winked at Tias, and studied the day as he bobbed in his saddle.

Lord Olin, squinting in the brilliant early sunlight,

found comfort in the noise of his army behind him. He glanced back often, pride swelling in his breast to see the long lines trailing far behind, dipping and moving and following over grassy fields and through glens, down and over hillocks. An army—a strong army. An army to retake his city and defeat sorcery.

He watched the road ahead, raised a gloved hand, and pointed to the northwest.

"Suthad," he told Sonja, "lies beyond that forest."

"Will we make the forest by tonight?"

"Easily. We'll make camp there. And by this time tomorrow, we'll see Suthad easily on the horizon." An eagerness, and a bitterness, seemed to rise in his voice as he said it.

Sonja relaxed. Pelides rode near them, as unconversational as ever. He might have been a statue, carved to fit onto his saddle, for all the vitality he exhibited this morning—lost, Sonja speculated, in his own brooding thoughts.

Sonja vowed not to worry about Pelides, and took instead to admiring the landscape—greener and brighter than the landscapes of her homeland in Hyrkania, which was a region of gray and brown fields and tall mountains, sharp cliffs, and deep lakes. Hyrkania was a vast and limitless land, it seemed, stretching on forever from one horizon to another. Koth was brighter, bluer and somehow, it seemed, younger than Hyrkania, where age, maturity, and toughness, were inherent in the very soil of the earth and the people who worked it.

"Sonja, why do you travel?" Olin asked. "What made you put on the sword and leave your homeland to join wars in other lands?"

"Do you think it unbecoming a woman, Olin?" Always that was the first thought in her mind, those the first words on her lips, whenever anyone asked. A woman with a sword . . .

"Not unbecoming, no." Olin smiled. "But—curious. Interesting. Every traveler has a tale to tell, every wanderer has a wealth of experiences behind him. It can make for passing the time on a long journey."

Sonja frowned—then threw back her head so that her rich red hair, windblown and wild, tumbled down her back. "My family in Hyrkania was killed when I was a much younger woman," she told Olin. "All of them were slain, but I escaped. My father had been a mercenary and a swordsman, one of the finest fighters of his day. He taught me the rudiments of swordsmanship, and after his death I learned to live by the sword, as he had."

How many times had she told that story? How many times had she joined this or that army, and explained succinctly her reasons for wearing sword and armor. *My father was a soldier. I learned the sword from him* . . . .

It made more sense than what had really happened . . . .

The road through the field dipped down into a valley. Sonja watched the trail as her mount rocked monotonously, and it reminded her of the many roads she had followed already in her career as a wanderer, and the many more she would doubtless follow tomorrow, and the day after, and . . .

I learned swordsmanship from my father . . . .

"Try not to struggle, Red-hair! You might find yourself *enjoying* it, wench!"

Pain. Searing, tearing pain. The walls of the house that had held so much love transfigured into a blurred chaos of mists and tears and shadows. The shadows—and the *face*. Through all of it, the face. Hideous . . .

The long, tortured sobbing and the feeling of clinging filth. The hideous face—skull-square, grinning, eyes dancing and laughing and black as swamp fevers—filling the darkness behind her closed eyes. The soft laughter, when she cried out in pain and in horror.

And then he had left. Sonja wondered why he hadn't stabbed her, why he hadn't killed her as he had her father and mother and brothers.

He should have killed her.

But, instead: "This place *stinks,* Horvak. Set the torch to it!"

The flames had finally roused her. Beyond the sounds of crackling wood and the engulfing heat, beyond the waves of black tarry smoke that boiled into the house, she seemed to hear hoofbeats, far away, receding into the distance.

Them. The mercenaries. The *face.*

Red-hair. Blood-hair. *Flame-hair.*

She had wrapped herself in soiled blankets and staggered from the inferno that had once been her home. She had run dizzily, tripping, stumbling as walls of burning fire sought to engulf her, as thick coils of smoke sought to devour her—as a murky sea of faces, all hideous, laughed at her from the flames and smoke and sought to pull her down again and cover her again with filth and breath and eyes and hands and sweat and burning pain and hatred.

But then she had found herself outside. The night had not been cool, but smoky and ashy and bitter with the odor of charred corpses. She had run, falling, once, twice, gaining her feet. And still she had run, until she had put the flames and the heat far behind her. Until she could run no more. Until . . .

She had found herself among the trees, among the tumbled stones of the ruin where she had played and dreamed so often as a child, talking and praying to gods and beings of her own imagining. And then she had seen it. Something lit up her vision with a blue light—not flames—and for an instant she feared it was the flash of an upraised sword. She looked up.

It was above her, high against the stars. A gleaming figure. A goddess. A vision.

Something.

Sonja cringed, and in that moment her agony was blotted out by an icy terror of the unknown.

But—

"You have suffered deeply, Sonja. Know now that there is *strength* born in suffering."

Her terror abated somewhat. There was a dazzling and humming in the air above her. What was it? What could it be—a vision of madness? Had she died in that fire—was she confronting her own spirit? Could it be a god?

"This strength is your own, Sonja, and has ever dwelt within you. But only *now* has it been awakened."

It *must* be a god! What else could appear so miraculously? Shaped like neither man nor woman, yet embracing all the strength and beauty of both, the vision spoke to Sonja and she heard soft music and deep thunder.

"If you but have the will, Sonja, you may use your strength to make the world your home. You may become a wanderer, the equal of any man or woman you meet."

A god—or herself? It seemed now as if this vision, human and more than human, male and female, lit a soulful light within her own breast, as well as transfiguring the night around her with its blue glowing effulgence.

"But first you must make a *vow* to me, Sonja. You must never allow yourself to be *loved* by another man—"

Sonja's heart beat. The pain in her seemed to reawaken afresh. She would make the vow!

"—unless he has bested you in *fair* battle—"

She would make the vow! Hard anger and the desire for vengeance welled up within her young heart.

"—something *no* man is like to do after this day!"

She would make the vow!

The specter seemed to loom closer; its blue light swept upon Sonja and she felt herself chill and sweat with fear and wonder and terror.

"Do you so vow, Sonja?"

"Y-yes . . ."

Yet why should she fear? Her terror bled from her as

she stared up at the wonderful vision. This god was a gift. Its vow was a gift. Did it not seem to fulfill her own desperate longings? Did she not seem to hear a secret voice—her own—deep within the wells of her being on this dark night, as she crouched before this stark being that filled her with warmth and strength and pride?

"Yes! With all my heart—with all my *soul—I do so vow!"*

How old had she been? How young had she been? A stripling child on the borders of a wild and reckless land, on the borders of a wild and reckless Fate?

The vision had reached down, then, and there was an instant of shimmering ice, flickering fire, coursing deep into Sonja's being as the ethereal blade touched her, tapped her shoulder. And the world went white and blue and orange and red.

Then the vision was gone.

The night was cold and damp with the foreign reek of smoke and burning wood and charred human flesh in it.

There was a sound in the brush behind her.

Sonja stood up, naked and shivering in the darkness. She took the soiled blanket and wrapped it tightly around her. It warmed her. And then she was warm with fury, warmed by the hot anger in her blood, seized with the fire of her own temper and longing for vengeance.

It was one of the mercenaries, coming through the brush, returning for that which his nameless leader had forbidden.

The brush parted. A panting, dark face with hard eyes appeared like a sudden growth through the tangle. The man laughed gutterally. "Well, it sometimes pays to be a straggler, I see."

Sonja stood up.

"Take heart, Red-hair. I'll thrill you more than our captain did."

She reached for her father's sword. It seemed natural to her that it should be there. Yet she could not remember . . . . Had she brought it with her, in the madness and the exertion of her flight? Or—?

She lifted her father's sword as if it weighed no more than a twig—the same sword she had not been able to lift in her defense only a short time ago.

The mercenary paused. "Take care, wench."

The blade was as light and welcome in her hand as a new limb. Sonja felt the true weight of it, seemed to sense every notch and bloodstain along its heavy blade. With the feel of that weapon in her fist she felt once again all the power of the vision seep into her heart and fill her body with strength.

The mercenary seemed to think better of his plan. He looked behind Sonja, looked away, glanced here and there as if expecting reinforcements.

"Tarim!" he muttered in a low curse.

And Sonja leapt at him. "Pig! Tarim *damn your soul!*"

The mercenary bounded back, yanked free his own blade, met Sonja's rush—it was as if he had appeared to test her vow.

The mercenary, overcoming his surprise, rallied to the attack. To him it was unthinkable that so hardy a rogue as he, who had sent so many foes to their doom, should now need to battle a stripling girl who but moments ago had been a whimpering bundle of tears and bruises, and had seemed easy prey. The fact angered him.

The swords clashed ringingly in the moonlit glade. The scrape and crunch of bootsteps, the panting of the mercenary's breath sounded through the night. Birds and small animals crouched in hushed silence, and the nighttime forest itself seemed to be watching and listening for the outcome of this strange match.

Sonja wielded her sword effortlessly, as though she had been born to wield it, born to be a warrior with the best of men. And the worst.

The mercenary drew back, gasping. Spit drooled down his beard. Surprise, anger, fear registered in his haunted eyes. "It cannot *be!*" he muttered,then lunged again with a swiftness born of desperation—and Sonja's blade slid through his chest, his momentum carrying him down the full length of the steel blade to the hilt.

A savage thrust, learned by watching her father, long-practiced under cover of darkness. Or was it, perhaps, a skill granted her by a vision?

Quickly she withdrew the blade and leaped back, on guard. The mercenary was clutching at a tree branch to keep from falling, too astonished as yet to realize that he was a dead man. His lips, writhing and twisting in his final spasm, almost seemed to smile in surprise. He stood a moment, staring at Sonja, surprise a mask on his face, until his knees buckled. His breath bubbled, his face twisted in agony. Blood gushed from his great wound.

And Sonja had felt—*exhilaration.*

"—did you?" Olin asked.

"What?" Sonja looked at him sharply.

Olin lifted his brows. "You've been daydreaming," he said. "I asked you if you heard anything I've been saying."

He noticed the sweat on Sonja's brow, the tension that had gripped her momentarily, the expression on her face—hatred, anger and—

"Aye, I *did* daydream," she told Olin, forcing a laugh until she found herself again.

"Were you thinking of your father?"

She looked at him. Olin's voice was quiet—caring. Sonja felt her eyes blur, remembering. "Yes," she said, looking away from Olin, staring at the road, shaking the hair from her eyes. "Yes. My father?"

"Is that his sword you carry?"

Sonja nodded. "Yes."

"Fine Hyrkanian steel," Olin commented. "Fine steel."

They reached the forest by late dusk, and camped there. The night sky was clear and cloudless and very warm; the high stars beamed down and wove broken silvery patterns on the mossy woodland floor. And the feeling of dread, the subtle influence of wizardry or dark fate that had accompanied the army during its march, seemed somehow to have lifted or evaporated.

It was inexplicable, yet Sonja felt it, as did Olin and the others of his retinue. While the soldiers pitched their tents, built their fires and posted sentries, Olin paced the forest uneasily, as if trying to sniff something in the atmosphere.

"Do you feel it?" he asked Duke Pelides, as Sonja stood by and overheard.

"A veil has lifted," came the iron voice, hollow and deep. "Or a doorway opened."

Olin looked beyond the light fringe of forest, searching for Suthad in the night. "It lies there," he said, "though we can't see it. No lights—no life—" He turned to Pelides and barked suddenly in an angry, urgent tone: "What has he done, Pelides? *What has he done?"*

Pelides did not answer.

"I can't see Suthad. Has he *destroyed* it utterly?" Rage shook in Olin's voice; his arms knotted, his hands clenched.

"He is not gone," said Pelides somberly.

"It is a trap—"

Pelides shrugged. "I think not. I know the feeling from before. Asroth is still here. He has merely drawn a coverlet over himself. His presence on the land may be lightened, but he and his sorcery remain." His words, heavy and ominous, carried the conviction of a man bathed in the fires of experience.

Olin walked off, to be by himself, to think and ponder and rage in silence. But Sonja, as she watched Olin vanish into the nighted wood, turned to Pelides.

"It feels as if the very clouds have lifted," she said. "Are you so certain Asroth remains?"

Pelides laughed hollowly. "Asroth can control even your senses. When it grows quiet without, be sure there is tumult within."

He turned on his heel and left. Sonja watched him go, pondering. The night was clear, the stars bright, their light almost as brilliant as sunlit dew droplets.

As brilliant as the droplets, she reminded herself, which had glistened under the sun only two days past, before the storm of winged ones . . . .

They sighted Suthad at midmorning next day.

It sat atop a high hill, surrounded by thin woods and a sea of rich pasture and cropland. Strong-walled, stark and alone, the city emitted no personality or aura to the approaching ranks.

"It is as we left it," said Olin. "Just as desolate . . ."

Sonja felt the tension and anxiety in the man as he crouched forward in his saddle, hands knotted on the reins, head craned toward the city, alert for any sign of sorcerous treachery. The morning was calm. The skies above were a clear azure and no birds flew. All around were the signs of fields abandoned—plows left in mid-furrow, hoes and planting sticks left where they had fallen.

"We rode this route when we left," Olin told Sonja. "Fighting ghosts all the way to the woodland . . . ."

Far off to the west, quite abruptly, a sudden low rumble of thunder reverberated, like a dragon awakening and stretching after a long slumber. Allas, riding close behind Olin and Pelides, commented absently: "A storm."

Olin shook his head, and Pelides, for some reason stirred by the comment, turned back to look at Allas and chuckled hollowly. Allas felt like a fool, to be so laughed at over something so minor.

The thunder rumbled once more, low in the west, as if to suggest to Allas that it was *not* a storm. The young warrior turned to Tias, and her eyes looked through him; she touched a light finger to his arm.

Asroth . . .

His legions waited, that was certain. But were they

within the city, or far to the west? Olin urged his horse ahead, until he rode well in advance of Pelides and Sonja and Allas. The lord of Suthad searched the landscape in all directions, scanning hill and field and farmland for some sign of ambush by Asroth's sorcerous forces.

Still the wizard remained in hiding, lying in wait.

Sonja grew more tense as they gradually approached the walled city; sweat trickled beneath her light mail. Suthad was no longer distant but lay clear before her, faceless, speechless; no figure on its walls, no noise carrying from its gates. Suthad was desecrated, dead. In Sonja's expectancy of attack at any moment, she imagined shudderings under the earth, storms in the skies, weird winds and ghostly eyes from somewhere . . . .

Yet there was no phantasm to meet their advance, no Asroth on the city walls with arms gesturing and robes flowing; no tide of sorcerous legions or swarming, unreal hosts to suddenly catapult upon them and meet steel sword with occult lightning. No monsters. No ghosts. No long-winded incantations to Hell. No devil in dark robes.

Only a city, its southern gates open—just as Olin and his company had left them in their bitter retreat many days before.

Olin called a halt as his forces reached the walls. He cantered ahead, sword drawn. Sonja waited beside Pelides; her horse snorted at something on the wind. She looked intently at the ebon helm, but Pelides continued to stare straight ahead, eyes on Olin.

Every moment Sonja expected a horror to descend upon Olin. Yet he rode, vigilant, to Suthad's gates, entered the city, disappeared behind the stone wall, and returned within a few heartbeats, signaling the army to advance. Horns blared and the low throb of thousands of horses' hooves welled toward Suthad, slow-paced and unwarlike.

"Asroth is not here," Olin announced to Pelides.

"Be not so certain."

"No, Pelides. No. He would have made his presence known to us."

"A trap," Sonja said.

Olin shrugged. "I don't think so. Perhaps he found what he came for. Perhaps our battle was for naught, our hired swords for naught—"

The thousands of troops and mercenaries followed his lead into the empty city. Everywhere, to their eye, was the sign of despoilment. The city, however, was not so vacant as Olin had presumed; there were still survivors left—old people, children, wounded soldiers; all with the stare of madness in their eyes, the taint of living death in their gestures. They sat, these few of Suthad's once thriving citizenry, upon the bricks of dried wells, on stone or wooden benches of the courtyards and squares. Old men sat clustered in gray knots, huddled together like frightened insects, One old woman tottered over the cobbles with a hand outstretched to the ground, clucking and chirping to attract nonexistent chickens with a handful of imaginary grain. Children crouched in corners, or in the limbs of small garden trees, growling, spitting, snarling at the passing warriors—wholly regressed, and reduced to madness. Soldiers, zombielike, wandered about with broken weapons.

"Are these—*all*—that have *survived?*" Olin whispered, emotion choking his voice. He swallowed thickly, and his hands shuddered with the reins. "To see Suthad, reduced to this—"

He turned his mount abruptly and led the way toward the central square. One of his commanders cantered up to him, saluted and spoke:

"I fear the mercenaries are grumbling, my lord. They expected battle, and there is none. Now they wonder if they're going to be paid at all."

"Watch them," Olin replied grimly. "They'll want loot. Let them steal the stores from some of the ruined buildings, but they must not harm the survivors."

"Aye, my lord."

Allas, trotting near Sonja, pointed out the steep rotunda of a polished dome just ahead of them. "There, Sonja—that is the city's palace."

Sonja was regarding the city wonderingly, disturbed. It was so utterly ruined. "How many people did Suthad once contain?" she asked Allas.

"Two hundred thousand." He wiped his forehead with his hand. "Two hundred thousand. And Asroth wiped them out in less than a day."

"He *slew* two hundred thousand people?"

Allas shook his head sorrowfully. "No. Most of them fled. While we fought his phantoms, our populace fled shrieking out the gates. And they'll never return, I fear. This land is cursed now."

Dead bodies, stinking, lay sprawled in the central square before the city palace. Packs of wild dogs moved around them. Hundreds of dead guards in dull armor had fallen in contorted positions. Swarms of insects hummed in the air, casting shadows like clouds. A few gray faces, gaunt and strained and frightened, peered out through windows and stared, then pulled inward to the shadows once more.

Olin dismounted before the open stairs of the palace. Behind him his retinue stopped, and his soldiers; but the mercenaries began to wander off, ranging through the wrecked streets and alleys at their leisure. The commanders passed the word to every soldier to keep alert and mark the temper of the mercenaries.

Though apparently the danger was gone, Olin drew his sword and slowly took the steps to the front portals of his palace. Sonja and Pelides followed him, and after them Allas, Tias, Som, and a number of others. Olin's senses tingled. Though no host of doom had met his army's approach, Asroth might still suddenly burst from the palace doors and cut him down as he advanced. Or there might be a trap awaiting him just inside. He reached the last step, crossed the portico, heaved open the doors that stood ajar—

Inside was dust and gloom and shadows—but no sorcerous army.

Olin's footfalls echoed as he slowly walked down the main corridor. The others followed him. There were more corpses, but otherwise this palace of marble and brick and gold stood deserted, untouched—as solemn and soundless as a tomb. Olin passed beneath the heights of the arched ceiling, walked down the hallway flanked by gigantic columns carved with glyphs and cartouches. He passed open antechambers and audience halls and feasting chambers, and came finally to the end of the corridor and his throne room.

Here he had dealt justice, declared wars, met with foreign ambassadors. Here was the heart of his city. Here was the core of his being—of his people, his realm, his army.

It was ruined. His throne had been toppled and lay shattered, chunks of stone and splinters of wood, littering the stairs of the dais and the flagstones of the floor. The sturdy tables and seats of his councillors were blasted and strewn in all directions. Pillars had been scarred, by flame or by sorcery; one stood, its middle section gaping starkly, cut in half.

The decaying limbs, men in armor who had fallen during the battle still lay as they had dropped—gray, dull, awkward, flesh rotting, and vermin crawling upon them. Arrases and hanging portraits had been torn down and burned. Incense braziers and food dishes lay battered and ruined. In the center of the chamber was a large dark circle, as if something round had been charred there. Or perhaps something had come up *through* the floor—something magical and immaterial. Perhaps Asroth had held council with monsters here, or had tortured those still alive in Suthad, or had turned the throne room into a stable for carrion from some nether plane. . . .

Olin silently walked toward his shattered throne. His fist tensed on the pommel of his sword, his muscles rippled, the veins stood out on his neck and forehead. Behind him the others held their breaths, hushed.

He stopped at the foot of the crumbled dais steps, staring at the devastation. Sweat beaded his face. At his boot was a tarnished bronze dish. He kicked it. It rang hollowly, clanged and rolled away with jarring spirals of sound.

"Where is he?"

His voice was hardly more than a whisper, but in that still room it carried like a monstrous clap of thunder.

"Where is he gone?"

Olin took a deep breath, turned and faced Pelides and the others. His sword trembled in his fist, as if straining for Asroth's heart, to murder him.

Tias cringed closer to Allas, frightened at this volcanic wrath in Lord Olin, frightened that it would erupt into the fury of Hell.

"Where is he gone, Pelides? Where is *Asroth?"*

The name echoed hollowly in the chamber. Pelides shook his ebon head once.

With a cry of outrage Olin turned on his heel and brought down his sword. An oaken chair, thick and hard, flew apart under the force of that angry blow. He cursed the names of Hyborian and Shemitish gods, then threw back his head and howled to the ceiling: *"Where are you, you foul—!"*

Then he caught himself. With an effort of iron will Olin checked his rage and brought it under control.

"This does no good," he panted, "to rant and rave and carry on. What else should I have expected? Did we not all suspect in advance that Asroth would have left Suthad in such a state of ruin?"

Calmer now, Olin approached his retinue, faced Pelides. "You were wrong—he is not here. He has fled. Did he find what he came for?"

"I know not."

"You knew him better than anyone."

"That counts for little now. But you may be sure he has not done with us."

"No. No." Olin looked around him, an animal at bay,

trembling with eagerness to kill, to rend whomever was responsible for his wounds. "No, he is not here. My sword would sense it."

"I cannot advise you," Pelides said.

Olin's eyes lit with new wrath at that fatalistic comment; but he checked himself again, snarled, and surveyed his throne room. "Find him," he announced. "Question everyone still alive in the city, search every building. Someone surely saw him go. Where would he have gone, Pelides?" He faced Pelides again. "Back to his fortress?"

Pelides shrugged.

Sonja wondered whether Pelides could be deliberately playing stupid. Somehow she felt that he knew more than he said. She was growing anxious; nothing could be accomplished here, listening to this arguing and speculating. Quietly she slipped away, backing out of the throne room while Olin, as calmly as he could, decided upon what options were his, what could be done, what should be done.

She walked down the corridor and out onto the palace portico. The noonday sun was hot but a breeze was growing to lend some comfort. The army was nowhere in sight; doubtless the mercenaries had scattered throughout the city to loot, the soldiers to keep an eye on them and see they did not get out of hand. It seemed a volatile situation which Sonja did not like at all.

She looked down on the desolation of Suthad. Never had she seen so large a city so reduced. It was as if the walls and buildings were mirages, created as an illusion amidst the Kothian field, but without people, without crowds—soulless.

She heard the distant sounds of mercenaries, men on horseback shouting and yelling. In the square, there was no movement to indicate life—only a few dead bodies. The breeze caused an open window shutter to clatter dimly. A cur prowled uneasily in an alley; Sonja saw its lean shadow upon the cobbles—

Not a dog!

Sonja tensed, watched the shadow as it curved around a corner of the alley. Then a gray figure emerged behind it and walked on, away from Sonja, hugging close to the wall of a building.

Sonja stepped ahead, nerves prickling.

It was a small figure—a man, from the way he walked. He was dressed in a worn gray robe, such as priests, ascetics and sorcerers used. He seemed to pay no attention to anything around him, yet he moved furtively, as if trying to escape—from something.

Sonja hurried down the steps of the palace. *"Hold, there!"*

The figure kept on, ignoring her cry or not hearing her. She trotted across the open court. The figure passed another building and headed for another alley.

"Hold!"

The man in gray slipped into the alley, taking his shadow with him.

Sonja drew her sword and began running. She reached the alley, looked down it, saw the man in gray outlined against the rectangle of light at the opposite end.

"Hold! Are you deaf, or just a coward?" She walked toward him, wary, sword out.

The man in the gray cloak turned to face her. From the dimness of the alley his eyes glowed brilliant yellow as he stared at her, and waited.

Chapter 5

Legions from Hell

"Who are you?" demanded Sonja.

His eyes played upon her like flickering coals radiating demonic light.

"My name is Sopis."

"A Stygian name. What do you here?"

He said nothing, just stood quietly, his hands hidden in the sleeves of his gray robe. Sonja fought back a strange fear; she gripped her sword more tightly, feeling an urge to strike and slay before this man could do—what? His aura was unwholesome and his attitude one of silent but sinister defiance, as if there lurked an occult threat behind his bland facade.

Sonja stepped closer to him, fighting her unreasoning fear of his strange eyes, and commanded him in a growl: "Come along with me, Sopis."

"May I ask why?" His voice was almost without inflection.

"Because I have a sword."

"Ah!" That seemed to amuse him. Nevertheless he nodded and moved forward; Sonja let him pass, then fell in behind him, directing him out of the alley and across the square to the palace steps. The man moved along slowly with short, catlike steps, unspeaking, and seeming unconcerned with her presence, and moving exactly as he had when Sonja had first seen him.

"Up there," Sonja told him, indicating the steps to the palace portico.

Sopis said slowly: "Lord Olin is returned, then?"

"Aye, you must have seen his army. What of it?"

Sopis was silent till he reached the portico. Then he turned to face her. "Why are you so frightened of me, woman?"

"I'm not frightened—I don't trust you. Make one unnecessary move, and I'll split you."

Sopis smiled slightly. "We do not make unnecessary moves."

They crossed the portico, Sonja gripping her sword with needless tension. The man's calm confidence was making her nervous; he acted like one proceeding on his own volition rather than as a prisoner.

"Through there," said Sonja.

They entered, Sopis leading the way down the corridor. Still with sword bared, she directed him into the throne chamber. Upon entering, Sopis threw back the cowl of his gray robe and Sonja saw that his head was shaven.

Olin and his retinue had set two tables and some chairs upright during the brief time Sonja had been gone. All were now seated with elbows forward, chins propped on fists, debating. They looked up as Sopis' shadow glided into the room.

"What's this?" Olin stood up and moved forward. "Sonja? Where did you find him?"

Pelides now rose also, and then everyone else.

"I found him skulking across the square, Lord Olin. I don't like the looks of him."

"Come forward, man," commanded Olin. "You're a Stygian, by your appearance. What are you doing here. What's your name?"

"I am Sopis!" The man bowed jerkily, as if in mock deference. "True, I am Stygian."

Olin studied him intently, then glanced for a moment at Sonja who still stood behind the man with naked steel. "And what are you doing here?"

"I entered here when your army had gone, Lord Olin," said the Stygian.

"Why?" The heavy tone of Olin's voice threatened violence. "Are you in league with Asroth?"

"In league with Asroth?" Sopis smiled darkly. "Lord Olin, Asroth is our deadly enemy."

"Our?" Olin walked forward, met Sopis's stare eye for eye. Pelides, too, approached more closely.

"There are others of my order, Lord Olin. Asroth is our enemy—he has tampered with things even he knows not the magnitude of. That is why I followed him here."

"And where are your fellows?"

Sopis did not reply, though his yellow eyes burned into Olin's.

"Where has Asroth gone? Tell me!"

Still Sopis did not answer.

"You'll tell me what I want to know," Olin threatened, "or I'll find the means to make you!"

Sopis shook his head. "Torture, Lord Olin? That is unbecoming a man with so wide a reputation for justice and leniency."

"Asroth has destroyed my city and my people," Olin answered him sternly. "If you know anything about it, you will tell me now."

Sopis did not answer. He simply stood, Olin and Pelides before him, Sonja behind, his hands concealed in his sleeves, his stance unaggressive, his attitude one of mild noncompliance.

Pelides grated in his hollow, iron voice: "Put him to the torture, Olin. He must know *something.*"

The tone of that remark caught Sonja's attention—an inflection of anxiousness or worry in Pelides's voice. Was he afraid of Sopis? Or was there something between them? She trusted Pelides no more than she did Sopis. . . .

A sudden commotion from outside interrupted them. Olin turned to Allas. "What's going on out there?"

At that instant a soldier entered. "Lord Olin," he cried. "It's the mercenaries—they've raised sword against our soldiers!"

"What?"

It's true," said Allas, who had hurried to an open window and looked out. "There's riot in the streets."

Olin ran to the window, gripped the stone sill fiercely. In the central square and down every visible avenue there was battling between the armored troops of Suthad's standard and the mounted mercenaries. Horses galloped, crowds of men surged against one another with steel clashing. Cries of the wounded suddenly rose to an alarming volume as the tumult escalated.

Olin swore furiously and ran from the throne chamber, calling his attendants to follow. Tias moved to Allas; together they stared out the window, Duke Pelides behind them, while others in the room crowded at other sills. Som, after taking one quick glance, voiced an oath and drew his two swords in a silvery blur of steel, then rushed out after Olin.

Sonja kept her eye on Sopis. The Stygian, still calm, looked back at her, his eyes glowing with an ironic amusement. He walked to one of the vacated tables and helped himself to some wine. Sonja watched him narrowly, uncertain whether to continue keeping guard on the man or hurry to join the fray against the mercenaries. She glanced out the window for an instant, then turned again to the table where Sopis was drinking.

Sopis was gone.

Sonja cursed herself and hurried across the chamber. He could not possibly have left the room within the space of a heartbeat . . . . No, she reminded herself—no *normal man* could have left the room in such a space; but Sopis had. He had the smell of sorcery about him. Sonja ran out of the throne room and looked up and down the corridor, but could see no one. On impulse she took the hallway to the right, past other rooms and antechambers, deeper into the palace. Behind her, the sounds of battle dimmed. The corridor ended at a wide fork, one hall leading to the east wing of the palace, the other to the west.

Was that a shadow at the end of the western corridor? Sonja glanced in the other direction, but again followed her first impulse. Racing down the marble hall, her mail clinking, hair flying behind her, she knew that she was betraying her presence with every stride and intake of breath.

She turned a corner and saw Sopis—walking, though surely he must have flown before—farther down the corridor. She hailed him. As he had in the courtyard, Sopis again chose to ignore her. Sonja ran after him, feeling more angry and frustrated and foolish. She caught up to the Stygian as he pulled open a heavy door at the end of a short side hall and began to mount a series of steps.

"Where do you think you're going, Sopis?"

"That is not your concern."

"You're coming back with me!"

"We think not."

"Tarim's blood!" Sonja cursed, grabbing his arm.

Sopis halted, turned fluidly, and although Sonja had clutched him tightly he slipped instantly and effortlessly through her fingers.

"Who *are* you, and what are you *doing* here?" Sonja demanded, the last of her patience gone. "Tell me, Stygian, or—!" She lifted her sword till its point barely touched his throat.

"Very well," said Sopis, still seeming wholly unalarmed. "I'll tell you—though truly it is none of your concern, Red Sonja."

When had she told him her name? Had he overheard it in the throne chamber?

"We are here to thwart Asroth," Sopis told her, his voice level and calm. "Now, let me pass."

"Then Asroth is here?"

Sopis did not answer.

Sonja pressed her sword point to the flesh of his neck,

indenting the skin; the Stygian's eyes glowed more brightly. Then his hand brushed away the steel, and a tingling shock passed down the blade and through the pommel into her arm.

She watched him, nerves taut . . . .

Low thunder suddenly pealed outside, for deeper than the sound of battle. Sonja glanced up the stairs to where a window faced west; from it came again the sound of thunder, the same sort of boom she had heard during the approach to Suthad.

Sopis's attitude seemed to change slightly at the sound; a touch of concern flickered in his impassive face. "Come with us, then, if you wish," he told Sonja. "But we cannot be responsible for whatever happens."

Sonja accepted the implicit threat. She nodded to the Stygian. "Lead on. But I warn you—"

"Do not warn us, Red Sonja. We face matters of importance now."

They proceeded up the stairs, Sonja as near to Sopis as his shadow. Thunder continued to rumble outside, otherwise the dank stairwell was as silent as a subterranean tomb. At the top of the steps Sopis opened an iron door—to more stairs which led further upward.

"Where are you going?" Sonja demanded.

"Asroth worked his most important magic in this western tower."

"And how do you know that?"

"We sense it."

He opened a gold door at the top of the second flight. Inside was a room—small and cramped, with shelves, a table, a chair and neatly piled articles of dark gramary—incense braziers, altlanors, prisms, parchments, and volumes. Carved and drawn designs on floor, walls and ceiling making mad and eerie patterns to assault a watcher's brain.

Sonja's immediate and puzzled impression was that the room had trapped her. It was insanely angled and had been deliberately built so. The floor appeared to slant downward to one corner, the ceiling to curve in a strange manner in the opposite direction. The walls were skewed. The geometry was wrong. Sonja sensed, somehow, that things—humans—forces—could be held within these angles of dementia as surely as a child could trap a dung-beetle in a wine jug.

Sopis glided to the table, whereon lay an open parchment and several rolled documents, a large crystal sphere, and an incense bowl filled with ashes. "Asroth left hurriedly," he said, bending intently over the parchment.

"When?"

"Yesterday evening."

"Why did he leave, Sopis?"

Sopis ignored the question and concentrated on the parchment. Its runic lines were archaic, of no modern language; yet the Stygian appeared to have no trouble deciphering them. And as he read he seemed to grow paler. His bony finger trembled slightly as it traced out the hieroglyphics of the scroll.

Sonja bent closer, looking down at the strange document over the Stygian's shoulder.

"Why did he leave, Sopis?" she repeated. "Did he find what he came for?"

"No."

Angered by his indifferent manner, she was about to curse and force him to pay attention again—when suddenly the man uttered a low hiss and lifted his finger quickly from the parchment, as if he had been scalded. Sonja saw that his eyes were wide with open fear.

"Sopis—what does it *say?*"

"Asroth left hurriedly—because . . ."

"What does the parchment say?"

Sopis straightened and averted his gaze from the parchment. He glared at Sonja with yellow eyes full of menace. More thunder crashed from afar; but to Sonja's ears the thunder did not seem to come from the skies.

The door of the chamber fell closed. Sonja looked at

it—had it closed of its own volition? She looked back to Sopis. The baleful glare had not left his pus hued eyes.

A strange, icy feeling trembled along Red Sonja's spine. She gripped her sword hilt more tightly. Sweat broke out on her brow. Abruptly she realized how far away she was from the others, realized, too, that Sopis was indisputably involved with the darkness. Would she have to slay him? Would she be able to?

"We will tell you why we are here. We worship a deity older by far than any god of this age. We worship Ikribu, and we are of a large cult devoted to Him—we whose duty it is to protect His worship from blasphemy. Asroth has committed sacrilege against our god."

And still the thunder, low and resounding and ever closer. Did the very walls of this high tower shudder? Sonja watched the Stygian uneasily, wondering if he meant to lull her with a tale, then suddenly strike her down.

"Asroth is not alive," Sopis continued, his eyes still streaming yellow and casting an unclear, sickly radiance upon his forehead and high cheeks. "Nor is he dead. Asroth walked this world a thousand years and more ago. Though mortal born, he became a legendary sorcerer so mighty that it seemed he meant to resurrect the dread empire of the Serpent. But he was slain, brought down by the magic of his enemies. For centuries he lay dead, his sorcery annulled, and had it not been for an error on the part of one of our Order he would be dead still."

Sonja listened, watching Sopis intently. Her conviction grew that he would never tell her this, did he not plan to kill her. Yet he seemed also, judging by his abstracted manner, to be relating this ancient tale for himself, as if to recall to mind a duty which bore on him.

"A short time ago, a wizard of our Order attempted a ritual of dark magic which was beyond him. He was blasted to utter nothingness for his audacity. Yet though we attempted to put down the forces he had unleashed, we were not entirely successful—and by the unutterable currents and eddies that control all necromantic power and intent, Asroth awakened and crawled back into this world. It is our responsibility to see that he is again destroyed."

Sonja was sweating. She tried to deny to herself that the Stygian inspired fear in her. But the effect of the weird room, the mad angles, the closeness, and the unnatural thunderstorm beyond, combined to breed instability, uncertainty, a warning of an impending torrent of horror.

"How do you intend to slay Asroth?" she asked.

Sopis held up his right hand; the sleeve fell halfway down his forearm and exposed a ring upon his middle finger. It was a very strange piece of art, large,alloyed of some golden-colored metal that appeared far brighter than gold. It scintillated with tiny gems that reflected writhing, wormy glints of light to make Sonja's balance almost fail. A ring of power, she *knew* instinctively—a device of sorcery.

"The Ring of Ikribu," Sopis proclaimed. "It was hidden here, in this city, ages ago—for Suthad is far more ancient than its Hyborian rulers suspected. Its very name is Stygian, and it was founded before the fall of Acheron. For here was first founded the revelation, and the high synagogue, of Ikribu.

"Today we who worship Him have no temples, no cities, no fixed location; we travel everywhere and revere in ruins, battle fields, caves, and graveyards. The artifacts of our worship are secreted in many locales known only to the initiated. Asroth learned that the Ring was here, in Suthad; thus he took the city. And thus we traveled hither—to keep the Ring from his hand."

Sonja glanced nervously about, at the closed door and into every twisted corner. There was no window. The increasing gale howled louder through the stone.

"Where is Asroth now?" she asked. "Is he still in Suthad?"

Sopis glanced at the parchment. "No, he is gone from here—no doubt back to his fortress. He could not find the Ring, and now he has worked further gramary to prepare a welcome for Lord Olin's army. His magic cannot harm us, however, for *we* possess the Ring now. We will live to destroy him—"

A hideously loud crash of thunder blasted directly outside the tower. Sonja started; yet Sopis only laughed dully and flourished the Ring as if it were a solid weapon.

"They come!" he crooned, his eyes like fierce beacons. *"They come*—as Asroth has commanded. But they cannot harm *me!"*

Sonja's heart thudded; she scowled and raised her sword threatingly. "Who are *they?"*

Sopis chortled.

Sonja stared at him. His attitude had become one of maniacal gloating, she knew he meant to murder her now. Thunder boomed again, lightning crackled; the walls of the tower shivered, and bricks loosened.

"Asroth set a trap!" Sopis shouted. "Olin and all his warriors are *doomed!* And *you* die—*here!"*

He gestured with the Ring. It glowed—

Sonja leaped, crouching, swinging; Sopis, laughing, slipped supplly out of the way. Then a gigantic crash made the room vibrate; Sonja's vision shook as she was thrown from her feet.

For a heartbeat she thought it was Sopis's sorcery. Then she was pelted with dust and rubble and felt herself sliding sidewise. She grabbed at the floor, heard rock and debris smash and bounce around her; a tornado whirlwind was tearing her from the floor. She gained her knees, still gripping her sword. Behind her, the wall of the tower was demolished, and through the dust and falling mortar Sonja saw other buildings, Suthad's western wall, a green-yellow sky—and *something* dark and glistening wet that just swept past the broken rim of the demolished tower wall.

Sonja rose and saw Sopis stagger against the inner wall of the room, gasping, blood coursing down his forehead where a stone or brick had cut him. The door was sundered from its hinges. Even as she heard another growl of thunder commence and felt the floor start to buckle, Sonja raced from the tower room and down the steps to the first landing.

She was thrown to her knees again as the thunder detonated. More dust fell and stones were dislodged. Behind, at the top of the stairs, she heard the absolute knell of the tower collapsing in great, harsh explosions of grinding stone and shattering timber.

And then other sounds. Rasping sounds, footfalls.

Sopis.

Sonja did not wait for him. She scrambled to her feet and continued down the stairs, even as they shuddered and cracked beneath her.

She gained the bottom of the second stairway, dashed through the door, and into the narrow corridor of the palace's western wing. She could hear Sopis behind her, coughing, cursing, and scrambling.

"Red Sonja!"

She ran until she reached the end of the corridor; the farther hallways did not appear to have yet been touched by the quakes.

"Red Sonja!"

She turned. He was injured; he staggered, holding the wall with one hand, slowly grovelling down the narrow hall.

"Sopis!" Sonja called out. "That Ring—use it. Defeat the power!"

Another upheaval pulsed up at her feet. Sopis was thrown to his belly. He cried out. Blood ran down his wounded scalp.

"*Sopis,* call—!"

The floor in the middle of the passage swelled up and erupted. Sonja was slammed back, and for an instant she thought she glimpsed enormous serpentine masses slither upward. Then the ceiling collapsed in a hammering flood of brick and dirt and stone.

The Stygian screamed.

Sonja clung to the corner where the passageways met. Thick dust and grit filled the air. Choking, she swiped at the boiling dust before her and tried to see down the passageway.

She could not see Sopis, yet she heard him groaning. Apparently he had been trapped on the other side of or beneath the fallen ceiling.

"Sopis!"

It was darker than midnight in the corridor. Sonja moved blindly toward the debris, feeling the way ahead of her with her sword.

"Sopis—!"

She came to the wall of fallen stone and brick that filled up the corridor wall to wall, with no chance of passage around it. She heard Sopis's labored breathing from the other side, gurgling, hissing. She felt at the rubble and kicked away stones, grabbed bricks and hurled them behind her.

"Sopis! Call up sorcery and stop this thing!"

"We—! They're—!" Sonja could hardly hear him. She choked again on the dust in the air.

"Sopis, listen to me!"

The floor rocked slightly beneath Sonja's feet, but it seemed to her as though the heavier earthquakes had passed. Trying to clear away rubble, she suddenly gripped something warm, soft, and wet.

"Mitra!" She instantly let go of it. It was Sopis's hand, blood-covered, with the Ring of Ikribu faintly glowing on its middle finger.

"Sopis, can you—?"

"They're—*they're here!*" he gasped painfully.

Sonja could see no more clearly now, though the dust settled and she became accustomed to the gloam. But she could hear, as the thunder died, the sounds behind the rubble.

"Sopis . . ."

"They're here!"

She heard mumbling or whispering noises, as if things without mouths were slobbering, slurping in an attempt at speech. And sounds of movement—floppings, writhings, like ropes of wet thick flesh slapping on stone; crawling, squirming nearer . . . .

Sonja heard but could not see. In dimness she could barely make out Sopis's bloody, twitching hand protruding from the shattered stone. She coughed, gasped, and wiped tears from her eyes as the swirling gravel stung her. Sopis was screaming more and more hysterically.

"They're *here—! Aya nagal ka nokomis kulum—!"*

Sonja's skin crawled. The acolyte was attempting a last protective spell, in the horrid forbidden Acheronian tongue. The Ring was *not* protecting him. Sonja heard his feet kicking on the stone. The deliberate crawling slobbering drew nearer, echoing hollowly, rumbling and sloshing against the stone just beyond the sound of Sopis's voice.

Ny harayat milak, aya nagal—Eeeyaaa!"

Sonja dug frantically, trying to tear away loose rubble. Why was she trying to save the Stygian's life when he would have taken hers? Because he was human and the Others whatever they were—from under the earth—were abominations.

"Help us! *Help! Red Son—!"*

She grabbed Sopis's hand, yanked at it as it squirmed and spasmed in a pathetic attempt at freedom.

"He-eeelpp!"

Sopis's voice cracked in sobbing ululation. Sonja heard the slapping squish on the far side of the rubble mingle with ripping, crunching breakage. Sopis's wail rose to a wild mewl of ultimate terror, then abruptly broke off.

Gristle rending—bones snapping—wet flesh slopping, scraping . . .

A dry brick fell clattering from Sonja's numb fingers. Sweat ran down her forehead, stung her eyes. The Ring of Ikribu glowed dimly on Sopis's hand.

Sonja grabbed the thing, wrestled with it, and tried to pull it free. It might protect her no more than it had Sopis, but perhaps it would defeat Asroth. Somehow.

The entire hand, dribbling blood, came free of the rubble. Gnawed bone protruded whitely from the severed limb.

Sonja tore loose the Ring, dropped it into a small pouch at her belt, grabbed her sword, and scrambled down the corridor. Munching, wet slavering, followed her from behind the charnel debris.

Red Sonja panted as she ran, as she broke clear of the corridor and its dust and damned darkness into the ill-lit hall that led to the center of the palace. The earth still rumbled, though faintly. It had ceased quaking. Did that mean They had withdrawn below ground? No, They were *above* ground now—and probably everywhere within the city, attacking and destroying Olin's soldiers and mercenaries.

She reached the central corridor. Far beyond, through the wide open front portals of the palace, she saw soldiers, mobs of them, swarming in the square. As she raced past the throne room she glanced in; only Tias was there, crouched under a table, Tias—and a fresh corpse.

Sonja ran to the girl. "What's happened?"

"Things—they came and—they—they're . . ." She was cowered beneath the table, staring straight ahead, her fingers stuck in her mouth.

"Tias!"

The girl looked up; a mad horror leaping in her eyes. *"What are they?"* she shrieked. "The—*things!"*

Sonja grabbed her by the arms and pulled her out from under the table. "In Tarim's name, girl! Come to your *senses!"* She slapped Tias's face; the girl wailed, lost her balance and fell crouching to the floor, sobbing and shaking.

"What *are* they?" she cried.

Sonja turned and left her. The lunacy was gone from

Tias's eyes; only fear remained. She would exhaust herself crying, but she would not lose her mind.

By a window lay the one body in the room—one of Olin's retainers. The soldier's face was bent back at an impossible angle, his mouth gaping, blood from his eyes drying upon his cheeks. Judging from the way his armor was buckled inward, he had been crushed to death, as if by a giant python.

Sonja turned from him and looked out the window. Roaring tidal sounds of unholy war surged from the central square, and she saw that every bit of pavement was crowded with moiling figures—thousands of men swinging swords, holding close in tight groups as they slashed at writhing, wet nightmares that curled among them. Great holes yawned amid the flagstones of the streets and alleys. Further east an entire building had collapsed; Sonja could see many carcasses trapped under the rubble; within the shell of the building knots of warriors were facing huge, black, warty tentacles; ropy feelers that reached around soldiers and pulled them into the air. To the west a line of warriors were fighting against a towering wall of convulsing, dripping limbs—obscene tentacles with huge suckers and bony horns—rearing and writhing up out of the earth like blind and mouthless serpents.

Yet the demon-spawn could be defeated, and without the will of magic. As Sonja watched, transfixed, she saw tentacles severed by many swords flailing on the ground. But the dead piled the arena of the square; lives were being lost in the sea of moving, jostling soldiers. Every moment some new warrior was lifted high above the heads of his fellows and flung, screaming, far out and away, to crash into the street or drop into one of the craters gaping in the earth.

A rasping yell rang out. A soldier, catapulted by a loathesome member, flew toward her—his body cartwheeling through the air. He arced downward, howling, arms and legs kicking helplessly, and smashed into the outside wall just beneath Sonja's window. She saw his body spurt grue as it crumpled against the stone, and slid down the side of the palace into the garden below.

Horror and red rage filled her; she whirled about, gripping her sword, and ran from the throne chamber. Behind her, Tias continued to grovel in fear on the floor, wailing for Allas.

The front portico of the palace was crowded with armed men. Two huge turgid rolls loomed erect before them as their working swords cut and brought stinking saffron ichor gushing from the rubbery flesh. Sonja fought through the press and, howling savagely, swung her sword two-handed against one of the tentacles, again and again. Yellow fluid spurted upon her and bled down her hair and face, half gagging her with its reek; but at last the appendage, hewn through by many blades, dropped flopping and spurting down the steps into the square.

The warriors cheered and bellowed, and all engaged the second thing. Sonja leapt down the stairs and hurried into the square. She saw Lord Olin before her, hacking mightily with his sword as he and a group of his men fought against a viscous pink member that was looping up from a hole in the pavement. Sonja howled a war cry and sprang to join the fray.

The earth trembled slightly, and then something gripped her violently about the hips and lifted her up. She gasped as slimy, rubbery flesh rubbed powerfully around her mail-clad breasts. Dizzied, she felt herself whipped round and round, felt the thrust of swords slicing the air near her head, saw red faces, upside down, skim past her. She heard Olin calling her name in a frenzy. Then she was brought around again and found herself briefly looking down into the square, where she glimpsed hundreds of men and swords and horses crammed and jostling and fighting the gray tentacles winding among them.

Sonja could not breathe. She struck frantically at the

thing that constricted her, felt her steel bite into its tough and turgid muscle, smelt the stench of its thick fluid. But the member only coiled tighter about her—and now a third tip of horrid limb looped about her naked waist to squeeze against her sword belt and the small pouch that hung from it—

Suddenly the thing jerked as if galvanized, and its coils loosened. Sonja was dropped lower, tilting backward so that all she saw was the sky. Behind her were the sounds of harsh voices, the clank of armor. And then other weapons hacked down near her, barely missing her, and such a reeking spray of gooey gel gushed over her that she feared she would drown.

Olin's voice came to her: "*Sonja!*"

Someone grabbed her under the arms and began to pull her from the coils of the thing that held her. She felt the defiling limb go slack but it was still hard to breathe through the stinking yellow film. She wanted to move her sword arm, but couldn't, and everywhere around her she heard chopping blades. She felt herself falling backward with no way to fight it—and then her mind went black.

Chapter 6

The Ring of Ikribu

When consciousness returned a moment or two later Sonja was on her feet, swaying, hungrily gasping in great gulps of air, reeling and leaning on someone for support. Blood surged with a tidal roar in her brain; numbness drained from her limbs to be replaced by agony; her chest and hips felt as if they had been twisted out of shape.

"She's alive," someone said.

Sonja felt the presence of a press about her. The pulsing in her ears ceased, replaced by fading sounds of war shouts and smiting swords further away. She looked up, saw Olin's grim-eyed face smiling at her, felt his firm arm supporting her. And then, charged by some violent inner reflex of battle energy, she jumped away from him and raised the sword she still clutched in her hand. Olin stood unmoving, looking at her with concern. She coughed, felt her forehead, and looked around sharply.

"It's dead," Olin told her.

She saw it—a long, smooth muscle of dappled gray, twice as thick as a man where its severed end dripped yellowish fluid. And around her, all over the square surrounding the palace dozens more of the severed, bleeding sections lay draped across and among mounds of armored corpses. Olin's army filled the streets, a sea of red, sweating faces and dripping weapons.

"Are these all that remain?" Sonja asked.

Olin nodded, pointed towards the west. The last of the things were backing down before the energetic assault of a line of thrusting swordsmen. Sonja saw knots of men severing and chopping at a half a dozen nearer tentacles while others, writhing, spraying mucus, were pulling themselves across the pavement and drawing back into the great burrows they had made through the stone and brick. Soon they were gone entirely.

They left a vision of insanity in that great square—the aftermath of yet another hellish battle against the ravaging powers of sorcery. The pavement was clogged with piles of bodies. The numbed soldiers and mercenaries who were still alive panted and growled and moved off in all directions to rest, to talk, to find some cause for it all. Immense severed tentacles of monstrous things lay fallen in tangles. The earth itself was ruptured, gaping with craters that extended down into infinite blackness—while faint, dwindling rumblings still came from underneath, as the minions of Hell retracted to whatever abyss had birthed them.

Sonja, wholly conscious again, surveyed the battlefield with revulsion. She faced Olin and the stern, exhausted men surrounding him.

"You were right, Olin—there was a trap. Asroth isn't here, but before he left he summoned these *things*—knowing that you'd come."

Olin's brows went up slightly. "You know that for a fact? I don't doubt that you learned it from that Stygian, then—he had a stink of wizardry about him. Where is he?"

"He's dead," said Sonja. "I followed him to the western wing of the palace. We found where Asroth worked his magic."

"Dead?"

"Part of the ceiling fell on him, and then he was attacked by—" She shook her head, pointed with her sword to the sundered muscles lying all about. She was about to tell Olin of the Ring, then decided against it. Not here, with every officer of his army present. But she felt for it in her pouch, suddenly worried that it might have dropped out in the melee.

She still had it.

A voice hailed her from across the court. It was Som, grinning, drenched with greenish-yellow ichor, a sword in each hand. "I hope our wizard has better sport than this for us," he growled. "One good slice slays these things."

His attempt at encouragement was lost on Olin's company. The survivors for the most part were sullen, subdued, and grim.

"I think, Som, you may find sterner work as we go on," Olin said. He turned to make his way up the corpse-cluttered stairs of the palace, when Sonja suddenly asked:

"Where is Pelides?"

"I saw him yonder," said Som, gesturing. "On the other side of that building."

"Fighting?" Olin asked.

Som shook his head. "He had his sword, Lord Olin, but he was not battling the monsters."

"Was he *running away?*" Olin asked sharply.

Som shrugged his giant's shoulders. "He did not join in the fight, Lord Olin."

Olin smote his gloved fists together in anger, glanced at Sonja, and saw a meaningful look in her eyes.

"Find him!" he ordered brusquely, addressing everyone present. Then he turned and led the way himself across the square toward the building Som had indicated.

Sonja, Som, and a few others followed him. Once past the building, Olin questioned soldiers as to whether they had noticed Duke Pelides along this way. He was directed further down the street, then across a broad boulevard towards Suthad's temple district.

"Have you seen Duke Pelides?" he asked a gruff man

with a large burn mark across one forearm.

"Aye, my lord. He just went into that temple over there."

Olin nodded and went on.

"Lord Olin—wait."

He turned and faced the man.

"Where do we go now, my lord?" Despite his rough face and his soldier's manner the fellow sounded concerned, almost dismal, at the prospect of future battles like the one he had just survived.

"We're going to find Asroth," Olin told him, "and send him back to Hell."

The soldier smiled wearily, not convinced.

Olin continued on, entered the temple with Sonja and Som close behind him.

The structure was abandoned, and evidently had been centuries before Asroth had ever entered the city. None in Suthad worshiped here, and none could remember to what deity the temple had originally been raised. There were other such in Suthad, and in every old city, marking the progression and decline of public interest in various gods and goddesses.

The building was not large. It was rectangular, with pillars lined along the walls, benches set about, and at the far end an altar stone and a statue of some bestial creature.

And Pelides, obscured by the enclosed half-lit dimness, his back to Olin and his companions, was rummaging through all the effects of worship behind the alter.

"*Pelides!*" Olin's voice rang out and echoed from the high stone roof.

Slowly Pelides turned about to face him. He stood where he was, ebon head held high, and waited for Olin to approach.

Olin stepped up to the opposite side of the altar. "What are you doing here, Pelides?" His voice was stern, measured, insinuating.

"Searching." His words rang hollowly, metallically in the empty temple.

"For what, Pelides?"

Pelides stood silent, seeming to ponder.

"Tell me, Pelides. Has it to do with Asroth?"

Pelides's voice, bitter but proud, sounded clear and level. "It is time that you learn why Asroth attacked Suthad."

Olin watched him narrowly.

"I came to Suthad to warn you that Asroth was about to descend on your city. He was searching for a weapon of sorcerous power by means of which he might control great forces."

"And what, Pelides, *is* this weapon of power?"

"A ring. The Ring of Ikribu."

Sonja, standing at the bottom of the steps, managed not to show her reaction. Events were now falling into order. Pelides, too, wanted the Ring. Again she felt for it in her pouch, found it resting there securely.

Som leaned toward her and whispered: "I'm thinking Pelides may be a sorcerer, too."

"No, I don't think so, Som—I have the feeling he's trying to protect himself . . . ."

Olin stepped around the altar. "Tell me about this Ring, Pelides."

Pelides sighed, his breath sounding hoarse from behind his mask. He turned his back to Olin, as if ruminating, then clenched his fists and placed them on the altar stone. "It is old," Pelides said. "Ikribu is a god of antiquity—an evil god. And the Ring has power to bring such a plague of death and madness upon the lands, that—"

He stopped abruptly, turned toward Olin, who met Pelides's iron visage with a stance of stern command.

"My life is a shambles," Pelides confessed in a prideful tone. "Outcast from my own land, unable to answer the destiny that called me. I found an opportunity with Asroth. I did not know how ancient and powerful he is; I sometimes think he may be a demonic force made flesh, and no true mortal at all. I do not know from whence he came, nor how long he has existed. But

I answered a strange summons one night, and made the long journey into the swamps of western Koth to his fortress. There, Asroth promised me an army if I would search out this Ring for him; he knew I was reduced to poverty—that my title and rank were meaningless and that I was desperate. I succumbed to visions of wealth and power, and agreed. With my army of bought swords I scoured the countryside, searching in material ways for the Ring even Asroth's magic could not locate.

"In the end, I could not find it anymore than could his magic. Asroth had grown impatient and was furious. In his rage, he did—this." Pelides touched his mask. "I swore vengeance against him. He mocked me. I learned that he supposed the Ring to be in Suthad, and came here to warn you."

Sonja found herself wondering how Pelides had learned this, but remained silent as he continued speaking.

"While you, Olin, and your councillors debated, I began to search every abandoned temple within this city, hunting for the Ring. I never found it. Then Asroth attacked. Only now am I able to continue the search—but I fear the Ring may no longer be in Suthad."

Olin stood silent, thinking. Som coughed, and Pelides looked at him abruptly as if threatened.

"Once you find the Ring, Pelides," said Olin, "what do you intend to do with it?"

"Destroy Asroth."

"Remember, Pelides, you are not the only one with a grievance against the sorcerer. And even if this Ring is as powerful as you say, what makes you think *you* can channel its forces? Surely you are no magician?"

"I must have the Ring!" Pelides affirmed doggedly. "With it I can destroy Asroth."

Sonja's heart beat faster at that comment.

Olin gestured impatiently. "Come, Pelides. I am returning to the palace. We must talk more. And let me make it clear that *we* will destroy Asroth, not just you alone. I intend to march on his fortress, and we'll destroy him—Ring or no Ring."

Pelides shook his head resolutely. "You do not understand these things, Lord Olin—"

Olin shrugged. "Enough. Come." Then, as a thought struck him, he asked: "What of this Stygian, Pelides; did you know anything about him?"

Pelides's ebony helm jerked up. "The Stygian? *Where is he?* Did *he* find the Ring . . . ?"

Sonja answered calmly: "Sopis is dead. Were you in league with him?"

Pelides laughed derisively. "Am I so great a fool? Surely he was some spy—perhaps he suspected that the Ring was here. Where is his corpse?"

Olin turned to Sonja inquiringly.

"He is dead," Sonja repeated. "I followed him, suspecting him of working with Asroth. But he was slain when those—*things*—attacked."

"How did he die?" Pelides asked quickly.

"A ceiling of the west wing of the palace collapsed upon him."

"Is he wearing a ring?"

"No," said Sonja without hesitation.

"You would not tell me if he *did* have the Ring, would you, Hyrkanian?" Pelides stared at her intently.

"Come," Olin reminded him. "I see you are still keeping secrets from me. Perhaps in my chambers we can all sit down and discuss things. And then, Pelides, you must tell me how we may march on Asroth's fortress."

Pelides complied. Some of the arrogance and stubborn will seemed to have gone out of his stance, perhaps because he had told his story of failure, or because he knew that he was unable to find the Ring; Sonja noticed it in his gait as he and Olin walked out of the temple before her.

He was a dangerous man, she felt—and he would probably become more dangerous should Olin follow his determination to attack Asroth's fortress. A single-minded, vengeful fanatic, ready at any time to use anyone else in his urgent desire to slay Asroth himself.

Olin must be told of the Ring.

As they returned to the palace, Sonja felt a new ominousness in the air. This time it was from the mercenaries. They were ranged about, in conference amongst themselves; their mood seemed dangerous. It was likely that, even more than before, they wanted no further involvement with Lord Olin's crusade against sorcery.

Olin ignored them as he and Pelides walked through the square and ascended the palace steps. His state troops—those who remained, who had not been slain by the Things—had lined themselves around the palace, in protection. They parted to let their lord and his company pass.

A number of retainers and soldiers awaited Olin in the throne chamber. Allas was among them; he sat off in one corner, with Tias beside him. She looked calm now, albeit pale.

"The mercenaries want to leave," Olin was told as he took a chair.

"The mercenaries can wait," Olin replied crossly.

"They're demanding gold again, Lord Olin," said another of his retainers, "payment for their services. And they'll resume fighting *us* if they don't get it."

Olin, at the table, rested chin on hand and scowled angrily.

"Can nothing else be done? We could promise them Asroth's treasure—"

"Perhaps," said Allas. "Whatever we do, we can't afford more slaughter, my lord. If we now have a thousand left we can count ourselves extremely fortunate. Our troops took the brunt of the fighting against the Hell things, and now we're outnumbered by the mercenaries, that's easily seen. Whatever those things were from under the earth, they've nearly demolished us."

Olin looked over at him, anger in his eyes, anger at the truth that he hated to recognize. Then he sighed. "Is Tias all right?"

"Just frightened," Allas told him.

Tias tried to smile at Olin, but looked as if she were going to begin crying again.

Olin said quietly, "I think we're all frightened, Tias. Allas, why don't you and some of the men get us some food."

Allas stood up and a number of the retainers joined him for a search of the kitchens.

"Now" Olin poured himself a cup of wine, faced Pelides across the table. —"Duke Pelides, you must speak frankly with me. I am going to hunt for Asroth, and I need all the information I can get. You must tell me—" He looked up; one of the soldiers from the hallway outside had entered. "What is it now?"

"The mercenaries, sir."

"The mercenaries, the *mercenaries!* Damn them for traitors!"

"Damn us all you wish," roared a loud voice, "but we'll fight no more for you, Lord Olin!"

Four of the leaders had entered the hall, hands on swords.

"We are in no mood to argue," said another of them. "Pay us in gold, so that we may quit this hellish place before all of us are slain by sorcery."

But Olin, too, was in no mood to debate. He rose, met their grim eyes with his own, called a soldier to him, and handed him a ring of keys. "Take a dozen men with you. To the vaults."

"Aye, my lord."

"Not you," said Olin tersely as one of the mercenaries made to move after the soldiers. "You and your men will be paid the gold promised to you. We agreed on a price, and that price will be paid. But I warn you now—all of you—don't think you're going to ransack this palace or loot the treasury." His stance and ready sword arm attested to his intention.

The chieftains broke into toothy smiles. "Hell, Olin, this city is already reduced to crap. What else are you trying to protect? Hey? You're a fool if you think this shit is worth defending."

Olin did not reply; his face grew red, his muscles flexed and twitched in his arm.

The mercenary captain read him well. Lord Olin was strained to the limits of his endurance. Battles against sorcery—intrigues—recruiting an army, managing it, leading it against storms of sorcery and winged monsters and things from underground—and now, his army outnumbered by mercenaries, his city in ruins . . .

"Why sit on this heap of a palace, Olin, when Suthad is—"

"You've looted everything else, Hedlar. Have done!"

"Aye. Not much here. I'll tell you what, Lord. Let's share and share alike. If you'll split up all the gold in your treasury between your army and ours—"

"Enough!"

All in the room blanched as Olin's temper, stretched to the limit, snapped at last. Before the ghoulish grin could fade from Hedlar's lips, Olin had leapt the table, blade rasping from its scabbard. The other mercenaries yelled in surprise and reeled back. Hedlar had his sword only half drawn when Olin's great blade flashed down. The whistling steel bit clear through the rogue's skull to the shoulders; brains and blood and bone fragments spattered in a crimson explosion in all directions.

Hedlar's body flopped to the floor and his pulped head smacked on the flags with a wet splattering. His comrades howled in rage. Olin crouched and growled at them, totally animallike in his fury—teeth bared in a snarl, eyes shot with red, body hunched forward in a stance of pantherish tension.

"Come ahead, you dogs!" he roared, swiping the air with his sword and sending an arc of red droplets whirling from its point. "You'll learn to fear this steel more than sorcery if you do!"

The mercenaries hesitated, wary of this madman. Their numbers might take Suthad's soldiers, but could they manage alone, here, against this raging demon with a sword, when all their troops were in the courtyard?

In the hallway outside, the state soldiers craned and peered into the throne chamber, then began to crowd inside. Some went for their swords, grumbling and muttering ominously, ready to defend Olin and the palace should the mercenaries attempt assault. But fortunately, at that moment the officer sent for the gold returned and wended his way through the press. The dozen soldiers who followed behind him deposited leather bags and small casks on the floor of the outer corridor.

"Take your damned gold!" Olin shouted. "But take nothing else—unless it be the corpse of this pig here!"

The three mercenary leaders backed away, wanting only the gold and their lives. Outside, the soldiers helped them carry away their payment to the outer courtyard; Sonja could hear them grumbling and squabbling over their portions all the way to the palace portico.

Allas and the retainers returned from the kitchens with food. The plates were set out on the table, and all—in deference to Lord Olin's state of mind—refrained from comment on the unsightly corpse upon the floor. Olin seated himself in his throne. It was knocked askew and one arm completely broken into rubble; still, it was his throne.

He refused food and drink, saying he would eat later, and while his company ate he brooded, his great sword still clutched in his hand with the mercenary's blood wet on the blade.

Sonja was not hungry, but she felt in bad need of a bath. On top of the grime of the road and the sweat of battle were blood and dust and the dried slime of the tentacle creatures. She asked Allas if there was a chamber where she could bathe in the palace; he showed her the way, then returned to his meal.

Whatever the condition of the rest of Suthad, the

bathing chambers were still magnificent. Sonja found one where two large pools were sunk into the floor; in the center of each, large fountains shaped like elephants spewed lukewarm water into the air. The scents of old incense lingered. With a little exploration Sonja discovered an antechamber where towels and cleansing oils were stored. Setting these by the side of the pool, she gratefully sat down and removed her filth-caked boots, then her armor, amused to note the bold line of contrast marking heavier dirt on her flesh from lighter. As she removed her sword belt she made certain that the Ring of Ikribu was secure in its pouch. She contemplated hiding it in her boot—but she would only be bathing a few moments, so—

She climbed into the water and immediately, welcome warmth and a sense of comfort enveloped her. She swam for a while, for the pool was easily large enough, floated luxuriously on her back, then finally returned to the edge and, emptying some oil into her palms, laved herself all over and washed her hair.

She had water in her eyes when she heard the door of the bathing chamber drawn open. Quickly she grabbed her towel and dried her face, automatically reaching for her sword as she looked up.

"Sonja?"

"Come in, Tias." She relaxed, eased away from the pool's edge and swam some more. "Are you going to bathe, too?"

Tias shrugged; but the water looked inviting to her, and so she began to remove the leather tunic she wore—a warrior's protective garment to be worn under mail, and too big for the slim girl. Quietly she slipped into the pool with Sonja, took some of the bathing oil, and smiled in contentment to be able to relax so completely.

"You didn't come here to bathe," Sonja observed. "Did you want to talk?"

Tias sighed heavily and studied Sonja, feeling somewhat intimidated as she always did in the presence of this warrior woman. "I don't know whether I can tell you."

"Speak your mind, child, else I'll never know." Sonja smiled. "We may be the only women left alive here—we'll have to look out for one another."

"I'm terrified."

Sonja could well believe that. She herself was frightened. Probably there was not an unfrightened warrior in Suthad right now, including Lord Olin. And Tias was young, little more than a grown girl, a timid city girl at that; no doubt she had been rich, pampered, well cared for, before the destruction of her city. Abruptly, Sonja wondered whether Tias might be like herself at a younger age, reared in different surroundings. Hard to imagine, but—

Tias shrugged in the water, sending little ripples away from her. "You're a strong person, Sonja," she said. "I know that. I suppose I really should have been killed during all this; I'm not strong enough to survive." Her voice was bitter; Sonja sensed that Tias might be jealous of her.

"Go on, Tias—I'm listening."

Tias said: "Allas—he—" But then she cut herself short, looked away and clambered from the pool, borrowed Sonja's towel and hurriedly dried herself.

"I'm just *frightened*—of all of this—Sonja! Maybe you can't understand that, but I—"

"Tias . . ."

"Olin wants to go to war!" Tias yelled suddenly. "He wants to go somewhere and find this *sorcerer—Asroth—!*"

"Tias, listen to me—"

"If Allas goes, he'll be *killed!* I don't *want* him to die! And I don't want to go along, but I *can't* stay *here!* Don't you understand—?"

"Ishtar! Tias, will you—?"

"Oh, never mind!" cried the girl tearfully. She hurriedly pulled on her clothes and ran from the bathing chamber.

Sonja fisted the water in exasperation. Tarim's blood! What a child! She had come wanting to talk, yet had never given Sonja a chance to share her concern, to offer some consolation or even argue with her.

Sonja shook the memory away. Languidly she eased herself back into the water and floated once more. Tias. Aye, only a girl, pampered and spoiled and wholly unprepared by her life for something like this. This destruction, this sorcery, this madness. And was she herself, wondered Sonja, in a much more enviable position simply because she was not like Tias, because she was a swordswoman and had fought sorcery before? Would any one of them survive this whirlpool of madness and doom that seemed to focus itself around the Ring of Ikribu . . . . ?

She sought to dismiss these pestering thoughts—these discouraging, self-doubting ruminations that aided one to no good end. She swam to the pool's edge and was about to pull herself up, when the chamber door opened again.

Tias, no doubt, come back to apologize. Sonja looked up—

Pelides's black shadow crossed the floor before him; his iron face rode frozen atop his dark armor and long cloak. Sonja stiffened and rested her hand near her sword hilt on the marble tile. Pelides came on directly towards her; reaching the edge of the pool, he stared down at her, his attitude suggesting neither embarrassment nor prurient interest.

"I see you haven't much respect for me, Pelides, to interrupt me like this while I'm taking a bath."

Pelides snorted through his mask, waved away her comment with a gesture of his gloved hand. "Your bathing does not interest me, Hyrkanian. I have been trying to retrieve the Stygian's corpse."

Sonja stared up at him, one arm on the wet marble, her body distorted by the reflective waters. "It's buried under a mountain of rubble, Pelides. You can't dig him free, and there's no reason for you to do so."

"I did find one dead hand—"

"I grabbed one of his hands out of the rubble, Pelides. It was torn off when I tried to drag him free. No doubt Asroth's monsters got the rest of him."

"Was there a ring on that hand?" Pelides asked flatly.

"I've told you once, Pelides."

She could see the gleam of his gray eyes watching her from within the black confines of his casque. Probably he was wondering whether to believe her. Sonja noticed that his boots, dirty and worn, were planted directly next to her armor and sword belt.

"Do you think *I* have the Ring?" Sonja demanded, putting fire in her tone.

"No." His voice was firm, even. "If I did, I would kill you now, while you are defenseless."

"I promise you, Pelides, I can reach that sword and stab you before you could draw your own."

"You boast, Hyrkanian. I think Sopis the Stygian told you something before he died."

"All he spoke were chants and madness. Perhaps even Sopis didn't know where the Ring was."

"The Ring brought him here. He needed it to confront Asroth, and he knew where it was."

"And how do *you* know that, Pelides? Come to think of it, how did you come to know Asroth was going to attack Suthad? I think Sopis may have told you. Am I right?"

Pelides barked a laugh. "The Stygian came to my tent the night I was cursed by Asroth. He told me he was in a cult of Ikribu, that he and his brothers had known of my search for it in the sorcerer's employ. He learned, by occult means, of my fall from Asroth's favor."

"Then it was he who told you the Ring was hidden in Suthad, and that Asroth would soon attack the city?"

"He and his brethren detected vibration in the spell surrounding the Ring, and knew thereby that the sorcerer had divined its whereabouts. Sopis instructed me to warn Lord Olin; evidently the acolytes want Asroth confronted with as much opposition as possible."

"Let's hope you have not played the fool," said Sonja. "Do you not fear they may be using you—and all the rest of us—as pawns?"

"Only the Ring can protect us from Asroth's sorcerous power. Without it, Olin is deliberately bringing his own doom upon himself by presuming to attack Asroth, and that doom shall fall upon all with him. Death by sorcery, regardless the form, is not pleasant, Hyrkanian."

Sonja reflected that the Ring had not been much protection to Sopis; yet she remembered also how the tentacle creature that had attacked her had recoiled upon touching her pouch containing it. Perhaps it protected against pure sorcery but not against destruction caused by material things.

"What did Sopis tell *you?*"

"If he had told me anything, Pelides, you may be certain that I would have gone after the Ring before seeking your counsel."

Pelides shifted his stance slightly, his boots nearly touching Sonja's armor. "I think you're keeping things from me."

"Aren't you leaving now, Pelides?"

He bowed slightly. "I must have the Ring."

"How do you know Asroth doesn't have it?"

Pelides chuckled hollowly. He walked away, reached the doors and opened them, then turned. "If he had the Ring, Hyrkanian, we would all be dead now."

He exited, drawing closed the portals.

Cursing in the names of Tarim and Ishtar, Sonja pulled herself from the pool and quickly toweled herself dry.

When Sonja returned to the throne room she found it vacant, save for Olin. He had apparently washed also, and wore fresh clothing. The room was lighted with a few scattered oil lamps and torches. Olin stood at a window; outside was dusk, quick-fallen and warm. The body of the mercenary chieftain, Sonja noticed, had been cleared away.

"Where have they all gone?" she asked Olin.

Continuing to stare out the window, he replied in a low voice: "To clean up and rest. We leave at dawn."

"For Asroth's fortress?"

"Aye, Sonja. Are you going?"

She paused at one of the tables, poured herself a goblet of wine. "What sort of question is that, Olin?"

Forgive me." He turned from the window, threw his hands behind his back. "Forgive me, Sonja. I am being deserted on all sides. The mercenaries have gone with purses full of gold. Even my own soldiers say our quest is futile. But I will fight Asroth alone, if need be. He must die."

"How many remain now that the mercenaries are gone?"

"Not enough, I fear. My retainers and the officers closest to me. Som is going along with us—I don't know why; he was hired as a mercenary. A few hundred soldiers of Suthad who want vengeance, and will risk death in the trying for it."

Sonja sensed a burden of discouragement in Olin's tone. "It could be worse, Olin," she said. "Angered men will make the most determined sort of fighters. The mercenaries with their fears might have proven to be a demoralizing influence in the long run."

"Duke Pelides says that without the Ring, we are a doomed army."

"Ah! Evidently you've talked with him since I left. He told me the same. Do you believe Pelides, Olin?"

"No." He walked toward her. "I believe in myself. I believe that no sorcerer is stronger than my sword arm."

Sonja lifted her goblet to him in a toasting gesture of approval, then swallowed a draught of the wine.

"I'm not sure I'd want that Ring even if I could find it," Olin went on. "Pelides mentioned some unsettling things which he says he learned from Asroth concerning its nature.

"This god, Ikribu—he was said to be a god of blood and battle. The black armies of ancient Kheba and Ishdaris worshiped him as a war god and sacrificed thousands to him in sacrificial battles, and even before then he was said to be one of the Elder Ones—those beings who created man and all other life forms in order to feed on the energies generated by suffering and death. Some of their artifacts were especially created to draw men into paths of madness and doom—to channel these energies the Elder Ones crave—the Ring is said to be one of these. A Ring of power, a Ring of madness!" Olin gestured impatiently, as if brushing cobwebs from his vision. "I know nothing of these things. I am a warrior, and would put my faith in steel above sorcery. Perhaps it is as well we cannot come by this Ring, even if it could aid us against Asroth."

Sonja's heart beat faster. She wanted to tell Olin of the Ring, yet felt a strange reluctance to do so. She must think—

"I'm hungry. Is there aught left to eat?"

Olin surveyed the remains of the dinner on the table. "Not much, I fear. But I can send—"

"Fruit is fine." Sonja snatched up a pear and began to munch. "I'll make do nicely with what's here. I've learned to eat well, Olin, when I have the opportunity, and to do without when times are lean."

Olin grinned. "Spoken like a true warrior."

Sonja finished her pear in a few bites. "How is Tias?"

"Tias?" Olin crossed his arms upon his chest, leaned and supported himself against the table, sighed. "I did not see her. Why?"

"She came to the bathing chamber while I was there. She's afraid. She doesn't want Allas to go with you."

"Allas is a fine young officer. But—yes, Tias. I knew

her family. She's very young. No one should have to suffer as she's suffered. So young . . ." Olin looked out the window again. Pale moonlight quivered on the sill, splashed a glowing rectangle on the worn stones of the chamber floor. "Where have all my people gone?" he said softly. "Gone to the ends of the world, I suppose. I cannot blame them. Why do I even make a pretense of fighting Asroth?"

If Olin were a lesser man, Sonja reflected, he would have broken down and wept—might have broken down and gone mad long before this. But somehow his broodings only seemed to make firmer his resolve.

"You're fighting for yourself now, Olin."

"Aye." He nodded, looked back to her. "Perhaps I am ridding the world of an evil, but I really want this revenge for myself—I want to slay Asroth with these hands!" He held them up; his face, gray in the dimness, was contorted fiercely in his anger.

But then he relaxed and wiped back his dark hair. Sonja watched him: a strong man, a determined man, nobly handsome in the dimness of the throne chamber.

"You had best be getting some sleep yourself, Sonja."

"Aye."

Olin's eyes rested on her; for a moment, his gaze lingered. The soft orange light of an oil lamp caught Sonja's handsome features and outlined them clearly against the darkness behind. The tousled mane of unruly red hair falling untamed down her shoulders and back, the darkness of her eyes, her lips still moist from eating the fruit, the swell of her breasts beneath her mail, the warm curve of her waist, all toned by torchlight. Olin looked again to her eyes; Sonja's gaze met his own.

"Sonja . . ." He held out his hand to her.

She swallowed, reached out, and took his hand. Something tingled up her arm. "Olin, I—"

He drew her to him. Sonja did not protest. Olin breathed a lock of hair away from her face and lightly pressed his lips to her cheek, then to her lips. More burning. Sonja quaked inside. Olin's hands found hers and held them, tenderly but securely. He pressed his mouth to hers, and Sonja met his kiss, felt Olin's tongue caressing her and met it with her own—

She broke away, so suddenly that Olin was startled. "I —cannot!"

"Cannot?" He laughed lightly in the dimness, then sighed. He stepped away, rubbed his face, walked tiredly to the window again. "So much death," he said. "Forgive me, Sonja. Perhaps you should take your rest."

But when he turned to see her go, Sonja was not there.

Chapter 7

Crossed Swords and Crossed Hearts

Sonja galloped her horse over the fields, away from Suthad. The warm night air whipped about her, cooling her body as the exertion of riding cooled her mind. She needed time to think, time to be by herself and ponder what had happened.

She galloped until she came to a small wood on a hillside. Dismounting, she led her mount to a thin stream that trickled there, then tethered it to a bush and sat down before a tall tree.

The high stars of night showed clearly through the sighing boughs and black foliage. The moon floated from behind a gray cloud and spilled silvery light down upon the wide, waving fields of grass, patterning strange, waving mosaics on the soft sward at Sonja's feet.

She tried to clear her mind. Olin's kiss had not been a rash action. Sonja had felt from him, all along, an attraction that all the turmoil of sorcerous battles and renegade mercenaries could not blot out. And she felt the same attraction for Olin, as well.

But what could it mean to her? She could never love a man. Never. Not only because of her vow, although her vow was her destiny—but because of herself. In all her wide travels she had met many men; most were only swordsmen or rogues or soldiers or artisans. There had been no spark of affection between her and any of them. Some had seen her only as a desirable woman, and their lust demanded that they attempt to possess her. These Sonja had met sword against sword—and she had never lost.

In all her travels she had seen the many poses and disguises love takes, from the simple and poetic attraction between two young lovers to the violence and brutality of lust and the frequent treachery and scheming between the sexes. Other women had been raped, as had she. Why, then, had they not been visited by that Vision and given their choice in life also?

It was something within herself, Sonja decided. There was something within her that she had only dimly perceived before the tragedy but which the Vision had seen, from afar, all along. And so she had been chosen, because both she and the Vision knew what was within her.

She could not consummate the affection she felt for Olin. She must guard her feelings. But—*did* she love him? Sonja wondered what love truly was, wondered if anyone really knew. She felt affection and sentiment, sometimes, when she looked at Olin. Yet though she admired and respected him, and though some part of her—almost foreign to her, now—wanted him physically, she could not allow herself to give in to such feelings. It was some rejected part of her that wanted Olin in that way. The world was wide and strange; were there not many Olins, and would she not cross paths with many Olins again and again?

And yet, Sonja had felt exhilaration when Olin had kissed her . . . .

She looked up at the stars, knowing they would give her no answer. They were the same stars as hung over Hyrkania, stars like on that night outside her burning homestead, the night of fire and smoke and blood, and—

There were many sorts of men: some brutal and vile, most mediocre, a few good. Her vow excluded them all. And yet, she had felt something different . . . .

Stars, as on the night when she had ridden, five years after the destruction of her home and family, through the Nemedian forest called Darkwood—a deserted, haunted place said to be the last remnant of a far vaster forest that had flourished during cycles of prehistory antedating even Acheron. Most people shunned it because of wolves, and because of older and darker things said to survive there from forgotten ages. Sonja traveled as she always traveled, with sword and horse, riding between some vague beginning and some undetermined end—or some end and a new beginning . . . .

Sonja sighed. She stood up and stretched, suddenly feeling tired and worn. Memories, and the battles of the past days, were catching up to her. She walked from the tree and looked down the hillside, away from Suthad, toward the east—toward Hyrkania. It was very far away now, as far away as her past, yet as near as her destiny. She sighed and turned, ready to mount her horse again and return to Suthad for a good night's rest—when suddenly she caught sight of many yellow lights to the south, far in the distance.

Campfires. Aye—the same she had spotted two nights ago.

A sound brought her about abruptly. Hand on pommel, Sonja snarled to see a dark horseman galloping toward her from the direction of the city. Heart beating, she instinctively returned to the tree—so that she could have it at her back in case of a battle—and waited.

The rider approached quickly. Sonja was certain that he had seen her, alone and outlined against the night sky. But then came the sound of a familiar voice:

"Sonja? *Sonja?*"

Her instantaneous reflex of self-defense bled away,

and she stepped from the shadow of the tree. It was Olin. He reined his horse to a halt, dismounted, led it by the reins as he came near.

"What are you doing out here? I thought you had gone to rest."

"I needed time to be alone, Olin—to think."

She saw him smiling worriedly at her in the moonlight, like some parent relieved to discover a wayward child. He walked his horse to the tree and tethered it. "It's not the smartest thing, Sonja, to be outside the city walls after dark."

She felt a certain resentment of his protective attitude. "I've traveled many dark roads in the middle of the night, Olin."

He nodded and grinned openly, faced her and placed his fisted hands on his hips. "I—I wanted to speak with you again, anyway," he began, talking in a low, intimate tone. "Sonja—I think we ought to talk about—"

She cut him off abruptly. "Look, Olin." She pointed to the south, stepped a few paces ahead of him. "Campfires—the same we first saw two nights ago."

He came up behind her, intrigued by the weird lights but at the moment more concerned to say what was on his mind. Yet Sonja's attitude prevented him; Olin sensed that if he dared to broach the subject of what he felt, she would halt him defensively. And why? Did he not feel the same thing from her, toward himself? Why was she such a child in a woman's body? Olin sighed; he turned from her, walked up the hill and crouched beneath the tree, sat down and picked up a stone, tossed it aside.

Sonja returned to him, looked down at him uneasily. Olin patted the grass; Sonja smiled and sat next to him.

For a few moments neither spoke. Olin picked up another stone, lobbed it down the hill. He said: "I had a strange vision, earlier tonight."

"A vision? You mean, a dream?"

"No. No. I was seated in my throne—what's left of it.

You had gone to the baths. My company was in a strange humor. I had just slain that mercenary, and the blood lust and the anger were still in me. I felt as if I would burst, I was so filled with an aching for vengeance. I wanted to slay and destroy—but where was my enemy?

"I had not drunk any wine—and yet I suddenly felt as if I had drunk to excess. I thought my heart had stopped, that I was suffocating. In my mind flashed a warning—that Asroth was trying to destroy me by means of a sending from afar off. No one in the room noticed what was happening to me; it was as though I were shielded from their sight by a mist or a blurring wall of smoke."

Sonja was listening intently now, watching Olin carefully as sweat grew on his forehead and he gestured excitedly.

"And then a vision appeared before my eyes. One moment my company were seated at table, dining and drinking; the next, they were blotted out in a strange veil, and before me rose the picture of a room—an ancient room of black stone blocks, high and shadowed. Far away, in a distant corner, stood a wizard or mage—perhaps Asroth—and he seemed as black and indistinct as the room itself, save for his eyes, which were yellow and burned like two lamps. Slowly his face came into view—skull-like, white but colored yellow by his glowing eyes. I faced him, and felt myself drawing my sword. Others were with me—you and Pelides, young Allas, a few more. Asroth—or whoever the wizard was—spoke something very quickly in a language I did not comprehend. I lifted my sword, for though at first he was far away, in an instant he had appeared right before me, and all I could see now were his eyes. There were no pupils—there was nothing to his eyes save the yellow light, as if he had no eyes but only twin cavities in his face that let the light of Hell shine through from behind. I . . . I raised my sword, and saw a vision within my vision—a memory of Suthad. Then I heard Pelides shriek, and though I did not look at him, I could see him howling in rage, and his mask was no longer a mask but his true face, contorted in pain and agony, a casque of living jet. Then he went down, and young Allas fell also, and a crowd of men behind me. Through all this I was in the midst of my sword swing, but as I brought down my blade it passed before the wizard's yellow eyes, blocking them for one fleet moment from my sight. And in that moment, the vision vanished; it was gone, as if I had snapped a cord with my hands. I was back in my throne chamber and my men were there at their feasting as before. I felt myself drawing in a breath, and realized that I had seen this complete tableau, vivid and real as life, within the space of half a breath."

As Olin finished speaking he raised a hand to his damp face, wearily massaged his forehead and eyes. Sonja breathed deeply to clear her mind, exhaled. She heard her horse whinny just beyond the tree, as if Olin's intense tale had raised a general aura of uneasiness there on the hilltop.

And Sonja was reminded of her own vision, so different from Olin's and so long ago, yet exciting the same rebellious, contradictory emotions within her. She asked Olin at last:

"Do you think this vision a portent?"

"I do not know . . . ."

"Do you think it a message from Asroth—a warning that you had best not attack?"

"I do not know." Olin looked at Sonja; her face was clear and brilliant, touched by the moonlight. "I have never suffered such a thing before, although I know that in fevers on the battlefield such enigmas occur to the mind, and pass when the fever passes. And yet, forecasters and seers often send themselves into fits and fevers, and their visions come to pass. I do not know."

"But you will not abandon your assault on Asroth?"

Olin shook his head sturdily. "Never. Though this be

a sign of my impending death, I will die fighting the sorcerer if such the gods decree. Yet many of my troops are against this venture; even those who have sworn to stay by me are doubtful of the outcome."

"Life is full of doubtful outcomes," Sonja replied, a strange bitterness in her voice.

Olin looked at her closely. Still flushed with excitement at reliving his strange vision, he reached out his hand to her—touched her hair, her cheek—

Sonja's first impulse was to draw away and damn him. Yet she could not; his eyes were tender, as only a strong man's can be in a moment of jeopardy and emotional flux. Contrary demands warred within her, and while her body trembled, indecisive, Olin ran his hand to her breast, drew her close, and again placed his lips against hers.

This time Sonja truly feared her own reaction. She fell back; Olin chased her with his kiss; but Sonja, suddenly filled with anxiety, warned him away, not scoldingly nor bitterly, but firmly.

"Olin, I could not love you, even if I wished to."

"Am I wrong then, Sonja," Olin asked, "in thinking that you *do* love me?"

Sadness filled her, and regret, immense doubt, and fatigue. "No, Olin, you are not—Olin, I cannot—"

"Cannot! *Cannot!*" he mimicked her brutally. "Do you think this armor disguises your sex, or that your sword—"

"Olin!"

"Sonja, I am not mistaken in what I feel, nor—do not be angry—nor am I wrong in thinking that you feel as I do."

"I . . . I *cannot.*" She sought to rise, but Olin gripped her arm and held her there beside him, forcing her to confront him—and, he hoped, herself.

"Tell me *why* you cannot, Sonja? Is there some fear? Is it some old hurt that has grown into a consuming passion? Or do you not care for men, as is the way of many warrior women? Sonja . . ."

Her heart was beating savagely, her pulse racing. She feared that were she to tell Olin her true nature, her past and her destiny, it would be as though she were violating a secret pact. Or perhaps her Vision and her destiny and her life's meaning would be brutally discounted by one moment of derisive laughter from him. Or he might try to convince her that her Vision and her past and her destiny were a fraud of her own mind, a mockery, an insubstantial thing that meant no more than—

"*Tell* me, Sonja," he pleaded, sounding more like a true friend wanting to aid her with a burden than a man trying to take advantage of her.

"Olin, I—"

Still she hesitated, wanting and yet not wanting to tell him all.

"Sonja, listen to me," said Olin. "You may trust me. I swear to you, you are the finest woman I have ever met. And it is not just because you fire my blood, but because you are so much a true person unto yourself. Yes, I desire you for your beauty, but even were you not a woman I would feel this admiration for you, for your courage and nobleness. And I would have your friendship even if it should chance that you cannot give me more."

"Olin, I suffer from a destiny."

"*Tell* me your destiny, Sonja."

She looked him in the eyes, read concern and love and torment there. She told him: "When I was a woman-child—when my family was destroyed by mercenary bandits—I wished that I could wield a sword and thereby equal my father and younger brothers."

"I know that."

"When they were destroyed, only I was left alive. The brigands forced me to endure their pleasure, then left me to die in our house. They set it afire, but I escaped."

"How does this—"

"I wandered into the forest, Olin, sobbing and broken

and bleeding, thinking I would soon die—*wanting* to die one moment, the next wanting fiercely to live for vengeance."

Olin said no more.

"I was visited by a Vision—a spirit or a god, perhaps. I do not know. It filled up my soul and gave me the strength to become what I yearned for in my heart. With my father's sword I slew one of the brigands, and in the following years tracked down the others. But within that instant of the Vision, Olin, I was transformed from a whimpering, broken young girl into a woman whose sword skill could equal any man's in the world."

Olin was silent, trying to imagine such a thing.

"I took up the wandering way. In my years of travels since then I have seen much, suffered much, been to hell many times, followed roads mired with gore and others paved with gold and splendor—but never, Olin, *never* in all that time have I given myself to any man. Were I to do so, I feel I would damn myself, sever myself from my destiny and my past. In return for my skill with the sword, Olin, I swore a vow of chastity to that Vision in the night. And no man has ever touched me since that night when I was defiled while my parents and brothers were slain and burnt."

"Sonja," said Olin gently. "Sonja. Can *no* love ever win to you?"

She looked him straight in the eyes, with an honesty that went beyond mere truth. "Should I be meant to love a man, Olin, then that will be proved by his besting me in swordplay."

"Sonja—"

"And that can never be," she added, already regretting that she had said so much.

But Olin stood up briskly, in a better humor. He looked down at Sonja and announced: "I love you. I can tell you that no more plainly in words. But if I must prove it, then I will do so."

Her eyes went wide. "Olin, do not—!"

His hand reached for his sword, gripped the pommel; the steel rasped from its scabbard.

"Olin—*don't draw your sword!* I must meet it, and it would mean the *death* of one of—"

But his sword stood free, a line of heavy silver in the moonlight. He backed away, smiling, certain of his ability, confident in his love.

Sonja stood up, angry and reluctant, scornful and sad. "Olin, why did you draw your sword?"

"Because I love you."

"I must match it!"

"Come, then." He played his steel before her, a wheel of light.

"Damn you, Olin," Sonja whispered, tears nearly coming to her eyes. She drew her own sword, slowly, not wanting to, hoping that Olin would somehow think better of this mad game and sheathe his blade once more.

"I do not want to slay you, Olin."

"You *won't* slay me, Sonja!" He laughed merrily, exuberant and happy to thus exhibit his love for her. "*Come!*" he urged, dancing on the hilltop and whirling his blade. "Match me stroke for stroke—and later, Red Sonja, we will match each other in gentler ways."

She lifted her blade fiercely, quickly, and stepped ahead. "Damn you, Olin!" she said again. "I don't want this to happen."

"*Come!*" he urged her, joyfully.

Sonja gripped her sword; the muscles in hand and wrist, forearm and bicep, charged and rippled with their familiar strength. Olin skipped before her, tapped her outthrust sword playfully.

Sonja reacted humorlessly, striking his weapon aside with a powerful foil.

Olin was not alarmed. "In earnest, then," he said soberly. "For love, Red Sonja, I will even go down in defeat."

"I am not playing, Olin."

"Nor am I," he responded sincerely. "*Nor am I!*"

He moved, thrusting for her heart, but Sonja could tell the thrust was not quite given in seriousness. Easily she stepped aside and knocked away his blade, crouched and moved back, feinted and lunged. Olin parried masterfully, caught the hilt of her sword with the tip of his; the blades scraped hissingly down their lengths, and Olin drew up before Sonja and smiled into her face. "*Again!*" he cried, sweating and panting.

Sonja's blue eyes glinted as coldly as hard diamonds in the depths of the sea.

They parted. Olin feinted, lunged, sidestepped, brought his blade around and up in a blurring display, then sought to catch Sonja off-guard. Another lunge. Sonja caught him; blade clacked on blade.

"Damn you!" she swore hotly, beneath the moon in the shade of the great tree. "Do you want swordplay, Olin?"

"*Aye!*" he growled, his lips drawn in a tense grin.

"Then master it!"

She charged, her blood up. Olin fell back, unprepared for the viciousness of her onslaught. This was no game-playing; Sonja fought with a furious surety and a dazzling speed. Her sword was everywhere, there was no clear-cut sight of it. Olin cursed, suddenly feeling for one moment that his life might truly be in jeopardy. He parried, parried again, saved a stroke, fell back, lunged, parried still again. But he fell back; Sonja's blade was everywhere. Once when he tried to anticipate her he felt out of time and was nearly skewered. Never had he faced an antagonist of such grace and surety and speed.

And Sonja never relaxed. The more energy she put forth, the more strength seemed to grow within her. She was forcing Olin down the hillside; he nearly stumbled many times. And though he determinedly sought to defend himself, to stall her advance and force her back to the top of the hill, his efforts seemed awkward. Frightened for an instant, Olin realized that the battle lust had come upon Sonja, and that if he failed in his defense by one heartbeat she would run him through before remembering whom she was fighting.

Then he felt anger rising within him. His strokes became more forceful and the sluggish feelings of doubt and amateurishness fell away. He saw Sonja's dark eyes staring grimly at him through the haze of their working blades, saw her dark hair foaming and jumping behind her head. With new surges of determination Olin met each of her thrusts, sidestepped feints, parried masterfully. Sonja laughed, brutally. Olin skipped back, out of her range for one moment, gained his breath, measured Sonja's advance and jumped ahead, meeting her blade where he had estimated. Sparks flew. Olin whipped his sword around, deflected Sonja's away, and did not hold back on his next stroke, meant to disarm her.

But her blade was there, tireless and certain. His edge caught again on her hilt and Sonja lithely slipped to one side as Olin's blade cut the air on the recovery. As he drew back—as his eye caught her next terse, graceful movement—Olin suddenly realized his own parry was an instant too late.

Sonja's eyes flashed and her blade drove in, sliding directly between Olin's arm and chest, never drawing blood.

Had she held back out of respect or love, meaning not to kill? Or was her own skill off by just a fraction, so that the thrust meant for his heart had missed by a hair?

Sonja never gave Olin a chance to worry the question. Never pausing, she drew back and thrust again, and Olin met her and caught the blow on his blade.

He was tiring. Blood drummed in his ears, his breath came in gasps, his arm felt weighted with lead. Sonja, too must have been feeling the strain, though she showed no signs of it. Then to Olin's ears came an outside sound, not his own racing blood or pumping lungs or the clash of steel, but the noise of their two horses whinnying and snorting.

"Sonja!" he yelled.

She did not hear the horses. But their frightened neighings grew louder. Olin dared not avert his eyes for a moment from Sonja's, and yet a feeling of dire peril suddenly gripped him, not the fear of her sword, but of something beyond them, outside the close-hemmed world of their working swords.

He glimpsed them—

"Sonja!"

With a frantic burst of energy Olin knocked aside her blade and leaped back out of range.

"There!" he yelled, pointing with his sword.

Snapping out of the battle trance, Sonja, too, heard the horses. She looked behind. There were yellow lights on the hilltop—small yellow lights atop moving, robed figures. *Eyes.*

"Tarim and Erlik!" Sonja cursed. "What in the Seven Hells—?"

The figures floated down the hillside toward them—six small men in dark robes, their hands hidden in their sleeves, their yellow eyes hovering like glowing coals suspended in the air. The horses had quieted somewhat but still nickered uneasily.

Nearly exhausted, sweaty, breathless, Sonja and Olin held their ground as the six shapes carefully surrounded and enclosed them in a circle, each man maintaining a safe distance from the gleaming pair of swords.

"Give us the Ring," muttered one of the yellow-eyed figures. The accent of his low, even voice betrayed his Stygian origin.

Sonja turned to Olin. "Priests of Ikribu!" she gasped.

"Aye," came a voice from behind another pair of eyes. "We know that the Ring is here. One of you possesses it. You will give it to us. Now."

"The *Ring?*" Olin breathed, still hungry for air and not averting his eyes from those of the acolytes. "Sonja?"

"I have it," she said. "I should have told you earlier. I lied to Pelides, Olin! Sopis had the Ring, and I took it from him when he was killed."

A pallid hand lifted from beneath the pair of eyes nearest to Sonja. "You will give it to me, woman."

"I'll give you steel, dog!"

The eyes began to glow more strongly, their yellow light spilling and spreading until the man's features were distinct—hollow, sharp, with bared, ugly teeth. Sonja felt her mind begin to go numb . . . .

"Beware, Olin!" she cried.

He moved, his blade upright, his back to her. "At them, Sonja!"

And even as the yellow eyes sought to steal her mind and strength, Sonja leaped forward to obliterate them with one lightning slice of her sword.

Chapter 8

The Road to Sorcery

The Stygian, his hands raised in a gesture of uncompleted sorcery, had not even time to scream out before Sonja's blade clove his head. His burning eyes winked out in the darkness like brilliant jewels suddenly dropped into a black well. Sonja felt his blood spatter upon her. Quickly she moved on; behind, she heard the thud of steel in flesh and the rage in Olin's voice as he howled at another of the acolytes to come ahead and face steel.

A Stygian near Sonja hove a knife aloft and hurled it; she caught its glint in the moonlight barely in time to bat it aside with her sword. She ran at him and lunged. piercing him through, and he fell groaning and muttering incantations, dragging himself along the grass, an unearthly vitality somehow keeping him alive despite his mortal wound. Sonja gripped her sword in two hands and savagely drove its point down through his skull. Tearing it free, she whirled about in time to hear Olin gasp in pain.

The remaining three Stygians had surrounded him and Sonja saw a lambent glow rising and spreading from their midst. Olin was on his knees before them, struggling to rise, his face and arms horribly limned by the pulsating red light. Cursing, she ran to his aid. The middle priest turned at the noise of Sonja's charge. She just glimpsed his lean, grinning face and the large, crimson gem he held in one palm before her sword swept down and clove him from shoulder to spine.

The Stygian shrieked as he toppled backward, spouting blood from his great wound; the red gem flew into the air, arced, traced a gleaming trail downward. A second priest ran for it; the third dashed away a few paces, then turned and faced Sonja, growling something ominous in an unknown tongue.

Sonja ran at him, howling. The Stygian's yellow eyes lit suddenly and brilliantly, like two torches thrust forward from the darkness. Sonja, nearly blinded by their intensity, was brought to an abrupt halt by a pulsing force that was not physical. Blindly she swung, hoping that her headlong rush had carried her near enough to her foe—

Her sword struck flesh with a slicing crunch. The glare vanished. Shaking off the blinding light that still seemed to cling to her brain, she looked down and saw the Stygian lying on the grass, his head lolling loosely, half severed.

Again Olin cried out. Sonja swiveled about, saw that he had regained his feet. The last priest had retrieved the gem and stood a short distance from Olin, holding the thing high above his head. From it pulsed waves of scarlet radiance, as visible in the air as the ripples caused by a stone dropped into water. Sonja saw the waves of expanding color strike Olin, and in that instant he dropped his sword and stood frozen in his tracks. She cried out and dashed forward, afraid that the gem's power would strike Olin down before she could slay the Stygian.

The priest saw her, twisted his cupped hand so that the gem's coruscations shifted from Olin's direction to hers. As the rings of red light enveloped her, Sonja was immediately brought to a halt. An incredible dizziness and fatigue filled her. The weight of her sword seemed immeasurable; the weight of her body on her legs, even of her head on her shoulders, seemed insupportable.

Trying to curse, she could only gasp. The world began to rock, red stars and red grasses tilting and swerving and trading places in her field of vision . . . .

Then she heard Olin yell something; the red light vanished, and the Stygian's voice lifted in a brief, high-pitched wail.

Staggering forward, Sonja felt her vigor increasing with each new step and breath. But she was still dizzy when she reached Olin, who knelt beside the Stygian's corpse and jerked free his dagger. A well-aimed throw had killed the acolyte.

"Are you all right?" he asked.

She nodded, shook off the last of her lethargy. "Find the gem, Olin."

He searched the ground, kicking at the grass with his boots. At last he snorted and dug his heel into the ground, shook his head and chuckled. "Dust," he told Sonja, walking back to her. "It must have shattered instantly as soon as it struck the ground. Or when the last of these creatures died." He nudged the Stygian's corpse with the toe of his boot, then put a hand on Sonja's shoulder. "Are you sure you're all right?"

She nodded. "I am now, yes. Can we be certain there are no more?"

Olin shook his head. "No. But I imagine those campfires are the answer to that."

"Aye. More will follow. They're after—this." She undid her pouch, opened it, and pulled out the Ring.

Olin looked closer, and Sonja handed it to him. A large ring, yet no larger than many ordinary ones. No one, however, could have taken it for anything ordinary. Its thousands of tiny gems caught the starlight and broke it into thousands of gleams of colors, shimmering and almost alive.

"The Ring of Ikribu!"

"Pelides must not know," said Sonja.

"Of course not. But this is a weapon we'll need, Sonja."

"Are you sure? Olin, you once said you doubted—"

"Aye. Pelides told me it is a ring of madness and doom, forged by an evil god. Yet he seeks it, also. I am not minded to cast it away now that the gods have given it into our hands. Whatever will help me against Asroth I'll use, risks or no. Still, it is your ring now, Sonja—you may do with it as you will. Shall I keep it, or you?"

She held out her hand. "I trust you, Olin, you know that. But I've guarded it so far . . ."

"Of course." He handed it back to her.

"Pelides does not suspect that I have it," she told Olin, "but he thinks I know where it is. He tried to dig through the rubble for Sopis's corpse."

"Umm. Well, he'll continue to guess until we decide otherwise, Sonja. Come." He held out a hand toward the hilltop. "It's time we were heading back. Keep that ring securely hidden."

She refastened her pouch and walked beside him to their horses. Their strange love battle had been postponed by the attack of Stygian magic, yet clearly not forgotten. Warrior and lord traded covert glances as they mounted, such glances as had been shared by foiled lovers throughout time. But neither Olin nor Red Sonja spoke. There was, in the haunted darkness, nothing to say.

Allas and Tias shared one of the small rooms in the upper stories of the palace's east wing, and while Tias slumbered Allas stood awake at one of the windows. His arms resting on the sill, he silently stared out at the gray, shadowed desolation of the city and watched the night sky. Far down a brick-cobbled avenue lined with black trees and marble buildings whose walls gleamed softly in the moonlight he could see the eastern gate, open to the fields.

A breeze played about Allas as if to lighten his heart, but he was too worried and depressed to be cajoled from his brooding. So much horror—and so much of the unknown still awaiting. Night birds called, and Allas wondered idly why he had not heard them earlier. Probably they were only now returning, now that the pall of sorcery no longer clung to Suthad like an invisible mist. The stars were clear, and Allas wondered at them, as he had often wondered at them since his childhood.

Tias stirred in their bed. "Allas?" she called sleepily. "Where are you?"

"Here." His voice sounded bold in the dark stillness.

She crawled from the cushions, and the soft pad of her feet neared Allas. "I thought you were sleeping, but—"

"I am restless."

"Have you decided, Allas?" She looked up at him with warm, liquid eyes, pressed closed to him, and moved one of his arms to hold her waist. It rested comfortably there. Lightly she stroked Allas's long hair. He remained silent; his attention seemed distantly focused.

"What are you watching for?" she asked presently.

"Sonja rode out the gate a short time ago."

Tias felt hurt, resentful. "Are you spying on her?"

"Olin followed after her. They've been gone quite a while."

"Are you *jealous?*"

Allas turned sharply, looked down at Tias with anger and disappointment in his eyes.

"Don't deny it, Allas."

"Deny it?"

"That you're attracted to that Hyrkanian swordswoman."

Laughter came to his lips, a brightness entered his eyes—a feigned humor that betrayed him. But then he swallowed stiffly and moved away. Tias followed after him doggedly.

"Isn't it true?"

"Once, maybe. Days ago, when I first met her."

"She doesn't care about *you.*"

Allas sighed. "You can't be jealous of the swordswoman, Tias. Please tell me what you really mean. Eh?"

She trembled, almost sobbed, and threw herself into his arms. Then a tightness gripped her, and an aura of maturity and reflection that belied her young years.

"I love you," she said flatly, "and I have for a long time. Damn you, Allas, Suthad is destroyed! Olin and Sonja and the rest of them are going off on some mad crusade against a sorcerer they've never seen, and you've nearly lost your life a dozen times over in the past few days. Doesn't that mean anything to you?"

"Lord Olin is—"

"Lord Olin is a *fool!* His city is fallen to ruin. All of our family and friends are—" She choked on her words, but pressed on. "And what has it all meant? The mercenaries were *right,* Allas! Don't you understand that? *Don't you?"*

"I'm a soldier!" he countered, his voice a growl of menace.

"Soldiers *die,* Allas! There's no more reason for you to be a soldier, the army is gone. Our city is gone. Whoever has survived this insanity—they've all escaped. They've *left* Suthad, Allas, to start their lives over again."

"I cannot forget what has happened."

"Then you'll *die* not forgetting!" Tias exclaimed, sobbing at last. "Would you rather be a proud soldier, and die in some wizard's fortress, than marry me and raise a family? Oh, you fool! You'd want your *sons* to be soldiers, and you'd send *them* to war as well, wouldn't you! *Wouldn't* you!"

"Quiet, Tias!"

"I *won't* be quiet! We had a *life* here, Allas. Two hundred thousand people lived in this kingdom one month ago. Where are they now? The city's reduced to rubble, and why?"

"And *why?"* Allas suddenly yelled at her; he seemed to grow in stature as his wrath finally vented. *"Why,* Tias? Because of *Asroth!* Speak the name, damn you! Say it over and over again. Asroth! Asroth! *Asroth!* One month ago you had a family and I had a family and there was no Red Sonja, no mercenaries, no monstrous things of sorcery. *Asroth* has changed that!"

"Allas—"

"*Asroth!* And now you're saying that since the wizard has come and gone, we should pick up whatever bits of rubble and slime he has left us and try to patch our lives together again? Tias! We can't ignore what has happened!"

"*I* can!"

"You're *selfish!* You think you can just close your eyes and have things the way they were before Suthad was destroyed. But Suthad *is* destroyed, and *I* can't ignore that. I've fought sorcery—I've proved to myself now that I'm a man, that I can live through slaughter and bloodshed and madness if that is what must be done. Now Lord Olin has taken me into his trust. Now we have a chance to avenge Suthad and slay Asroth. Only animals cower from the storm, Tias, and when the damage is done rebuild what was shattered and forget the tempest."

"And is that so *bad?*"

"*Yes!*" he answered fiercely, eyes shining. "We are men! We're human beings! If a storm comes down on us, then we're no better than animals if we scurry and hide, and afterwards only try to get away. And Asroth isn't a storm, a natural disaster. Asroth is *evil,* a—a disease, a pestilence; and the innocent people he's murdered —our *families* and *friends,* Tias, our *families* and *friends* —their ghosts cry out for vengeance. I hear the ghosts in Suthad, crying 'stop Asroth before we'll be at peace!' We're capable of *revenge.* That's why I'm not an animal —that's why I place trust in Mitra or whatever other gods rule the skies and the earth! If Mitra saves us from death, then we'll come back to pick up our lives again. If Mitra permits me to die in the contest, then I've died a *man,* for a just cause!"

"You're a *fool!*" Tias wailed, frightened half out of

her senses that her arguments had been for naught, that Allas would choose to die and shatter her hopes of loving him and living with him in sanity and safeness. "You *want* to die!"

"No!" His voice was full of anger and certainty, as grim and ringing as the tolling of a brazen temple bell. "No—I don't want to die, Tias. But I'm a soldier, and I want no one else to die as those poor dogs did in the square today—if I can do anything at all to stop it from ever happening again."

She cursed him, crying and gnashing her teeth, and kicked at his legs like a furious little girl. Suddenly she turned and ran from him, pulled open the heavy chamber door with a strength that surprised Allas, and ran out of the room, sobbing.

But Allas had made his choice, and felt justified in it. He returned again to the window, looked out—and saw two figures on horseback cantering into the eastern gate. Sonja and Olin. Then they had not been killed!

He had feared for them.

Tias, embittered and humiliated, ran down the corridor until she came to the end of it, then gasped, stopped in her tracks, and stammered some outcry of surprise at seeing Duke Pelides loitering alone against a window embrasure.

"Can you not sleep?" he asked Tias in his hollow, metallic voice, not turning from the casement.

Tias looked at him, too shocked for the moment to answer. Pelides had always frightened her; he seemed like a creature of living night, not human, emotionless and resolute, stiff, eyeless. He never ate or drank in the presence of anyone; his words seldom betrayed any extreme of emotion, neither tenderness nor wrath. She found herself unable to face him and looked around the dim hallway, which was lit only haphazardly with widely spaced torches. Her argument with Allas was immediately forgotten; she suddenly longed for the protective comfort of his strong arms and light laughter.

"Tias."

"Y-yes?"

He turned and looked at her—cold mask, immobile, horrible. "Are you afraid of me?"

She could not answer him.

He continued when she remained silent. "All of us are restless tonight. We have come to a crossroads. We are a company, now; the gods have weeded out the unfit, those whose destiny it was not to travel the road to sorcery." He looked out the window again, as if communing silently with someone or something outside.

Tias's heart ceased its wild beating. She found herself telling Pelides: "I—I just don't want Allas to *die* . . . ."

"Trust more to yourself," Pelides told her, still looking out the window. "Love is only a word, no better for two persons than wings for a fowl, unless each has strength enough to supplement the other. That strength must come through independence."

Tias stared at him wonderingly. Was this the Pelides of stone and ebon visage, the man cursed by sorcery, bitter in heart, black of soul?

"You stare at me," he said, turning to her again. "Do you think that I never loved, never learned aught from life, before—this?" He touched his mask in a rapid gesture.

Tias had no answer. What was he saying? *Why* was he telling her this?

"I grow thoughtful on the eve of a great departure," said Pelides. "And you can no more hold Allas from his path than you could hold back a storm. Endure it. Rise above it. Trust to yourself."

"I—I don't understand."

She heard Pelides breathing behind his mask for a moment. "We are all of a company here," he said finally. "Each of us united for our own reasons, each brought to Suthad by our own wayward paths. Some of us can be trusted, others cannot. Each of us has a secret, each a fear, each heart burning for vengeance or with some other great desire that transcends us. Perhaps the gods are playing a game, and we are the gaming pieces. Take this."

From his belt he unstrapped a long, heavy dagger and handed it, blade and sheathe, to Tias.

"Learn to use it," he told her soberly. "Wear it. Put it on now, carry it at your side. Before this journey is over it will become part of you."

"I—I don't want it." She held back her hands.

Still Pelides proffered it. "So far you have survived weaponless," he said somberly. "Now I offer you this weapon—it may someday help you survive. Ask someone to instruct you in its use. Do you think that, once refused, you won't one day regret it?"

"Pelides, I—"

"Take the knife. It is a gesture, Tias, and a symbol. I may not be in this mood again. You have not needed a weapon at any time in your life, but you will in the future."

Tias swallowed nervously. Suddenly it seemed to her that by taking the knife she was crossing some unmarked division, that her soul was somehow striding from one path to another. One path was in Suthad, perhaps, ending as Suthad had ended, the other leading toward a new horizon. She must take the knife and turn herself to the new road for the old road was no more. The feeling was so strong that it frightened her.

"I don't want it," she told Pelides again. "I feel there is some sorcery—"

Pelides sighed in his mask. "No sorcery. The weapon is of good steel, no more, and I offer it to you for your own protection. Take it if you will."

"I'll take it, but—" Hesitantly she wrapped her fingers about it, and a strange sensation seemed to ripple over her. She looked up at Pelides, but as soon as the knife left his hand he turned from her once more, clasped his hands behind his back, and resumed his staring from the window.

Tias, trembling, slowly backed away, then turned and ran on pattering feet back down the corridor to her room.

They left Suthad the next morning—Olin's small army on a crusade against black sorcery, to face a monster whom none of them, save one, had ever seen.

Allas wondered that Tias did not protest wildly at their going. She breakfasted quietly, saying little, then mounted a horse without ado and rode beside Allas out the western gate. He noticed the dagger she wore on her belt, and recognized it as one of Pelides's, but he did not presume to ask her the why and wherefor of it—not presently, considering her changed mood and attitude.

Olin rode at the head of his company with Duke Pelides on his left and Sonja on his right. Neither he nor Sonja spoke to anyone about what had happened the previous night, and if anyone in the company had noticed their absence, they did not broach the subject.

A few gray faces watched from windows as the thousand horsemen passed through the streets, on their way from Suthad. But none hailed or called after them; and as the horses passed by and clattered on down the cobbles, the gray faces pulled closed their shutters again and backed away into their dark rooms and their apathy.

West of Suthad the hilly plains and fields of grasses gradually sloped downward and gave way to thicker and thicker woodland and forest. This unpopulated territory had not yet been tamed by the Kothians, and in all directions forestland yielded to swampy waste the further west one traveled. A low mountain range situated between Argos and Koth was the beginning of a thin watercourse that flowed eventually into the Western Sea; but this unnamed tributary followed a tortuous path, and flowed only sluggishly through the western region of fens. It was not a huge area, and caravans and mounted armies could bypass it in a few days; nevertheless it was extensive enough, and a home of death and pestilence and unclean things. And it was here, so Pelides had told Olin, that Asroth had his fortress, which sat atop a low cliff on a rocky hillside on the other side of that stagnant river and the murky, deadly boglands.

A day's ride brought Olin and his small army to the end of the grassy fields. They camped comfortably in the grasses, under the protection of scattered trees at the edge of the woods. Only another day's ride would take them into the deep forest, and yet another into the territory of the sorcerer.

"Can you feel it?" one soldier asked another, sniffing the air.

"Aye—it's changed."

Nor was it their imagination. The aura of the place was the same they had at first known in Suthad, a feeling that brought gooseflesh upon the skin, that affected the senses, that seemed a harbinger of unnatural, impending tempest . . . .

The campfires were made, and while the troops prepared their evening meals Lord Olin stood before his tent and watched to the south. The sun died in the west and sent lengthening shadows across the fields. Hills slowly became inky silhouettes, valleys filled with gloom, and at last the black horizon of the land was merged with the descending night. Stars filled the great ceiling of the skies and to the south, where Olin watched, other lights glowed.

Sonja, standing beside him, commented: "They're closer than they were last night."

"Aye, and tomorrow night, I think, they'll be closer yet. They want—" He caught himself.

The crunch of boots had caught their attention. Pelides approached, noticed the lights to the south, and shook his head.

"More of them," he murmured in his strange voice. No longer did he make any pretense of not knowing what the lights were. "Asroth is before us in his citadel, watching by magical means, while behind us camp the priests of Ikribu, who want both Asroth and us."

"Us?" Olin asked.

"The Ring," Pelides ammended tonelessly.

"Caught in the middle, perhaps," Sonja growled, "but we're not cornered, Pelides.

"Not if we have the Ring," he replied.

Sonja did not deign to respond. Instead with deliberate casualness she returned her gaze to the south. After a silent moment Pelides withdrew, entering Olin's tent.

Sonja turned. After a few moments, she heard sounds coming from the tent—strange sounds, like chewing and gurgling, eerily unhuman. The faces of the two soldiers Olin had stationed before the tent flaps were impassive.

"Olin?" Sonja said.

"I have never seen his face," he told her. "I do not want to. I allow him to take his meals in private."

"Out of respect for him?"

Olin shrugged. "Or myself, perhaps." He stared at the distant campfires, then said: "He suffers strange dreams as well."

"I can almost feel pity for him, Olin."

He looked back at her, smiled awkwardly, then sighed. "I still feel like when we first entered Suthad. Can you feel that—*malignancy* in the air?"

"Yes, but I did not feel it today, during our ride."

"Nor did I. Pelides swears the atmosphere will become worse as we approach Asroth's fortress. This—*sorcery*" Olin slapped his hands together in an abrupt display of vitality, not wanting to bow to this encroaching feeling of inhumanness. "I do not—"

He was interrupted by howls from the troops camped below. The soldiers' cries carried up clear and distinct on the evening air—cries of alarm.

"Stop him! Grab that—!"

"Emros, no! *No!*"

"Get—away—!"

"Take his sword! Take his *swor*—!"

"*Mitra!*" Olin cursed and ran down toward the commotion, Sonja at his heels.

A knot of perhaps thirty men had collected at one

corner of the camp, and at the center of them Olin and Sonja saw a single warrior with blade drawn, snarling, dementia in his eyes. Olin recognized the man and knew him for a stalwart rogue who would never crack under duress.

A number of the men gathered there stepped aside when they recognized Lord Olin.

"We don't know what happened, sir," one of them told him. "One moment he was simply talking about a feeling in the air, and how he didn't want to fight a sorcerer. And then he grabbed his sword and tried to kill the man next to him."

Olin stepped ahead. "Emros!" he called, holding out his arms, weaponless, in a gesture of trust. "Hand me your sword."

Emros backed away, bumped into a tree. "I see you!" he snarled, spittle drooling down his beard. "Sorcerer! You'll not take me! I'll drive this steel through your black heart before you can—"

Then he jumped ahead, howling and waving his sword. Olin drew back hurriedly, and others with him.

"We'll have to slay him!" cried a soldier. "He's a mad dog—doesn't even know us, or himself!"

Sonja ran forward, pushing soldiers aside and drawing her sword.

"Don't kill him!" she shouted. "If I can disarm him—"

"She-demon!" howled Emros, his eyes flaring, teeth snapping. "Sent by *Asroth,* eh? I see the magic staff in your hand—but you won't get *me!*"

Again he leaped ahead, swung his sword in a wide circle. Sonja crouched and parried his slice, then retreated, deftly drawing Emros back and away from the crowd of onlookers. Emros shrieked with rage.

"You won't kill me with that staff!" he howled, fighting madly to get past Sonja's blade.

Sonja swore. Emros had a madman's strength to pit against her skill, and at every blow she felt a jarring numbness growing in her arm. The fool was fighting wide open, berserk! Expertly she feinted and lunged, trying to take Emros in his weapon hand. He sought to charge, slipped on a wet patch of grass; his blow went wild and Sonja unintentionally cut him along the upper arm.

"*Yiiie!* Bitter by the staff!" Emros shrieked. "Poisoned by the she-devil's sorcery! I'll not die by poison sorcery!" he shrieked. "She-demon—wizard—pack of demons! Mitra, take my soul!"

And he twisted the sword around in his grasp—and fell on it.

A chorus of moans and yells went up from the gathered troops—all, now, hunching forward wide-eyed in the field to witness the insanity. Emros pitched forward face-first into the turf; his sword, plunged hilt-deep through his chest, protruded like a silver-red tongue from between his shoulders.

Shaken, Olin yelled out to his men: "Back to your tents, you gawkers!"

Sonja stood there a long moment, staring at the corpse, until someone touched her arm and called her by name. She looked up. It was Som.

"Come away," he urged her in a low tone. "Naught else can be done for him. Perhaps suicide was the wisest thing. I think there was a spell on him."

Sonja shook her head and slowly walked off, back toward Olin's tent. Olin joined her, and together they climbed the grassy slope as the soldiers behind and below them drifted away in mumbling groups. Two or three of them took charge of Emros's body, dragging it away from the fires to inter it out of view.

Olin's expression was fierce; his jaw muscles twitched and his lips curled back from clenched teeth.

"What *now?*" he asked Sonja, and himself. "Will Asroth slay us all with his sendings, as he did Emros? Or will we each go slowly mad and murder *ourselves?*"

"Perhaps that's what he wants us to do," said Sonja, "to feed on our own fears till we destroy ourselves. I think we should disappoint him. As for Emros, perhaps it was best that he died by his own hand rather than be a slave to sorcery."

Olin shook his head.

Then they saw Pelides standing motionless, watching the field below. He turned to them as they made their way up the slope to the campfire and sat down before Olin's tent.

"Not the first," Pelides muttered darkly, arms folded across his chest. "Nor the last."

The forest grew thicker as the army moved on next morning, and the air became more humid. Soon it was necessary to ford small streams and trail-break through the undergrowth of rushes and reeds at the banks. Trees grew ever taller and closer together and began to take on a more sinister aspect, their great boles and heavy branches looming on all sides and reaching away into a shadowed vastness high above. Mists clung to the ground all morning, catching errant beams of sunlight and forming gray, murky swirls of fog that intermittently hid portions of the moving troops from one another. From far off came the noises of forest creatures, growls and thrashings of large beasts, and the weird cries of unknown birds. Flocks hovered high in the foliage above them, as if trailing the army or spying.

But no one reacted with madness. The only effect of the land they traveled through seemed to be a depression of the soul. Among the soldiers there was growing an unusual sullenness that produced flashes of sudden anger at trivialities.

Tias complained bitterly and often about the route and though Allas tried to keep his emotions in check, her constant worrying made him tense and overanxious. Som rode with them, telling jokes or recounting stories of his past exploits in an attempt to amuse Tias or turn her mind from the drudgery, and the ominous surroundings. But his efforts, though vigorous, did little good.

Olin kept a sharp eye on the trail ahead, trying to probe the shades and shadows and indistinct forms as mists drifted in the oblique sharded light. The broken path turned to soggy, mossy carpeting that sloped gently down to more placid streams, through dry ground close-hemmed with trees, by stagnant pools where the air was as warm with mosquitoes and gnats.

"How much farther?" Olin would ask Pelides, more and more frequently as the journey came to pall on him.

"First we must enter swampland."

"Can we cross the swampland in one day?"

"If we press. The bogs are dangerous. It might be better to go around—"

"And delay our journey by how long?"

"Two days, three."

Olin shook his head determinedly. "I want to see Asroth dead as soon as possible."

"But we must take care as we cross the swamps. *Things* are there—"

"What things?" Olin asked irritably.

"Asroth knows of our coming, his minions await us."

"I have an army," Olin reminded him, "and each man remaining with us is worth two of those who abandoned the quest."

"Asroth has his army," Pelides replied, and then withheld further comment.

They made camp that night on a rise of land that was more or less dry, in the heart of the great forest. The stink of the swamplands carried; the air felt heavier than it had the night before, with its cloak of mist and shadows and dampness.

There were no stars to be seen beyond the thick boughs of heavy foliage; and though campfires were hurriedly lit in the descending dusk for warmth and light and cooking, the air of the deep forest seemed to encroach upon the flames as if wanting to subdue and smother them. Conversations were hushed; tempers grew shorter all around.

As Sonja cooked a fowl over her open fire, Olin sat beside her. He had become temperamental, irritable, angry. "Damn Asroth!" he fumed continually. "I'll bring his head back on a pike and hang it from Suthad's western wall."

"I think you're as worried about Asroth as you are about the feel of this land," Sonja told him.

"And what does that mean?" Olin asked sharply.

Sonja smiled dryly. "Only this—a line I once told Allas, and which I think is true. A Khorajan poet told it to me—that a magician's strength is in illusions of fear, and that if he can make his enemies reveal their souls to him, then half his magic is accomplished."

"As with Emros last night, you mean?"

"Aye, perhaps. But with all of our army as well, Olin. Look at them—depressed, tired, quick tempered. This land is doing it to them, and their expectancy that at any moment *something* might occur. At any moment a storm might brew, an army emerge, or Asroth himself appear to stay our advance. Such fears work into the mind like maggots in a corpse; they fester and boil and work to no good. That is Asroth's advantage."

"Aye." Olin felt his own temper calming even as he realized the truth of her words. "Aye, Sonja, you're right. My mind is become so burdened with thoughts of foulness that I weaken myself and make myself defenseless *for* the foulness."

"We must all keep our minds from thoughts of gloom and defeat," Sonja told him. "We're strong, each one of us, and we have swords and armor and the will to triumph."

Olin felt cheered at her words. He stood up, clapped a hand on her shoulder. "It might be best were I to make the rounds and speak with the men in small groups, steel them and work them up to better spirits."

"Aye." Sonja placed her hand, briefly, on Olin's. There was warmth—friendliness—a shared concern, each for the other. Sonja smiled.

Olin went off, trudging over the mossy ground to other campfires.

Red Sonja ate her roast fowl, with good wine to wash it down, and relaxed. She would sleep well tonight, she felt, even in the middle of this weird forest.Her thoughts skittered briefly over what had happened so far on this quest—the faces and events, the words and looks. To her memory came the evening of her swordfight with Olin—the dispute of love whose outcome had been left in abeyance. She wondered whether Olin, once done with this crusade, would again remind her of his love and their interrupted battle of wills and swords.

Their interrupted battle . . . Sonja's mind flashed to the priests of Ikribu, and to the Ring still in her pouch. She stood up and guardedly looked around, stretched, then sauntered away from her campfire. The coolness of the air was a welcome contrast to the blazing heat of the fire, though mosquitoes and ghats hummed in the dark, muggy air. Once away from the light of the fires and the company of the soldiers, Sonja took the opportunity to pull the Ring from her pouch and briefly examine it in the half light. It winked and coruscated, shining as if with an intelligence of its own.

She heard footsteps behind her; expecting it to be Olin, she casually replaced the Ring, then turned with a smile to ask how his speeches of encouragement had gone.

The footsteps stopped. Before her stood Duke Pelides, ebon-visaged and black-armored, with an uncanny, angry hue lent to his false face by the backlighting effect of the fires.

Chapter 9

The Face of Sorcery

Sonja's brain raced. Had Pelides seen the Ring? Had he noticed the light of it, playing in waves in the surrounding darkness? For a timeless moment she stared into the black mask, the black eye-sockets that gave no clue to the intelligence within. Sonja's heart went cold. Instantly she decided that if Pelides made one move toward her, if he made any mention of the Ring, if he sneered or laughed or began to growl, she would draw blade and cut him down, end his charade here, in this forest.

Pelides stared at her in a drawn pause, almost as if he were reading her mind and deliberating what to do, what to say. Then he ended the wordless conflict with a nod at the forest and said in his low, hollow voice: "The lights from the south are clearer."

Sonja did not look to see. "What do you want, Pelides?"

He did not move. "Olin is speaking with the soldiers," he said quietly, "urging them on for the fight."

"What of it?" Still her hand rested tensely on her sword, and she knew that Pelides sensed her readiness.

"Foolish to assume that a thousand swords can defeat Asroth," said Pelides. "Madness and suicide to fight our way through the swamps with only steel to protect us."

Sonja watched him, blue eyes sparking.

"We need the Ring, Hyrkanian—else our cause is doomed."

"I grow weary of hearing you recite that theme, Duke Pelides."

"And I grow weary of game-playing. I want the Ring."

"So does Asroth."

"You know where it is. The Stygian told you before he died."

"He did not."

"You're *lying.*" Pelides's voice was a low growl, like that of a beast at bay.

Sonja stood her ground. "Make one step, Pelides, and you will never set eyes on Asroth's fortress, I promise you that."

She could hear him breathing within his hollow mask. "You are sending all these men to their deaths!" he whispered hoarsely. "They trust you and yet you are their butcher. These men will die in agony, blasted mercilessly, all because you, she-demon—!"

"Enough, Pelides!" cried Sonja, startled by his use of the same epithet Emros had used.

'—because *you,* will not reveal where the Ring is hidden."

"Say no more, Pelides, or I'll cut off your tongue!"

He laughed hollowly. "You won't," he said in his hissing whisper. "You need me. Olin needs me. Your sword cannot slay me, Red Sonja, not with Asroth's spell upon me. You know where the Ring is, and you'll tell me before we reach the fortress."

Sonja shook her head once, eyes narrowing.

Pelides, finished with his demands, made as if to draw away. He half-turned, then paused, faced Sonja again and told her: "I will tell you what I suspect, Hyrkanian. I will read in your eyes if I speak the truth. I believe that the priest told you where the Ring was, that you discovered it before we left Suthad."

Sonja stared at him.

"Someone in this camp now possesses the Ring.

Asroth does not have it, that I know. Sopis went to Suthad to get it; he knew where it was and would have had it by the time you met him. He might have secreted it before he died, or—"

"Perhaps one of the cultists of Ikribu has it, Pelides."

"No," he replied with assurance. "They are after *us,* as well as Asroth. They can do nothing to harm the sorcerer without the Ring, even as *we* can do nothing against him without it. No. Sopis told you the location of the Ring, or you found it somehow. That doesn't matter. What matters is that I don't believe Olin is fool enough to pit only muscle and steel against Asroth. He has seen what Asroth can do, and he would lead his troops to battle such a power only if he were certain that he could protect them. Therefore, the Ring is here."

Sonja swallowed tensely; her hand itched to draw her sword.

"You're crazy, Pelides. Even if you were right, what *use* would the Ring be to us without the knowledge of how to channel its forces? We are not sorcerers."

"Nor am I."

"Then what good will the Ring do *you?*"

"You know the answer," said Pelides contemptuously. "The spell that protects the Ring from sorcerous divination and attack will likewise protect its wearer Only the acolytes of Ikribu know how to penetrate its defenses. Once I have it, I will be able to enter Asroth's fortress without fear of being detected by his magic or deterred by the illusions he conjures to protect him. Then I will need no sorcery to slay him."

"Perhaps so—but why just *you,* Pelides? Are there not others who have as great a grievance against Asroth—?"

"No!" barked Pelides; then, in a quieter voice: "Not even Lord Olin, who has lost a city and a kingdom, has suffered more from Asroth's sorcery than I, who have lost not only my very humanity but perhaps even my soul. Only *I* deserve to slay Asroth, and for that I will need the Ring's power."

"Perhaps you deserve a chamber in Hell, Pelides,"

said Sonja crisply. "You are not here to help Olin and the rest of us; you are here to *use* us all, in any way you can, to accomplish your own personal revenge. Now, get away from me—or I'll send you to Hell quicker than Asroth will!"

Pelides chuckled mirthlessly. Instead of obeying, he stepped ahead a pace, rubbing his palms together. "I will not use Olin and the rest of you, Hyrkanian, because I do not *need* you; all I need is the Ring." His voice became harsh and vibrant with hatred. "Do you know *why* I am so avid for revenge, Red Sonja?"

"*Begone* from me, Pelides!" Sonja growled.

"No." His voice dropped to a whisper. "I will let you judge for yourself."

Sonja drew a breath. Pelides lifted his gloved hands to his face, reached behind his casque, and pulled. Her heart froze. Two small clicks sounded loudly in the muggy dimness.

Was he going to bare his face to her? Sonja's imagination raced. What new ploy was this? Was Pelides trying to disarm her? Was it true that to look upon his face inspired madness . . . ?

Pelides's mask twisted and came free in his gloved hands; there was a moist sound as he pulled it from his head. Sonja averted her face to one side, watching Pelides askance, wanting to keep him in view yet not wanting to look upon his legendary, hideous features.

"You see?" he said.

His voice was garbled, as if issuing from between pulped, swollen lips. His head was backlit by the fires of the camp so that Sonja could not distinctly see his misshapen face. A breeze, suddenly blowing through the trees all around, made the flames flicker so that his naked face was swept with moving, blurry shadows. His eyes showed clear, but that was all—the whites of them gleaming crystalline from the black blotch atop his neck; one seemed to droop lower than the other. . . . A fringe of hair matted and coarse, clung to the sides of the neck;

free strands, blowing, seemed to pick up gleams from the fires behind. But the face—the face was unclear, indistinct, and it inspired a huge loathing, a monstrous revulsion in Sonja, as if that face were somehow the accumulation of all the horrors and fears she carried within her heart. It was as though Pelides's black, distorted face, betraying lumpiness and hints of raw veins, hinting at dissolved muscles or destroyed details or unhuman protuberances, was somehow a mirror in which Sonja could read the uttermost fears of her childhood, the horror of her family's destruction, the awfulness of things she had battled in other lands, the tremulous icy grip of other-worldliness that had sometimes possessed her in her travels—midnights spent alone amid wild mountains, in deserts or in deep forests. She imagined soft tar pliantly molded by some mad artisan's fingers, magically imbued by some sorcerer's will with the ability to suggest frightening and soulless patterns of cosmic terror, so that those who looked upon that image instantly recognized the fears of their own souls, bared. Her own phrase came to her mind: a magician's strength is in illusions of fear. She realized suddenly that Asroth —whoever he was, whatever he was—had made Pelides into a living vessel of hellish illusions, and she wondered what nightmares tormented Pelides. What hideous visions must assail him, knowing that he, himself, was a walking, breathing, *changing* tool of such insane grammary!

She looked away, unable to stand looking at Pelides even indirectly.

"Enough, Pelides," she grated, a strange catch in her throat. "You cannot inspire me to pity."

"No," came his reply in a voice now sibilant. "Not to pity, Red Sonja. Perhaps to understand, perhaps to new heights of fear and hatred and desire for vengeance. Did you see yourself in my face? My face has been known to drive men mad."

"Spare me, Pelides," she growled warningly.

"I *have,* Hyrkanian," Pelides replied, "as well you know."

She waited, listening to the sounds of the mask replaced. Cold shiverings pimpled her flesh, and even when Pelides told her that she could again face him, she was wary. Perhaps he lied, perhaps she might now be able to see *through* the mask, now that she had seen him without it . . . .

"I continue to watch you, Hyrkanian," said Pelides, the old vitriolic harshness in his tone once more. "You know where the Ring is. Does Olin have it? The youth, Allas? Yourself? Or are you all trading it carefully, to divert my suspicion from one to the other?"

"Your face has affected your mind, Pelides."

He chuckled darkly. "Oh, yes, Red Sonja; quite correct—but not in any way you could understand. I think that perhaps that mindless giant, Som, now holds the Ring. We shall see."

Sonja swallowed again; the ice thawed in her nerves, melted from her arms and legs.

"I am watching," Pelides warned again, and then he walked off, slowly, as if measuring each footstep he set upon the ground.

And Sonja, still panting from the repressed fear of looking upon the shadowed face of naked terror, remained behind a few minutes until she was sure that Pelides had passed through the camp and retired to Lord Olin's tent.

Later she sat by her campfire. Olin had joined her, but she had not told him what Pelides had done; Pelides had already retired, as had most of the camp. She and Olin talked of other things; he, once or twice, broadly hinted at his affection for her while skirting the issue of their swordfight on the hilltop. But for the most part, they spoke of minor things and not at all of Asroth and the Ring, or Pelides, or death and sorcery, or Olin's quest for vengeance.

Yet now, as their talk quieted and trailed off like the

fading glow of the campfires and the hushed, fitful breezes amid the forest, Sonja found herself staring into the flames and reflecting upon what Pelides had said to her, and what he had done. She was almost resolved to mention the matter in private to Olin, when a soldier approached noiselessly and asked in a whisper:

"My lord, would you come with me?"

"Why can't you speak aloud?" Olin demanded.

"I don't want to arouse the men, sir."

"What has happened?"

The soldier thought a moment, as if considering the best way to explain, then said simply: "Four men have died, sir."

"What are you saying?" Olin got to his feet, and Sonja rose beside him.

"Lord Olin, they died quietly. I didn't notice it at first, till I asked Mors a question. He didn't answer, so I thought he'd fallen asleep, but when I shook him and he rolled to one side—Lord Olin, there was such a look of *fear* on his face, that I—" The soldier stopped, shaken, raised a trembling hand to wipe sweat from his brow, then continued: "I—I thought I had best to alert you."

"Are there others at your fire?"

"Aye, sir."

"Lead me."

As quietly as possible the man led Olin and Sonja on a winding course through the encampment, stepping over sleeping men, passing by dying fires until he came to his own.

"Four," said a soldier nearby, standing up. "Four dead, Lord Olin."

"All in their sleep?"

"Aye, sir. They died soundlessly."

Olin knelt low, felt for the pulse of one of the men, found none. He reached out and closed the corpse's eyes; the drawn, frozen expression of utter terror stamped on the dead soldier's face sent icy chills down his back. Olin arose again.

"Awaken some of the others nearby," he said. "If all

are dead—" The thought of several hundred sleeping men lying about the field—sleeping, to wake no more—brought a shakiness to his voice.

But on the ground nearby a man, prodded from his slumber, sat up and croaked: "What the hell's going on? Are you going to let us sleep or—? Oh—Lord Olin, forgive me, sire—"

"Pay me no mind, man. Are you well?"

"Well enough to butcher wizards," he answered sternly, recalling Olin's speech of earlier in the evening.

Others awoke also, complaining at their rousing and asking Mitra to make their fellows leave them in peace for a needed night's rest. Olin breathed more calmly, tapped Sonja on the shoulder, and motioned her back toward their own fire. The soldier who had originally come to him followed a short way, confessing to Olin: "I am afraid to rest, my lord."

"I think you have nothing more to fear, soldier. If this is Asroth's sorcery, he is probably done with it." He studied the youth's face, saw that the lad was young—too young, by far, to be experiencing such events as these. Olin's heart went out to him. "What is your name, lad?"

"Sarinth."

"Return to your blankets, Sarinth. I think no more harm will visit us this night."

Yet his tone was not entirely confident, and Sarinth was by no means assured that death would not grip him silently and swiftly in his dreams. But he nodded reluctantly to Olin, then returned to his fire.

Olin sighed heavily as he and Sonja made their way back to their own fire. "Little by little," he said bitterly, "one by madness, others in their sleep—one by one. How long will it last? Will there be ten men left when we finally reach his fortress?"

"If a magician can make his enemies reveal their souls to him," said Sonja in a cold whisper, "then half his magic is accomplished."

"And in dreams," Olin replied, "men's souls are freer than birds on the wing, visioning great delights and great terrors both—true?"

"Aye, Lord Olin."

They reached their fire, which had dwindled to orange cinders that glowed with a gentle heat. It was late; both Olin and Sonja stretched and yawned, then smiled at the simultaneity of it.

"Time for sleep," Sonja announced, covering her mouth. She turned to her rolled blankets and began to unlace them.

"Sonja—you may sleep in my tent, if you wish," offered Olin.

"No." She knew he meant nothing untoward by his offer, yet found herself resisting her own sudden desire to accept it. "I thank you, but—no, Olin. I prefer to sleep in the open, alone. I have always been that way."

"Very well, then, but—" Olin looked down at her, and his tone changed. "Pleasant dreams, Sonja."

He meant—just that.

"Aye, Olin, aye—and you."

Blackness—a void, chill and damp as the Pit itself. Sonja stood alone, the darkness about her so real and tangible that when she reached out to feel through it, it seemed to stick clammily to her fingers, like soft tar. Yet the blackness she stood upon, though she could not see it, felt real enough beneath her boots. The sword she gripped in her hand seemed to cut away enough of the viscid darkness for her to maneuver, but she could see nothing. She moved forward, and as she walked carefully, sword before her, an itchy sweat grew on her flesh. A fear began to grow in her as she realized that no matter how far she walked the blackness would not lessen, no light would ever come to her.

Her pulse quickened. The blackness seemed to suffocate her in some impalpable way. She walked ahead but saw no relief from the darkness, and so turned about purposefully on her heels, making sure of the hardness beneath her feet, then strode back in the opposite direction. Or was it the opposite direction? She could not tell. The darkness was complete. She could not see her own hand, could catch no glimmer from her mail armor, no shining half-light from her sword blade. Panic began to grip her and the suffocating feel of the darkness seemed to close in more densely about her. The clammy feel of horror began to weigh her down like a physical pressure.

Yet she trudged on. Now she began to feel a breeze blowing—a stirring in the viscous blackness that grew into a violent wind. She was being blown backwards, yet her feet remained solidly on the blackness below. She was tumbling backward, the darkness was tumbling with her; but there was no way to tell, nothing to see and nothing around to feel . . . .

She felt her boots blowing away, disintegrating, turned to old parchment, shredding free of her feet and whisping away in brittle bits behind her. Her armor dissolved likewise, rusting into insubstantiability, the linked scales withering dead leaves bound by rotted grasses, blowing away, evaporating, leaving her naked to the frigid gale that blew yet harder.

Then even her sword was gone—transformed into a brittle reed, a useless twig that passed as dust. Her fist gripped clammy, cold tar.

Fear stole over her—icy, utter, with nothing to focus on save the blackness, the interminable *blackness* outside and inside her as well. Her mind went black; her eyes went black. There was nothing to see, no direction to go—

She fell to her knees. Her wind-whipped hair, flying behind her, turned gummy and flaked from her skull, vanishing in the wind. She tried to cry out but could not; her gums and teeth were soft; her arms and legs, her breasts and feet dissolved into streams of black, gummy tar, and there was no way to fight, nothing to see, nothing to face, only the blackness turning everything liquid and putrescent. She felt her face beginning to melt into dripping gummy tar, and though she wanted to scream she had no voice, she had no mind. She was a flowing, dissolving wind of blackness—

"Sonja!"

—dissolving and flowing and she could not—

"Sonja!"

Light! The wind had brought light from somewhere. *Light* bled towards her as the wind died down, as—

"Sonja!" Something gripped her, warm and firm; not tar. She was trembling and shaking, but she was real, she was real—

Something enveloped her, and the light became orange. Suddenly she felt herself lying on cool dampness and the orange became dying faggots in the fire. She lay on her own sweat-sodden blankets and she was looking over Olin's shoulder, breathing the scent of him, manly and trail-worn and sweaty, and he was hugging her, holding her and rocking her—

"Olin!"

"Mitra!" he gasped. "Gods! You were suffering in your dreams—you were *dying*—almost like . . ."

"Olin!" She was awake now, her hands on the grass, her armor on her body, her sword in its scabbard lying at her side.

Olin let her go, knelt beside her. He was shivering, and his voice was shaking. "Oh, *Mitra!*" he breathed.

"I'm all right now, Olin! I'm all right!"

"I nearly fell asleep," he confessed to her, horror in his tone at what might have happened had he done so. "But I was roused by Pelides—"

"Pelides?" Now she could hear low groans issuing from Olin's tent.

"He is dying in his sleep," Olin told her quickly. "I wanted the Ring, to try to save him, but I found *you*—!"

"The *Ring?*" Sonja was on her knees now; she strapped on her sword as Olin got to his feet and started toward his tent; then she sprang up and ran after him.

"We cannot allow him to die, Sonja. I know you distrust him. I do not trust him either—but we need him. He must face Asroth with us—"

"Yes, yes!"

"Perhaps the Ring can save him—it is our only chance. He has suffered these dreams nightly since I've known him, but tonight—when all of us are *dying* in our dreams . . . !"

Sonja hurriedly searched her pouch, pulled free the scintillating Ring. "But I don't know how to use it, Olin."

"I hope that does not matter. Its strength may be enough by itself. We must hurry, but Pelides must not know."

They reached the tent. Olin tore open the flaps and entered, pulling Sonja behind by one hand.

Pelides lay on his cot, his ebony helmet turned away from them, his body stiff and shivering as with an intense fever. He was moaning hoarsely, and Sonja immediately guessed him a dying man.

"The *Ring*, Sonja!" Olin nearly shouted.

She held it in one palm, stared at Pelides as she approached him. A sudden seizure gripped him and he thrashed on his cot, kicked and groaned in utter agony. Sonja stood beside him looking down, Olin directly behind her.

"Touch him with it!" Olin directed her. "Place it on his chest!"

Wary, staring at the writhing, twisting figure on the cot, Sonja did so, gingerly dropping it upon his breast. Its scintillating light spilled in clear waves upon Pelides's mask and armor.

His shiverings ceased. Pelides's arms fell slack and weary from his sides, his legs straightened on the blankets. A low moan issued from behind his visor, and Sonja saw—through the eye slits—that his lids fluttered, his eyes opened.

Instantly she took back the Ring, stepped away, and stood beside Olin, shoving it again into her belt pouch.

Pelides sat up groggily, leaning on one arm. He turned and looked at the pair staring at him.

"What—?" His voice sounded hoarse and croaking.

"You were seized again with a violent nightmare," Olin told him, "worse than other nights, Pelides. A number of soldiers have died this night, from nightmare sendings from Asroth."

"You—" Pelides sat up on his cot, tried to stand but rested a moment more. "How did you save me?" he asked. "Asroth had drawn my soul beyond the point of —" He stopped abruptly and a light entered his eyes; Sonja and Olin could see the intelligence glint in them even from behind his mask. "The *Ring!*"

"No, Pelides—"

Pelides got to his feet, fierce hatred knotting the muscles in his limbs. "You have the ring. *Give* it to me!"

"No!" Sonja yelled at him. "You fool, we've just saved your *life!* Plague us no more about the Ring."

"I will *have* it!" Pelides howled, reaching for his sword. With a lurch he drew it free, then crouched against his cot and faced them. "Which one of you has it? You'll give it to me, or *die*—I swear it!"

Olin stepped ahead, glowering. "Put away that sword, Pelides!"

Pelides drew back, sword held menacingly. Olin retreated a pace, still refusing to draw his own blade in confrontation.

But Sonja readily freed hers. "Damn you, Pelides! If it's the Ring you want, you'll have to kill *me* for it!" Steel glimmering luridly in the dim lamplight, she jumped ahead a step and swung her sword down at him.

Pelides ducked, saved himself with an awkward parry. Olin cried out, but Sonja—furious and exasperated—had had enough. Once, twice, once more she lunged at Pelides, not sparing him despite his grogginess. Pelides howled wrathfully, stumbled upon his cot, sought to move around it—but Sonja held him at bay, forcing him to meet each one of her strokes while deftly preventing him from making any worthwhile counterattack.

"*Enough!*" Olin cried out, drawing his own blade.

Pelides made a lunge. Sonja caught it. Their blades snaked and scraped, moved downward with points crossed near the ground—and in that instant Olin brought down his own, the edge clanging into the crotch of the crossed swords, pinning them into the sod.

"No more!" roared Olin. "Pelides—put away your blade! Sonja—get outside and cool your temper!"

For a heartbeat, each ignored Olin's command, wanting to shove him aside and continue this duel to the death. Yet, realizing the absurdity of it, and feeling the force of Olin's anger, each slowly relaxed and drew erect, both silently vowing to finish the conflict another day.

Sonja backed away from Pelides and Olin, turned and went through the tent doors, shoving her steel home in its scabbard when she was outside in the cool air. A crowd had gathered but Sonja pushed through them, ignoring their comments and questions as she made for her fire.

Allas followed her there. "What happened, Sonja," he asked.

"He wanted the Ring—" she began, then checked herself.

"The *Ring?*" Allas breathed. "Then you have it?"

Sonja whirled and faced him, her temper still with her. "Tell no one, Allas, do you understand?"

He was taken aback by the ferocity of her tone. "I—understand—"

"No one is to know! This is between Olin and Myself—and Pelides, now."

"I understand, Sonja."

"Then get back to sleep. Dawn will be here soon."

He stood a moment, surprised at the violence of her temper, then turned and went away. He passed Lord Olin emerging from his tent but said nothing.

"You men return to your sleep," Olin commanded harshly. "Go on!"

Sonja ignored Olin as he sat down beside her. Neither said anything. A soldier approached.

"What is it?" Olin snapped.

"Sir, I'm—I'm afraid a dozen more men have—died in their sleep."

Olin did not answer him. Wearily he bent his head to his chest, wound his hands through his hair, and sighed an immense, labored sigh of impotency. Sonja, angered, stood up swiftly and kicked her dying fire, scattering it in a shower of orange coals. Then she stood staring defiantly at the night, legs wide-braced, clenched fists shivering at her sides. She wanted to curse, but felt the futility of it.

The soldier backed away, returned to his fire and his comrades.

From far off, deep in the thick forest and the swamps, birds were raising their first shrill cries to the graying east.

As dawn broke grim and pale through the low, clinging mists of the forest, it was discovered that seventy-seven men would not be joining in the day's march through the western swamplands. Each lay rigid in his blankets with face contorted into a mask of fear, limbs frozen in positions of agony. One of them was Sarinth.

Although some men muttered of turning back and abandoning the quest, none faced Lord Olin with the challenge. All mounted up, while seventy-seven other horses, riderless, were taken along in tow as spare mounts. Olin rode at the head of his slowly diminishing army, with Sonja at his right. Duke Pelides, however, did not take his customary position at Olin's left but held back, riding just behind Allas and Tias and Som. His black mask turned continually in Sonja's direction, who showed no sign of being aware of him; but Som, sensing that something was up, and trusting Pelides no more than he would a swamp adder, rode close by and kept a keen eye on him.

Late in the morning the terrain shifted suddenly; the

mossy, damp carpet of the forest floor sank under the horses' hoofs, giving way to soggy ground and fenland. Olin slowed the pace of advance.

"Keep in line here," he ordered his men. "Three abreast."

The horsemen following behind him staggered their mounts and the army transformed itself into a long, winding caravan that dipped and twisted through bogs and camouflaged stretchs of soft mulch and quicksand.

The army had not gone far when one man in the rear strayed from the path and blundered into a quagmire. His horse whinnied and shivered; a dozen of his comrades dismounted and waded into the treacherous bog, trying to lend aid. The rider, keeping his wits about him, managed to grab hold the limb of an overhanging tree. His horse panicked and sank the quicker; within moments its nostrils slipped under the soupy muck.

The man hung on to the branch. A friend began to climb the tree to aid him, slipped on moss and damp vines and nearly fell in the muck himself. Someone else produced a dagger and tried to carve handholds with it. Ere he could reach his comrade, however, the man on the branch made a desperate move to save himself and threw his legs up to clasp them about the limb . . . .

The limb snapped.

Soldiers cried out as their comrade fell head first into the quicksand. His shriek was cut short as he sank to his boot tops, legs kicking, and within another breathless moment his boots also were sucked under, leaving behind naught but bubbles and slime on the rancid surface of the pool.

The spirits of the company sank even lower into depression and desperation.

Carefully Olin led his army, halting often to judge the safety of the earth ahead of him. He would try one route, only to call a halt when his horse sank above its fetlocks in some quagmire; then he would slap it in another direction and the troops behind would wend their way clear of the dangerous spot.

All around them lay festering forest, stagnant and misty, full of noxious odors and enigmatic sounds: the caws of carrion birds, the splash of toads and water lizards, the crash and crackle of some large creature stumbling through the thick brush ahead. Once or twice men cried out that they had seen a ripple, the white of an eye, the flash of a jaw, coursing beside them in the deep, greasy waters of the fen.

The swamp existed in perpetual dusk, the air rank and dismal, the light uncertain and treacherous. More men were lost on the way. By noon—which Olin and Sonja had to guess, for the sunlight never reached through the overhanging ceiling of vines and hanging moss—at least a dozen men had blundered into swamp waters and quicksand and drowned, or had been bitten by adders and large, poisonous spiders and centipedes.

More reminders of their perilous situation were not needed, but more were nevertheless forthcoming. Early in the afternoon Olin spied ahead of him some bulky objects floating in a wide, stagnant mere. He tried to discern their nature in the half light.

"What are they?" he asked Sonja as they drew nearer.

She watched the things, uncertain, then made them out and passed judgment. "Corpses."

The bodies of soldiers—mercenaries. Olin stared at the profusion of them as they rode past, at the hundreds of cadavers sprawling puffed and mutilated and discolored all along the bank of the pool, and he recognized them, by some of the armor they wore, as men who had quit his company after the battle in Suthad!

"But why would they ride here?" he wondered aloud. "It was sheer madness. What could they have—?"

He stopped short at the sound of Duke Pelides, close behind, clearing his throat. He looked to Sonja, and read in her eyes the same wondering, unanswerable question that formed in his own mind.

Chapter 10

Death

And yet more men died, by misjudging the terrain and riding into quagmires, by foolishly dismounting to better make their way and being bitten by serpents or swamp spiders, and by sudden fevers—chills that struck abruptly and within moments dizzied them, sickened them, and dropped them dead from their saddles.

And mutilated, rotting, bloated mercenaries were strewn all over the swamp. Had they stupidly tried to make their way home by passing through the swamplands? Had Asroth somehow affected their minds and drawn them to him, to certain death, for the part they had played in aiding Olin? Had they suddenly decided to attack Asroth himself, for whatever reason, perhaps imagining his castle was full of untold treasures?

The questions whirled in Lord Olin's mind as he looked upon the crowds of corpses sprawled about the banks and shallows of the swampland.

With each new death, each new discovery on that march, the men of Olin's company continued to reassess their situation. Thoughts of mutiny built up within them, yet for the time no one voiced those thoughts. For it was too late; those who saw ahead an endless trek through mist and swamp—hemmed in by huge trees concealing Mitra only knew what new horrors—realized that behind them lay only the same dismal prospect. They had traveled too far into the swamp, and since they had ventured in it seemed as though a curtain had been drawn to shut them off from the world behind. There could be no turning back, no mutiny, for if any of them tried to pick up their backtrack and return by it, they would doubtless come to the same end as had the mercenaries whose bodies littered the route ahead of them. Depression and somberness gave way to actual fear and terror in the minds of many; only the feel of their swords in their hands, the movement of their horses beneath them, gave them any feeling of security.

Allas was growing more and more restless. He rode at the front of the line, beside Som and Tias and just behind Duke Pelides. More and more often he glanced to Som, as if the big man's demeanor were a measure for adjusting to his own emotions and doubts. Som gave no indication that any of the dangers around them, real or imagined, had in the least dampened his determination. He rode his horse proudly, one hand on the reins, the other resting on his sword pommel, gently guiding his mount over the treacherous terrain. Once, when a large serpent hanging from a tree watched him as if about to dart into his face, Som only chuckled and cursed, warning it to stay back or suffer the sting of steel. Another time, his horse mistakenly stepped into soft mulch and nearly threw him in a sudden panic, but Som gently cooed to the animal and patted its neck, talking to it of days past when they had together braved dangers far worse than a stretch of swamp. Occasionally, riding through one of those too-infrequent patches of securer ground, Som would notice Allas eyeing him—a young soldier looking for guidance from an old trooper. Then Som would lean close to him and, conspiratorially, as if sharing a secret that the gods might steal could they overhear, tell him some ribald jest to lighten his heart or some tale of danger that he had lived through and that had been a thousand times worse than this. That sort of talk steeled Allas's heart. He was a young man—and now, riding through this earthly hell, he seemed very young even to himself. He had never fought in wars before, had never faced sorcery, had never killed. He needed to borrow some of Som's courage, needed to feel that Olin and Red Sonja were in control of the situation. When Allas felt that, he was a proper young soldier gradually gaining the experience to one day become a veteran himself.

Som told him: "The reason those men behind us are dying is that they have no control over their thoughts. You must keep things balanced right in your mind. What usually happens when one swordsman has to fight three? Most men would cringe and say: 'Three swords—and I have but one!' Yet the way I look at it, there are *only* three swords, and I am a match for them."

Allas smiled. Som's boasting had a contagious cheerfulness about it.

"The same with this swamp," Som continued. "Those poor, floundering bastards who died back there—they saw this swamp and started immediately to lose their heads. They're the same kind of fools who, in times of peace, lose their heads and want to go to war. They think they'll like warfare. So they get their war and join the fighting, then panic and want out. They're always the first to fall in combat. They have no control.

"Now, as for this swamp—you can start to panic as soon as you get into it. But, just stop and think—it's not going to go on forever, is it? Look at the maps—the rest of the world isn't swamp. This festering mess will take a day, maybe a day and a half to cross. That's not so bad. Don't panic, stay aware, and you won't get hurt. Same thing if you're facing three bastards with swords."

Allas considered all this, and Som's words cheered him; Som was right.

But when he looked to Tias, his mood changed again. Tias had altered; she wasn't the girl he had always known. Seldom had she spoken to him since their leaving Suthad. She wore the dagger Pelides had given to her, and for some reason that worried him. What did it mean, Tias accepting a gift from Pelides? Had something passed between them?

As she rode, Tias kept her eyes on the route before her, but Allas watched her and sensed that her mind wandered to a thousand other places. Whenever corpses were sighted, or word came that a man behind had blundered and died, Tias would shiver. She would not look at Allas, would not turn to him for aid or search his eyes for some slight comfort; instead she would ride straight in her saddle and shudder, as if her fear were something shameful and immoral, not to be shared with anyone. At other times she would slump down listlessly as she rode, drawing into herself. In those moments Allas would canter near to her, ask if she were all right, smile in an attempt to lift up her spirits, but Tias would only shrug or grumble, not looking at him.

"I'm all right, Allas," she told him on one of these occasions. "Anyway, I don't really have a choice, do I—?"

"We'll be all right," said Allas. "This swamp can't go on forever, can it?"

"Well, we can't go on forever either, can we?"

"Keep your hopes up, Tias. We'll be out of here soon."

"I never wanted to come here in the first place," she reminded him. "But now that I'm here, Allas, I'm not stopping for anything." She said it bitterly, angrily, as if he were to blame and she had not decided to come along in the first place out of love for him. Resentfully she went on: "Maybe the rest of them will die, Allas, maybe you'll even die, in the middle of this swamp—but *I* won't. I never wanted to come here in the first place, so I'm not going to die."

Allas was hurt; he looked at her, pain in his expression. This was not like Tias at all. He sensed that she regretted speaking to him so harshly, yet she would not apologize or retract anything she had said. Such speech seemed to bolster her own strength, and she gripped the reins more tightly, watching the bobbing horses ahead, trying to ignore the constant menacing sounds of the woods around her.

Allas sighed and followed beside her closely. Ahead he saw Olin and Sonja and, somewhat behind them, Duke Pelides. He sneered when he saw Pelides, partly to deny his own fears for each time he looked upon the enigmatic Pelides he was reminded of the sorcerer Asroth and the supernatural dangers of the quest they were all upon. He thought of the Ring. He knew that Pelides wanted it, and since Sonja had told him that she had it, Allas had spent many idle, worried moments wondering if, and when, Pelides would try to steal it from her. And now he wondered why, if the Ring were supposedly so potent, it did not protect them all, or even Sonja, from the rigors and dangers of this ride. Could only a sorcerer wield the Ring? And were there others in the swampland, now, who also wished the Ring?

He kept his eyes on Pelides, and on Sonja.

A man behind screamed; someone else who had blundered into a pit or bog. The sounds keened wildly through the forest, quivering on the mists, but Allas rode steadily on, beside Tias. Som and Pelides, Sonja and Olin also rode on, never looking back. What could be done? Another scream for help rang out—perhaps from a man who had tried to help the first one. Still the column rode on, never looking back. What good could they do? Was this not a sorcerer's swamp? Perhaps those men had been fated to die here, fated to die at just the moment their screams had risen to the canopy of foliage . . . .

A strange fatalism was spreading over Olin's company—a growing, shared feeling that seemed to seep into them from the very air of the swamp. Whereas the sorcerer's fortress had originally been the goal of the march, a new sense of purpose now became apparent.

Few cared any longer about finding the fortress; they cared only to make it through the swamplands. They were together in intent only because they had entered this hell together and now rode together, but all were individuals. Each thought only of his own destiny, his own determination to fight clear.

Olin felt the uneasiness of his men, as did many of the officers who rode near him.

"I fear it is a sending from Asroth," he said. "Do you notice that the men no longer try to aid one another? Soon they may be slaying one another. We must fight this influence. Ride back along the lines, all of you, and tell the men this mood is but an illusion. We must not lose our morale or we cease to be an army."

When the officers had gone, Sonja leaned close to Olin and whispered: "I fear it is indeed a sending, for I do not feel the mood you describe."

"What? But, how—?"

"I carry the Ring, and evidently it is protecting me from this influence. I feel a sense of oppression from these swamplands, but no more than that. Here—grip my hand."

Olin reached out and did so. Immediately he felt his sense of fatalistic gloom dwindle and vanish. When he released Sonja's hand the feeling began to creep back over him, yet not as strong as before.

"Ride close to me, Olin," she urged him. "Touch me when you feel you need strength. Without you this army could not hold together. Tonight, when Pelides is not watching, I will give you the Ring; I should have done so before now."

The army plodded on, their mood of predestination persisting. Only one thing seemed to be able to shatter the apathy, and that was a man's own knowledge of his imminent death. A rider finding himself suddenly mired in the muck with his panicking horse, sinking deeper and deeper, would shriek out in stark fear, convinced the gods had made a mistake and that some other, not he, had been meant to die—until he sank under the soupy, bubbling mud.

But the living knew nothing of the feelings of those who died, and so somewhere in the line men would privately consider that, one more alloted soul having been slain, their own chances of escaping were thus increased by one.

They came at last to a break in the swamp. The marshy, poisonous ground gradually shifted upward and Olin and Sonja found themselves riding on secure, dry turf. Ahead, the terrain sloped down again into further reaches of forest and swamp, and all around this knoll or island stretched deep, stagnant waters. But for a time they could plod on without worrying whether the next step their mounts took might plunge them thigh-deep into bog or quicksand—and death.

"Look!" Pelides pointed ahead. "The foliage is parted just enough so that you can see a distant cliffside. Do you see it—low there?"

Olin and Sonja both nodded. Allas cantered ahead so that he, too, might see.

"That large black rock-mass atop that cliff," Pelides continued, "is the fortress."

Allas looked; he could see it clearly now.

Olin turned to Pelides. "How much farther? We dare not stop to eat or rest, and the afternoon is half gone. Can we make it through this swamp by dusk?"

Pelides shrugged. "I cannot say."

"You cannot say?" Olin abruptly shouted, the tension and weariness and worry getting to him. "You *know* these lands!" He ceased, at a look from Sonja, then grunted in disgust and motioned his army ahead.

Pelides held back. Sonja took advantage of the pause to look behind her, once, to glance at him. Pelides was gazing straight at her, and she knew that he but waited for the slightest chance to take the Ring. She muttered an oath to the god Erlik and rode on.

Behind, someone cried out.

Neither Sonja nor Olin paid much heed. Another death—another blunder into the bowels of this devouring Hell. But then still another wild shriek carried to them, and then others. Olin quickly turned about. From many throats came one terrifying, howling clamor of alarm!

"They've come back!"

Olin cursed, glanced at Sonja, reined his horse about. The line of soldiers—dipping back down the knoll and winding far back into the shadowed, misty recesses of the forest—was partly hidden from view. All the men had pivoted in their saddles and were looking behind them. The yells from the rear echoed and rose up anew.

"They've *come back!*"

Cold sweat bathed Olin. "Gods!" he swore, then slapped his steed down the knoll and galloped past his line of troops, dashing into the swamp as if daring it to swallow him up. Further howls sounded from the rear.

Sonja kicked her mount and followed in Olin's path.

Allas turned to Som; the great warrior's face was sheeny, his eyes glowing. He muttered in a growl almost too low to hear: "The mercenaries."

Ice clutched Allas's heart. "They're—*alive?"*

Came Pelides's hollow, iron voice: "And slaying our troops."

Tias whimpered.

Olin crashed on through brush and brambles, nearly lost control in a tangle of roots, splashed up muck and fetid water. Near the end of the line he suddenly reined in as he came to an impassable clump of his own soldiers. Sonja, following him, pulled up so shortly to avoid plunging into him that she was nearly thrown.

"What is it?" she yelled, drawing her sword.

Her answer was the battle before her. The troops, perhaps two hundred of them, were swording wildly against a dark army much more numerous than they. Some of Olin's men had dismounted or had been thrown from their saddles; dozens of horses had panicked and were rushing directionless over the low swamp, trapping themselves in bogs and pits, shrieking and kicking and sinking under. A number of soldiers, betrayed by their own fear, had tumbled from the safe path into stagnant pits of mud; they waved their swords uselessly, kicked and howled, and were slowly sucked under.

But the army those soldiers faced—Olin sucked in a breath that felt cold in his throat.

The dead mercenaries had risen from the swamp sling —bloated, butchered, their armor caked with dried grime, their faces eaten with rot. They shambled, unliving, wielding their weapons stiffly. Lurching from the dense shadows and the clogging mists, they advanced, relentless automators, taking on Olin's troops with blind, mute malice. Horses shrieked and whinnied; troops jumped to the unsure ground and raised sword and buckler, fought against the dead meat, and were cut down. Here and there a number of Olin's men managed to defeat the juggernaut corpses, but only by pushing them back into the pits and bogs, where they became trapped to their waists in the muck.

"Sound the horns for battle!" Olin cried out.

He rushed ahead. Behind him his troops, frightened, bewildered, uncertain, reined their mounts about and spread out gingerly over the deadly terrain.

The mercenaries stomped through the muck, scything their swords even though they had not reached their foes. Frantic screams and whines rent the air. Sonja galloped ahead, nearly trapped herself in a bog, reined about, and struck one of the dead. Her horse stumbled and she was thrown, landing on soggy ground but luckily not sinking in. Her horse galloped on and was lost in the shadowy mist. She rose to her feet, lifting her sword.

The demonic carcass staggered toward her and she met it, appalled by the sightless white stare of its eyes, the blind sweeping attack it made with its sword. She easily sidestepped a lumbering blow, swung her own blade, and severed the thing's head from its neck. Instantly it sank down in the mud and lay still.

But the warriors around her seemed to be doing less well; their blows apparently had little effect on the things. Sonja saw one man sweep the head from a walking corpse exactly as she had done; the head flew through the air and splashed into a pool, but still the corpse came on swinging its blade, an aimless killing machine. Yelling with fear, the soldier jumped aside and savagely kicked the zombie off balance; it stumbled into a bog and sank under, still swinging its sword against the quicksand, thrashing the muck into a froth.

Sonja heard a rising commotion behind her. She turned and saw the rest of Olin's army advancing, on foot and on horseback. But the rotting horde of the dead marched on.

Olin battled the zombies fiercely, still atop his nearly uncontrollable horse, which was wild with fear. A group of the things had surrounded him. He hacked off arms and hands, split head, drove steel through breasts. The dismembered things writhed on the ground, moving horribly, writhing like maggots, still trying to kill. His horse was slicked with blood where dozens of strokes had wounded it, front and side. At last Olin abandoned the poor animal, leaping to the ground to face a mindless stampede by three grasping corpses. He sidestepped them, beheaded one, and carved open the back of another. The third swung a blow at his throat; barely avoiding it, Olin sworded the thing through the heart, drew back, and lunged again. The mindless clay didn't stop. Olin jumped back, gripped sword with both hands, and with a wild swing severed the thing's arm from its shoulder. The arm flew and tumbled, still clutching its sword, humping back to the fight, while the slaughtered mercenary nevertheless continued to go for Olin, its remaining hand clutching for him. Olin sliced off the hand, slashed at the legs, until finally the creature, its muscles and tendons severed, fell back into the swamp where it wriggled and sank.

Olin's soldiers were going down in great numbers. From all directions amid the obscuring shadows and fog came the clatter of swords, the splashes of bodies falling into pools and bogs, the howls of wounded and dying men. Olin saw two of his men go down before a mercenary, saw the swords of their comrades hack and rend the living corpse until it was headless and limbless —and still it struggled horribly, a bloody torso only, squirming in the muck. A soldier shrieked as a putrescent cadaver, whose sword arm he had hacked off, locked its teeth in his arm. Frantically he sawed through the thing's neck, but still the grinding jaws hung on. The man dropped his sword and stumbled away, howling, trying with one hand to tear loose the head, then screeched as he blundered into a quagmire and sank, thrashing.

Olin saw three of the dead skewer a soldier. A berserk rage possessed him; roaring, he leaped into the midst of the fray and within seconds had hewn two of the corpses to pieces. The third raised steel to hack him down, but in that instant something moved behind the walking meat, a shadow in dark armor, and its sword hand went flying from its wrist. Another blow sent its head tumbling to the mud. It stumbled on, sightless, and Olin saw Pelides standing there with the bluish, stagnant corpse-blood rilling down his sword and iron visor. Then Pelides turned and took on another zombie, while Olin ran ahead to engage yet two more.

Sonja's sword rose and fell ceaselessly; her armor, flesh and hair were filthy with blood and swamp slime. She swung her blade tirelessly, taking on one corpse at a time, two at a time, often three. And she learned that skilled swordplay was not necessary. The graveyard spawn were nearly blind; if they were guided by anything it was simply the sounds of combat. Moreover, she found that they died at the mere touch of her sword—or even at the touch of her blade against theirs—in contrast to the inhuman vitality they displayed in combat against all others. Against Olin's troops they never tired; showing no skill, they simply hacked, swung, lunged, and struck where they would. Such unthinking brutality unnerved men who were used to fighting in a soldier's way against foes who would defend themselves.

Sonja realized it must be the Ring in her pouch that was enabling her to slay these fiends so easily. Screaming a Hyrkanian war cry she moved on among them like a whirlwind of steel, smiting down all she could reach.

Olin had quickly learned to side-step the nightmares and hack off their sword-arms. At every opportunity he beheaded them, so that whatever vestigial senses they might still possess would be lost, then prodded them off balance into brambly thickets or pits of quicksand. All around him, his troops were learning the same advantage; too many of them, however, were stumbling or being dragged into the bogs themselves. He saw one young soldier shrieking and struggling in a pit with a headless marauder, trying to pull himself by climbing the corpse like a floating log. It did no good; the trunk and oozing neck of the lich sank and the lad went with it, kicking and suffocating.

Olin was forced to engage another of the unburied horrors. At the same moment he heard something slogging up behind him; he tried to swerve, but the dead mercenary he faced was delivering clumsy strokes in all directions and he could not maneuver. Then a voice cried out:

"Smite him, Lord Olin—I'll take this one!"

It was Allas. Olin roared and charged, battered down the corpse's blade with one great blow and beheaded it with another. He whirled to see Allas struggling with another foe; his sword was lodged fast half-way through the body of the sword-wielding carrion. Olin swiped off the thing's weapon-arm. Allas yanked his blade free; they nodded to one another, then dashed off to fight still others.

The sounds of battle had diminished. Red Sonja, her arm tiring from smashing down more walking corpses than she could count, saw that most of the zombie killers were put down: hacked bits, twitching arms and still biting heads lay everywhere, rolling on the sodden ground; mutilated bodies struggled spasmatically amid the bogs and quicksand pools. But the nightmare terrain was also littered with Lord Olin's troops—suffocated in the swamps or mangled by the mindless, animate dead. Horses lay savaged, nostrils white and flaring, chests laboring in quick gulps. A nauseating miasma of rotted flesh, spilled blood, and filthy sweat mingled with the stench of the marsh gas and stinking, stagnant puddles.

Olin stood alone, exhausted, grime-encrusted. He yet gripped his sword fiercely. Wearily, Sonja sought him, and together they stood panting, flexing their aching muscles; sharing, for a moment, desperately needed breathing space. Still, men died around them, even as Olin's shattered forces sundered the last of the undead.

"We'll be lucky if a handful reaches the fortress," Olin gasped. "We're wiped out. No horses. No men." The immensity of the catastrophe seemed to outweigh even the moans and curses of the wounded around him. "Do you still have the Ring?" he whispered.

Sonja nodded.

"The damned Ring," Olin snarled, shaking his head. "A Ring of madness and doom. I think it, not Asroth, has been our bane. How long did it lie in Suthad, spinning its hellish web? The Ring has sacrificed my people to Ikribu—lured us into this unending nightmare, this depraved horror, just so our suffering could feel the appetite of some malign Elder One. Ikribu—is it glutted, did it sate itself on my people—or did the screams of thousands of souls being ripped from their hearts just whet the damned thing's taste? Mitra—what the hell more does Ikribu want? I should just tie the ring to an arrow and shoot it into Asroth's hands. Let him *have* the Ring's power—in the end, Asroth will find his own corrupt soul being ground up in Ikribu's jaws."

"Olin!" Sonja cried, "Don't give in to such thoughts—they may be but another trick of Asroth's. The Ring is our only chance!"

Olin shook his head. "No—our doom."

Red Sonja turned to see a zombie smashing at an older veteran who was mired thigh-deep in a stagnant pond. She rushed the abomination, half-severing its swordarm, and instantly it flopped face-down in the waiting water. Immediately Sonja extended her hand to help the soldier out of the fen—and something rose from the water. A slime dripping stalk of flesh with a bulbous eye on the end of it.

The soldier felt the moving water, half-turned to see—and went white. His mouth opened; he bellowed, frantic; he kicked and splashed, grabbing at reeds and roots as he tried to pull himself free. Sonja leapt forward as a tree root rose from the bank, serpentine, groped around the soldier's chest and dragged him down. Wading knee-deep in the ooze, she slashed at the thing, chopping sodden chips and drawing sap. A submerged vine, as thick around as a python, whipped out, lashing, and Sonja barely managed to leap to the bank in time to avoid it. The vegetable horror wrapped around the screaming soldier, covering his face, pinning his arms to his sides. The man was dragged under; the surface of the pool bubbled a moment, then went glassy.

At that instant, the remaining undead corpses dropped, stopped moving, returned to clay; and as the living looked about in wonder, all realised that the entire land had fallen into utter, unnatural silence. Not only had the thrashing of the dead and the moans of the wounded ceased—the world itself had stopped. No animal moved, no bird crowed, no insect buzzed. More ominously—not a leaf nor grass blade rustled, not a single dew drop fell.

Then silently, slowly, but with ever-growing force, the swamp began to pulse. Vast, rhythmic throbbing, far below the thresholds of sound or thought, the awesome heartbeat of a god. Olin's company, gripping their swords, looked about, and felt an indescribable dread more terrible than all the nightmare sendings of the last days. Something was being knit, bound, birthed. Something that drew together within it the deformed flora and misbegotten creatures of the mire's dank and vicious world. Something enormous, omniscient, all encompassing. Something unholy, unearthly, unspeakably alien. Something possessed of a dark, absolutely malefic sentience. It pulsed, it spread, it grew. It hated.

It became the swamp itself; it became every plant, every mold, every algae; it became every insect, every lizard, every beast. It became the hideous landscape; it became the oozing slime; it became the lichen; it became the moss; it became the parasites, the fleas, the chiggers; it became the leeches, the spiders, the snakes; it became the buzzards; it became the rats; it became the rabid weasels. It sprawled, it hated, and it became all.

Then it attacked.

Never had a mad artist painted a vision of gruesome delirium; never had a fanatic poet captured the cadence of frenzied apocalypse; never had a syphilitic musician wailed a cacophony of final doom. Rank weeds roped a soldier while burning slime surged up his legs; weeping willow boughs snagged up another in a straitjacket cage and flung him straight to a churning heap of vipers; carpets of moss dropped in strangling blankets while heavy roots flailed and lashed; batrachian hordes drove some into the smiling jaws of crocodiles while others were butchered beneath the teeth of boars and ferrets.

It could not be said that some screamed—everyone screamed all the horror in their hearts with all the power of their lungs. It could not be said that some panicked—everyone ran blindly from the inescapable terror. For everything which lived, moved; and everything that moved, killed.

Of the company, only a few reacted not with panic,

but with a raging desperation to survive. The power of Ikribu's Ring protected the Hyrkanian warrior from the worst of the grisly attack; but Red Sonja's sword, which had dealt already so much destruction, whirled again in a simmering dazzle of sharp death. Sonja heard slithering; boots smucking in the mud; the dead sound of blades frantically striking the wet flesh and pulp of monstrous, silent foes; the piteous whines and groans of the smothered; the hysterical shrieks of terrified mortals.

Smashing and thrusting almost randomly about her, Sonja heard a bestial snarl, and turned to look at Olin. She saw the red madness building in his eyes. His entire body shook with a wrath too great for one man to contain. Catching her glance, Olin stopped briefly, bravado before the wall of horror. He forced his mouth into a grim smile; he lifted his sword in salute—a length of reddened steel trembling in the fierceness of his grip; he forced enough sanity briefly into his eyes for Sonja to sense his love for her, the terror for his men, the iron of his will and the immensity of his hatred toward the monstrous evil that fed on the agonized souls of men. Then Olin abandoned his humanity, gave himself to a berserker fury of feral passion. Howling, the Lord of Suthad launched himself into Armageddon.

Tears blurred Red Sonja's vision as she watched him disappear into the thick of his troops with an inarticulate shriek of madness, hacking at hellspawn with unrelenting violence. Pelides rushed past, his black armor blotched with gore, his sword out. A bearlike bellow issued from a strangling cocoon of branches—Som. The giant, not trying to escape, rushed the trunk of his unthinking attacker, wrestled furiously; a loud crack boomed; the huge warrior snapped the man-eating cypress in two, threw the tree like a lance, and ripped the still-living stump from the ground by its thick, twitching roots. Som, using the tree trunk as a mace, flailed at a dozen spiny vines that coiled toward him, trying to pull him to bloody death in a huge, writhing thorn hedge.

Even so, Som was among the luckier—he, at least, had something tangible to battle. Not so the poor devils who were gagging on gelatinous masses of crawling mold; who wailed inside a cloud of millions of vampiric mosquitoes; or rolled on the ground, futilely trying to crush thousands of blood bloated leeches and vermin. Some soldiers no longer looked remotely human, so completely were their bodies and armor covered by revolting masses of black spiders, worms, and maggots. Many gave up and tried to end their lives by diving into quicksand—but even they were denied merciful death. For from the deadly pits erupted scores and scores of curling, everwrithing tentacles, guided by alien eyes that rose on waving, fleshy stalks. Beneath the noxious suck—impossibly—nameless beings lived and hungered.

Red Sonja, swinging her sword in mad, double-handed arcs, tensed to charge after Olin, into the chaos. Then someone screamed her name.

"Sonja!"

She turned, and spied Tias and Allas on the bank of a pool. Something, wrapped around Allas's leg, was dragging him into the mire. He had dug his sword into the earth and was clinging desperately to the hilt. Tias had her arms wrapped around him, but unstoppable, gray, sucker laden tentacles were wrenching Allas from her hold, tearing his sword from the too-soft ground.

Tias looked up as Sonja came running. *"Help him!"* she hollered.

Allas had wounded the thing; pink ichor drooled from deep gashes in the twisting limb. Red Sonja leapt into the shallows near the bank, and savagely flogged one of the wounds. The tentacle parted; its stump slid into the pool; pink fluid boiled up, spreading luridly on the surface as the other tentacles released their holds. The nameless quag-dweller retreated. Sonja grabbed Allas and hauled him bodily up the bank. The severed member that still coiled and sucked around his leg spasmed. Sonja kicked it into the water.

"Are you all right?" she gasped.

"It burns!" Allas grimaced while tearing open his legging. Venom infected welts wealed up the length of his calf.

"*Do* something!" Tias wailed to Sonja, tears running down her cheeks. "Help him!"

Sonja stared at Tias; what more could be done? She knelt beside Allas to eye the wounds more closely—then shot to her feet as a horrified cry chorussed from the soldiers.

"LORD OLIN! OH GODS—LORD OLIN!"

Red Sonja ran, striking down anything in her path. A bloody, blinded trooper staggered before her; Sonja killed him with a single stroke—but assassination was a kindness compared to what gnawing rats had done to the soldier's face. Sonja stumbled and almost fell across a still living young man whose grotesquely swollen body was being endlessly penetrated by countless hornets—to him, too, Sonja dispatched a fast and blessed end.

After seconds that stretched like eternities, Red Sonja staggered to a murky bog, where a crowd of men were frantically thrashing the water with their swords. Sonja reaced forward, spurred by a heart wrenching fear. All she could hear was a litany of hoarse throats shouting: *"Lord Olin! OH GODS, OH GODS! LORD OLIN!"*

The knot of soldiers bobbed in Sonja's vision; then she was in the thick of them, shoving them aside, slamming them to the ground.

"Where is he?" she heard herself shriek. *"Where is Olin?"*

She glimpsed a hand that clutched and closed on air, disappearing under the surface.

Red Sonja dived into the murk, scrambling for the place where the hand had been pulled under. As she surfaced, she howled, "Olin!"

Then she dived again, again, and again. She could not see; reeking mud gummed across her face, and her own tears blinded her. Unseeing, still she dived, but found nothing. Taking her sword in one hand, groping with the other, she kicked, paddled and treaded further into the stinking waters.

"OLIN!"

A ripple cut the surface; the tip of a gray tentacle bobbed and waved obscenely. Snarling, Sonja threw herself at it, stabbing and spearing the water furiously. A stub of slimy, severed gray limb erupted from the pond, coiling and spouting pink blood, then vanished.

With ferocious violence Sonja stabbed and battered the pink-stained bog, shrieking Olin's name. Further out in the water a scum coated eye-stalk slid from the surface, coldly regarding her; then arose a tubular limb ending in an orifice full of gaping red fangs. Sonja saw it; she howled and thrashed to make for it, slashing the water in convulsive fury.

"Sonja!" a voice behind her bellowed.

She paused. Her heart was pounding so hard and quickly, she was deafened.

"Sonja! Come back! By Mitra, woman—now!"

She turned, vaguely, unable to swallow, unable to think.

Water reared in a crunching splash as someone crashed into the pond beside her. Without looking, Sonja shrieked in raging grief and pain, and began again spearing the roiling water.

Bellowing her name, Som grabbed her arm, tried to pull her to him. Sonja whirled, teeth bared like a wolf's, glaring through eyes of crimson rage. She tried to cut the waters again, but Som crossed his sword beneath hers, and grabbed her once more.

"Stop it!" he roared, "Damn you, Hyrkanian, stop it and get out of here!"

"Olin!" she raged. "Find him! Must find Olin!"

"He's dead."

"Lying dog!" Sonja whirled about, screaming, "OLIN! OLIN!" Suddenly her head rocked as Som delivered a fast slap. The swordswoman lashed out, kicking the giant, and glowered, hate-filled. She pointed her sword at him, daring him to move or repeat his words.

Som returned a steady, red-eyed gaze. "Olin is dead," he said softly, his voice hoarse and broken. "It is over."

Sonja could hear the gentle dripping of swamp water, water from her own drenched hair and face and sword, dribbling into the pool. She trembled in a sudden ague; the shivering water around her swirled.

"Come, Sonja," Som said gently. "It is over."

She looked around the deep, stagnant bog, stunned, benumbed, unbelieving. Her head shook uncontrollably; she mumbled, unable to form her thoughts.

"Come," Som urged, taking her hand, pulling her toward the submerged bank until their legs found and plodding in the clinging mud at the pond's bottom.

Sonja's mind was fog; she could not see, could not hear. The attack had ended; the order of nature returned; the survivors were gathered at the edge of the pool, but Sonja could not see them. She could barely breathe; her body was leaden; her soul tottered on the razor edge of an emotional abyss; and Red Sonja was consumed with a searing, absolute realization.

She loved him.

That was the ultimate loss. His death brought into focus the tremulous, fiery love which had been burgeoning, blooming hidden within her. Melting, joyous emotion her warrior's heart had never felt as a woman; nurturing, soothing beauty her woman's heart had not known since she was a child. Red Sonja had fallen in love with Lord Olin of Suthad; and with distant, dry-mouthed horror, she understood the fullness of that love only at the moment she was being dragged from Olin's grave.

Was this why she had come so far—why she had been born and raised in Hyrkania and travelled homeless and unfriended and without family and accompanied only by the memory of her vow to a strange diety? Was this why she suffered carnage and conflagration enough for three lifetimes—to see this man broken and destroyed by sorcery, by monstrosity, in some nameless swamp? Was this the meaning of her vow, her geas, her curse, her bravado—not that she would never love, but that he Sonja loved must die?

She loved him.

She remembered the last look Olin had given her, a look that now reminded her so much of her father's eyes—devoted, stern, mad with anger against evil, yet sure that once the evil was vanquished the world would be safe and secure and soft again.

She had reached the bank, but now she tried to fight her way back into the water. She had to find Olin, had to tell him, she had never told him . . . Som held her back, gripped her arm so strongly he feared he might injure her if she persisted. But at length Sonja sank to her knees on the earth, exhausted, speechless, dizzy, and unable to think.

Red Sonja laid her sword in front of her. It was notched and stained crimson from tip to pomme. Why, she wondered dismally, why, why had she been able to kill so many, why had she been able to save others and herself so many times, why had she been apart from him, why had she not been there, why had she been helpless to aid him when he was grabbed, screaming, by fat, writhing tentacles and pulled forever and ever and ever down to the depths of a bottomless mere?

She had loved him.

Chapter 11

Life

Red Sonja sat for a long time near the edge of the knoll, with her grief and her memories, her aching muscles, and her bloody sword. Dusk fell thick and dark upon the swampy forest. Behind her, at their fires, were the handful of soldiers who had survived that day—Som, Pelides, Allas, Tias, perhaps thirty others at the most.

The battle was long over. The swamp monsters had oozed away to their hidden lairs directly after Olin's slaying; with his death they had accomplished their purpose. Now hundreds of slaughtered, mutilated bodies lay in heaps all over the swamps, clogging the meres and bogs, lying headless and limbless and blood-drenched upon every slope, tangled in roots and brambles—Suthad's soldiers and the dead mercenaries crowded together amid the hacked relics of swamp monsters. And the wounded—groaning, dying, their awful cries filling the air—sent as great a chill through the others as had the death screams and the roar of battle.

Som approached Sonja, stopped and stood before her.

"Come away, Sonja," he said quietly.

She sighed heavily and looked up at him, then rose to her feet. Som offered her his arm but Sonja did not take it, she sheathed her sword and followed Som, sat down beside him at a fire he had built. There was no food, nothing to drink all had been lost in the battle.

"A number of the men are boiling water," Som commented, "and butchering some of the horses for meat. We'll have something to eat soon."

The groans of the wounded went on interminably.

Allas lay by another fire, resting his head on Tias's lap. Tias stared silently and blankly into space, horrific visions still before her. Allas wiped sweat from his face, whispered some words of comfort to Tias, lay still.

The woods and swamp had become very dark and quiet, save for the gurgling sounds of streams and pools and the far-off noises of swamp denizens.

Sonja sighed heavily and looked over to Allas's fire. "Are you all right, Allas? How is your leg?"

He turned to look at her, saw her through the flames of his fire. "I'm—all right," he answered.

But Tias glanced at Sonja sharply and muttered: "Little thanks to you for that, Hyrkanian!"

Sonja caught it. "What did you say?" she asked Tias, her voice rising with a hard edge to it.

Tias demurred; she looked away, not wanting to face Sonja. But then something gripped her—a resentment—and she again faced Sonja and said crisply: "What do you care about Allas? You, who ran off to help the doomed madman who got us all into this horror!"

Instantly Sonja was on her feet, white with fury.

Som stared, disbelieving what Tias had said.

"Tias! She saved my *life!*" exclaimed Allas. "Sonja, listen—she's upset. She did not mean—"

But Sonja drowned him out. "Tias, you damned child, what did you say to me? *Answer me!*"

"Allas almost died!" Tias shot back, tears streaming down her face. "Another of those things could have got to him and—"

"To help a *madman?*" Sonja yelled, her voice carrying wrathfully through the darkness. "Is that what you said to me?"

"Yes!" Tias shrieked. "Yes, damn you—*she devil!* You and Olin brought us into this! Were you crazy? Look what has *happened* to us!"

Sonja leaped, grabbed Tias by the hair, and slapped her once, hard, across the face. Tias wailed. Sonja held onto her hair, yanked her head back, and glared into her eyes.

"Never say that again!" she hissed. "You worthless little tramp, what the hell good are you? *What are you, Tias?* You're no good to us—all you've done is whine and bleat, while honest soldiers were fighting to save your useless, petty life!"

"Stop, *stop!"* Tias shrieked.

"Stop it, Sonja!" yelled Allas.

Red Sonja threw Tias's head down; the girl covered her face and sobbed in shame and humiliation.

"Look at yourself!" Sonja shouted. "Hundreds have died and still *you're* alive, damn you! *Olin* is dead and—!" She stopped, choking. The fury still not gone out of her, she stomped away, came to a corpse by the knoll's edge, and yanked a sword from the rigid, white fingers. She brought it back to Tias, hurled it into the ground beside her, barely missing her thigh.

"Learn to fight!" she hissed. "Learn to look after yourself, damn it! Learn to do something with yourself, and do what the rest of these fighters have done today, and then you'll have the right to complain. Damn you, you're *alive!* Allas is alive! But all those poor bastards out there"—she waved an arm toward the dark forest—"they don't have the chance to complain. They died helping protect *you!"*

She stopped, out of breath, red-faced, trembling. Unable to go on, she returned to Som's fire and crouched there, chin on hands.

Tias's sobs carried fitfully throughout the small camp, though she tried to stifle them with her hands.

"Hush, Tias," Allas told her, patting her hand. He recognized the truth in much of what Sonja had said, realized that the fury and scorn she had heaped upon Tias was all she had left after Olin's death. Allas felt the same fury at the pointlessness of it all. He, too, was alive, and feeling guilty about the fact. "Hush, Tias, be quiet, be—"

"I'm so sorry," Tias whimpered. "I don't belong here —I'm—"

"Shhh . . ."

Silence settled upon the camp. The smell of cooked horse meat rose on the air and exhausted soldiers began to eat ravenously. There was little talking. The small fires burned fitfully, their flames seeming to suffocate in the humidity, hemmed in by the night. The woundeds' moans had diminished; a few had slipped into fitful sleep, the rest into eternal rest. Now and then the abrupt, frightening slither or splash of something in the swamp waters caused heads to turn, hands to grip sword pommels.

Sonja turned to Som and said in a low voice: "We must decide what to do. We can't stay here to fester and go insane. Have you any idea how many men are left alive?"

Som shook his head doubtfully. "Thirty, perhaps."

"No more than that?"

Som shook his head again.

"Thirty," Sonja whispered wonderingly, "five days ago we had five thousand."

"And Asroth is not done with us yet, I'm sure. His evil shadow still hangs over us, inciting us to pointless hatreds and irritations against each other."

"We must decide who shall lead us," Sonja told him. "Will you, Som?"

"I'd rather you did," he rejoined. "Yet it may not be for us to say. We are mercenaries, and more used to fighting than commanding. It is likely that the soldiers will prefer one of their own officers. It must be put to a vote—"

"Wait!" Sonja had just remembered someone else.

"Where is Pelides? Was he slain?"

She stood up and scanned the campfires, looking for a glimpse of the black helmet.

As if called by name, Duke Pelides arose from beside a distant fire and faced Sonja. A shudder went through her. All these brave men, and the villain Pelides survived.

Pelides approached silently, and as he moved toward Sonja and Som the eyes of all the surviving warriors followed him.

Sonja stood waiting, tense. Som arose; Allas, still lying beside his fire, twisted his head in Tias's lap. Tias ceased her sobbing and watched. Other faces, too—haggard, battle-scarred and gray—looked up to see what was happening.

Pelides stopped before Sonja, legs planted wide in a defiant stance, hands locked on his belt. He was covered with clotted blood and dried ichor, caked mud and gore; his armor was dented and stained, his cloak ripped nearly to shreds.

"Lord Olin is dead," Pelides said in his hollow, metallic voice.

Sonja watched him.

"I want the Ring, Hyrkanian."

Now other faces looked up, perking at this new development. A ring? Some of the men began to mumble. Allas struggled to sit up despite Tias's protests. He sat awkwardly, supporting himself on his hands as he listened and watched.

"The Ring."

"No," said Sonja.

Pelides moved his hand to his sword pommel. "The army is dead," he said slowly. "Olin is dead. The Ring has done you no good. None of you will make it to Asroth's fortress."

"But *you* will survive, Pelides?" Sonja's voice was mocking.

"*I* will survive, Hyrkanian. The Ring."

Som interrupted. "What ring, Sonja? What is this?"

Others approached, crowding in around them, mumbling and gesturing. Allas called out weakly: "Defy him, Sonja! Don't give it to him!"

Neither Sonja nor Pelides looked at him; their eyes were locked, each on the other.

The men surrounding them muttered and whispered. One of them called to Sonja: "What's this about a ring, Hyrkanian?"

Sonja took advantage of that. Immediately she stepped back and faced the crowd, held up her hands for silence and order.

"You men will decide what is to be done," she called to them. "Listen to me, and I'll tell you why Asroth attacked your city and why Pelides came to Lord Olin and began this quest.

"*Listen* to me!" she insisted, against a growing rumble of voices. "The sorcerer is searching for a magical Ring. He attacked Suthad because he learned the Ring was hidden there. Lord Olin did not know this, but Asroth knew—and Duke Pelides knew also, for he was in league with Asroth before the sorcerer damned him and put him under the curse that ruined his face!"

Angry growls carried from the crowd, and angry faces turned toward Duke Pelides. But Pelides held his ground. In a low voice full of hate he said: "Give me the *Ring*, Hyrkanian."

"*Listen* to me!" Sonja called to the warriors. "*I* discovered the Ring accidentally in Suthad, and told Olin of it. We had to keep it secret from Pelides, for *he* wants it in order to accomplish his own private revenge. We thought it would protect us on our march against Asroth, but we were—*Quiet,* and *listen,* you dogs! It did *not* protect us—one must have sorcerous power to use the Ring. Duke Pelides does *not* have that power—but nevertheless he has threatened my life, and Lord Olin's, in his demands for the Ring.

"He demands it *now*—he says he will take it himself to the sorcerer and destroy him with it, to even an old score. *I* say we should carry the Ring to Asroth ourselves, and justify the quest Lord Olin died for!

"But you men all have a stake in this; I will leave it for *you* to decide. We must *all* decide whether to go on and face Asroth, as Olin wished, or turn the Ring over to Pelides. You know how I feel, but I can't speak for you. What shall it be, soldiers? Do we carry on Olin's cause and insure that he and all these others did not die in vain, or shall we give the Ring to Duke Pelides? *You* must decide!"

She stopped, sweating and trembling in the firelight, looked at Duke Pelides, and smiled grimly.

"Don't give it to him!" Allas cried weakly. "Pelides—did you lead us into this swamp to have us all killed, just so you could get your murdering hands on the Ring?"

Pelides turned to him and said coldly: "You fool, be silent, or I'll sword you where you lie!"

"Coward!"

Tias held his face, covered Allas's mouth. "Be *quiet,* Allas!" she pleaded. "Please, be quiet! The *men* will decide . . . ."

Sonja glared at Pelides, wishing he would give her an excuse to spring and slay. She knew that if the men voted to keep the Ring, he would try to murder her that very night. He would do anything to get his hands on it.

The soldiers broke up their discussion. Some returned to their fires looking weary and discouraged; others clustered about a spokesman, who presently stepped forward to let Sonja know their judgment.

Silence settled over the camp. Insects hummed and buzzed; the fires crackled. Sweat trickled down Sonja's face and arms and legs. Something splashed distantly in the swamp; a slight wind blew up but could not disperse the heavy stench of blood and death.

The spokesman, grim-faced, said to Sonja: "Give Duke Pelides the Ring."

Sonja stood dumbfounded, stunned.

"No!" Allas cried out. *"No!* You *fools!"*

Tias tried to hush him. The spokesman turned his

back on them, returned to his fire.

Pelides advanced. "Give me the Ring, Hyrkanian." His voice was expressionless.

Sonja growled; instantly she reached for her sword, refusing in her heart to betray Olin's trust in her. Then, even as she tensed to draw blade,she caught a look from Som. He nodded to her curtly, once.

Again Sonja was stunned. Som, one of the backbones of this entire quest—Som from Izak's tavern, who had admired her swordplay and demanded the right to fight beside her—Som, who had battled for Lord Olin against winged men and earth monsters and swamp things . . . .

Sonja whispered to him in a trembling voice: "Olin would not do this, Som."

"Olin is dead, Red Sonja. Nothing but evil has come to us from this Ring. Let Pelides have it."

"The Ring, Hyrkanian," Pelides repeated, a hard finality in his voice.

She reached to her belt, felt in the pouch, and pulled free the Ring. It glowed in the dead blackness of the swamp. Sonja stared at it.

Pelides held out his gloved hand.

Sonja found she could not give it to him. She looked at Pelides's ebon visor, black and hard and angular, barely saw his eyes, gray and white, glinting through the slits. The light of the Ring played upon his mask in reflective waves.

Pelides reached out and plucked the Ring from Sonja's fingers. Then he turned and walked away, head held high, quickly shoving the Ring into one of his gloves.

"Dog!" Sonja muttered at him, but some of the force of will had gone out of her.

"Fools!" Allas cried out. "You fools! Traitors!"

Sonja returned to her fire and sat down tiredly.

Pelides mounted a horse, rode from his campfire and paused in the center of the troops, right before Sonja's fire.

"This campaign is at an end," he announced in a flat, hard voice. "I will destroy Asroth. You could all have saved yourself much agony and grief had I been given the Ring in Suthad; you may blame Red Sonja and Lord Olin for the deaths of your compatriots—and perhaps your own deaths. But my vengeance is very near at hand. I will see you no more."

He reined, whirled his steed about, and quickly galloped out of the camp.

Tias stared after him, not believing what she had heard.

"Dog!" Allas yelled at the darkness where Pelides had vanished.

Tears coursed down Tias's cheeks. "You lied to me, Duke Pelides," she whispered, touching the knife that hung from her belt. "You lied to me. . . ."

Sonja turned to Som. "What can we do now?"

He shrugged. "Wait till dawn. We'll all need sleep—we must rest now. In the morning we can all decide what we want to do next to get out of this hell swamp."

"Aye," she said. "Aye . . ." And then, softly, a curse that was barely audible: "Tarim and Erlik!"

"He lied to me . . . ." Tias whispered.

"Quiet, Tias," said Allas soothingly.

The others in the camp were trying to sleep. The pain in Allas's leg had eased somewhat and the swelling had subsided, but still he could not sleep; he was thinking of Olin and how he had died—Olin, and the mugginess and darkness of the swamp, the sounds coming from it, threatening . . . . No, Allas could not sleep. He watched his smoking fire burn lower and lower.

"He lied to me," Tias said again.

"Who, Tias? Keep your voice down."

"Duke Pelides . . ."

"Who?" Allas nearly shouted it, and strove to sit up again.

But Tias held his head still in her lap. Tonelessly, recalling the thing that had wounded her, she told him: "The night before we left Suthad, Allas—we argued, remember? And I ran out into the hall. Duke Pelides was there; he saw me, he spoke to me. He was in a—strange mood. He was kind, almost tender. I couldn't understand it. He started talking about how all of us were destined to be together, and how each of us had a secret fear and a secret longing. He said some of us could be trusted and others could not—and many other things. He was—*kind,* Allas. I couldn't understand it."

Allas looked up and saw the expression of worry and disillusionment on Tias's inverted face.

"He gave me his knife. He told me that I'd better learn how to use it, how to protect and look after myself—that I had to change, because we were all destined to go on this journey. There was—*pain* in his voice, Allas"—Tias sounded surprised at the memory of it—"but not because of what the wizard did to him. He was so very alone. I—I felt sorry for him."

Allas made a small sound of disgust.

Tias shrugged. "But he lied to me. He led me to think he cared about what happened to me, but—he lied. He doesn't care if we all die—all he wants is his revenge."

Allas told her tiredly: "Go to sleep, Tias. Here—lie down beside me. Go to sleep. We're not going to die."

Tias swallowed, carefully moved Allas's head from her lap, stretched out beside him, and hugged him.

Within a few moments her exhaustion had put her to sleep; Allas, however, still could not relax. He listened to the sounds all around in the forest, watched the low campfires on the knoll, listened to Tias breathing in her sleep and thought of Lord Olin. Olin . . .

In her dream Red Sonja rode with Olin through a countryside of plains and fields and sparse woods. They were happy, riding thus together, searching for adventure, and they were in love. Olin had a wooden leg; he had lost one leg in a battle against swamp demons, and

Sonja admired his valor, for the wooden leg did not stop him from continuing his career of adventure.

Dusk came down, and they found a place to camp. As the last rim of the sun descended in a fiery sea over the western horizon, they built a fire and cooked their food and tended to their horses. Then they sat together, and Olin professed his love for Sonja. She replied that she could never love any man, that she had seen a Vision, and that only the man who bested her in swordplay could demand the right to possess her. Olin stood up, laughing, and drew his sword, demanding that Sonja fight him. She was reluctant, but Olin urged her and jeered at her until Sonja's blood was up, and with a curse she drew her sword and fought with Olin beside their campfire.

But as soon as they began trading strokes, Olin transformed. He began to glow with a blue aura, and Sonja felt herself being defeated by his sword strokes. Olin became a godlike being, part man and part woman and more than both, a luminescent being of tenderness, strength, and insight. Sonja's sword flew from her hands and she cried out ecstatically. Olin transformed again into his original shape, but this time he had lost his wooden leg and had both his original ones. He led Sonja to their campfire.

The fields and sparse woods that surrounded them were now transformed as well. The trees became larger and denser, thick and shadowed with huge boles and heavy, overhanging foliage. No moonlight or starlight showed through those trees. The grassy ground that Sonja and Olin lay upon became soft and mulchy, and soon they were lying in a swamp. Sonja could hear strange noises all around her; the campfire seemed a very weak refuge indeed against the encroaching darkness and the sounds and feelings of evil in the air.

But Olin told her that their love could overcome even the evil of this land. He lay down beside her and gently, with many caresses, removed her garments and then his own. He kissed her passionately and lingeringly, and she responded; she held him to her hungrily, and her entire body trembled. Their campfire seemed to glow with a brighter and brighter fire, dispelling the darkness and driving away the noises and the luminous, unblinking eyes that stared at them. Olin protested his love more and more, and Sonja felt herself sweating, felt her muscles loosening and tightening in her passion. What must it be like to make love? She called Olin's name and held him to her tightly, never wanting to let him go, and all the while he likewise called her name passionately, ecstatically, lovingly, and . . .

"Sonja!"

—and Olin rose—

"*Sonja!* Gods—*wake up,* Sonja!"

She opened her eyes, sensing the terror in the voice. It was not Olin's.

"Sonja, *please* wake up!"

It was Tias. Sonja stared up into the girl's face. Instantly her hand was at her sword pommel.

"What—what is it—Tias?"

"Sonja! *Look!*"

The girl nodded toward the swamp. Sonja sat up and looked. Deep in the forest, in the direction from which they had marched, things were moving. Lights, dozens of yellow lights.

"Torches!" Tias exclaimed. "Someone's coming!"

"No, not torches," Sonja muttered. "Get back to Allas."

Tias scurried away. Sonja rose and went to Som, who lay snoring and wheezing by his smoking fire.

"Som!" She kicked him in the legs "Wake up, damn you!"

He cursed eloquently as he came to life, sitting up and staring at Sonja with sleep-crusted eyes. "Damn *you,* and—Sonja!" In the next instant he was up, adjusting his armor and sword belt. "What?"

"Look."

He peered in the direction where she nodded and saw the yellow lights coming through the forest.

"Torches?"

"No, Som. Stygians. Olin and I—we fought these beings once before. Their campfires have followed us since we began this quest. They are sorcerers—cultists."

Som swore violently. "Awaken the men!" he yelled.

He and Sonja quickly made the rounds of the camp, kicking men awake, yelling that death was approaching, anything to jar them out of slumber.

New sounds came echoed from the swamp—the swish of footsteps through water, the suck and squelch of boots in the muck. And the lights—the eyes—glowing, bobbing, casting a yellow mist before them . . . .

Sonja and Som stood with drawn swords, and behind them some thirty men, tense and expectant. Allas and the few others of the wounded who had not died lay watching apprehensively by their fires.

Figures emerged from the forest, three abreast, others behind—perhaps thirty in all. Silently, save for the sounds of their feet, they lined up before Sonja and what was left of Olin's army. The foremost Stygian advanced—a small man, his hands lost in his sleeves, his body almost lost in the darkness because of his black robe. His head was bald and brown, gleaming in the firelight, and his yellow eyes glowed with a light of their own. He paused a small distance from Sonja and said in a thick Stygian accent:

"We want Ikribu's Ring."

Sonja said nothing. Grumblings arose from the men behind her. Som shifted his weight, balanced the two swords in his hands.

"Woman, we know you have the Ring—our divinations have shown it. The soul of Sopis, languishing in Gehenna, has told us you took it from our dead hand. Give it to us or we will take it—and all of you will die."

Sonja told him boldly: "I do not have the Ring."

"Which of your party does, then?"

"We do not have it."

Those behind the spokesman now stepped ahead; they muttered darkly together, and those few words Sonja overheard she could not understand. Then the priests parted; hands reached into robes and rested there, as if gripping hidden weapons.

The spokesman said again: "Give us Ikribu's Ring."

Before Sonja could respond, a shriek rang out behind her and a young soldier ran forward, waving his blade. "We don't *have* it, you dogs! *Leave us alone!* Haven't you killed enough of us already?"

Maddened, he leaped forward, sword raised to strike. The acolyte darted back with a hiss, drawing from within his robe something that glowed upon his palm. With a wild yell the soldier swung his blade; incredibly, the priest caught the arcing steel in his naked hand—and instantly the swordsman screamed in pain. A red glow erupted up the length of his sword, slipped over his body and dissipated; the youth fell back, smoking, dead.

The lead acolyte reversed the sword, gripped it in his free hand, and weighed it with a gesture of a man who knew swords.

"The *Ring!*" he hissed.

Sonja charged and swung steel with lightning speed. The dread priest reacted a fraction too late; Red Sonja's slash cut just beneath his groping right hand. The Stygian screeched as the hand that held the glowing source of his power flew into the air, trailing red droplets. Red Sonja's next stroke clove his skull and splattered his nearby companions with a spray of blood and brains.

"Kill them!" Sonja cried, waving her sword.

Immediately Som and those behind him took up the yell and charged. The two factions closed—soldiers with swords and acolytes with occult rings—and once again the forest rang with the clangor of battle.

Chapter 12

The Cult of Ikribu

Roaring, Som dashed into the thick of the fray, his two swords whirling, and two acolytes went down with severed limbs flying before they could react. He kicked them aside and made for a third priest, who crouched to meet the attack.

Sonja moved like a whirlwind, never still, offering no target for their magic. Around her fought the tired, bloodstained soldiers, howling and cursing, swiping and striking. Sonja saw an acolyte reach into his robe, glimpsed a glowing gem in his emerging hand; quick as thought she swung, cutting him open from scalp to jaw. Pivoting, she barely sidestepped another who sought to ensorcel her from behind and slashed him across the belly; he collapsed and folded over, vomiting blood as his insides spilled out in a tangle.

She saw a soldier go down choking, entrapped by the spell of a swiftly moving Stygian. Sonja howled and charged; the acolyte gestured at her, yelling out an incantation, and a nimbus began to form around his hand. Cursing, Sonja lunged desperately; the acolyte shrieked as he was gored through the chest, and Sonja yanked free her blade and ran on.

Som, backed against the margin of a black pool at the foot of the knoll, faced three of the weird priests. One charged slightly ahead of the others and Som skewered him through with such force that the hilt thudded against the man's breastbone. Som hurled him aside and the acolyte shrieked as he splashed into the pool, Som's sword still in him, Som stumbled on a slimy root and with a grunt went down on his face. The other two priests were immediately upon him, evil rings gleaming in their fists. Som caught the ankle of one and jerked awkwardly, sending him tumbling into the pool, but the other shot waves of crimson pain shuddering at the giant warrior's back. Som bellowed, heaved himself up with the strength of rage, and caught the acolyte's wrist as the man began a second stroke. Bones snapped; the robed man shrieked. Bellowing loudly, Som lifted the Stygian from the ground, yanking the arm from the man's socket as if he were a rag doll; the man screeched as his shoulder joint cracked and his limb was torn away, then flopped to the ground and writhed in a welter of blood.

Som threw the torn arm upon him and left him to bleed to death. He staggered up the bank and sank to his knees at the base of a tree, gripping the bark for support.

The soldiers, battling fiercely, were finding the acolytes to be more formidable foes than they had anticipated. Sonja, now facing two of them, found she had to draw upon all her skill to battle the hypnotizing eyes and the swift, cobralike movements of their weapon arms. One she skewered through the chest, then pivoted barely in time to avoid the other's narrow-beam magic force; completing her whirl, she buried her blade in his side, yanked it free, jumped—and just missed being caught by the flashing Ring of a third robed assailant.

One sorcery-wielding acolyte darted through the line and leaped upon a wounded man who lay defenseless upon his blankets. The man shrieked as the Stygian's power crushed his forehead, killing him instantly.

Allas, yelling in rage at the priest, struggled to draw his sword. Tias cringed in fear as the Stygian turned in their direction.

"Fight an *armed* man!" Allas yelled as the priest ran at him. He managed to pull free his sword, but was still unable to stand and could maneuver but poorly by pivoting on his left elbow. The Stygian circled him like a spider about to spring, his face inhumanly calm, watching for an opening.

Tias, wide-eyed with fright, spasmodically tore Pelides's dagger from its sheathe.

Suddenly the acolyte rushed Allas, horrid Ring forward, eyes blazing. Allas swung his sword, cut only empty air as the Stygian dodged easily away and swung about for another shot.

Tias crouched forward, knife in her fist. The Stygian's back was to her now—

"Allas!"

Even as she cried out she leapt and struck with all her strength. The long dagger stuck deeply into the acolyte's back; he shrieked, throwing up his arms, and fell forward. Tias whimpered, her hand frozen on the knife hilt, watching the man at her feet as he struggled and his blood seeped out the wound in his back.

"Again, Tias!" Allas howled, trying to rise. "Strike again!"

Tias screamed as if in pain, jerked the knife up, and brought it down again and again and again. Beneath it she sensed tissue rending, felt warm wetness streaming over her hands, running between her fingers.

"Enough, Tias!" Allas yelled, finally getting to his knees and crawling to her. "Enough!" He caught her wrist, took the knife from her hand, drew her to him.

Tias hugged him and cried, blood all over her hands.

The fight seemed to be subsiding. Twenty soldiers remained standing; the others lay dead or dying, streaming with blood, some with throats slit, a number with weird yellow glows ebbing and fading from their bodies. A dozen of the acolytes were yet on their feet; the others lay about in heaps upon the knoll and the surrounding bogs, beheaded or carved open.

A last soldier went down, two priests knifing him at the same time. But then one of their number—evidently in command—cried out:

"Stay your weapons, servents of Ikribu, ere he reaps us all in a harvest of sacrifice! We'll give these fools a last chance."

The men in black withdrew, gathered together, and stood with yellow eyes glaring. The soldiers faced them grimly, wondering what was coming next.

All at once Sonja glimpsed Som panting in a pool of blood against the tree to which he clung. Allas saw him, too; he tried to rise, but the pain in his leg was yet too great.

"Tias," he gasped, "I'm all right. Go help Som—I think he's badly hurt."

Tias wiped tears from her eyes, nodded, and ran to Som. She tore the cloak from a fallen soldier and tried to staunch the blood pouring from Som's back—but it was no use. The giant warrior slumped forward, teeth chattering and limbs shaking, and lay uncomfortably on one side, panting, watching the confrontation.

"The *Ring!*" hissed the gray-cloaked spokesman with the yellow eyes. "Give us the *Ring,* Red-hair."

Sonja glared at him and howled out angrily: "You assholes—we don't *have* it!"

The priest stepped closer. *"You fools,"* he told Sonja and the few soldiers still standing. "It was not our intention to harm you. We know you have the Ikribu's Ring, and you are wasting your own lives in refusing to give it to us. It is of no use to you. Now, cease your lying and give it to us."

"Dogs!" Sonja spat on the ground and pointed her sword at the priest menacingly. "Idiots! Lord Olin was right—the Ring is a focus of insanity and death, drawing all who seek it into the chaos of his sacrifice. Aye, even you, his priests—as you know better than most, I'm sure. We do *not* have the Ring, nor do we want it anymore. What must we do to prove that to you?"

"No?" sneered the priest. "Who has it, then?"

"Pelides has it. Last night he rode with it to Asroth's fortress."

The Stygian paused for a long moment upon hearing that. He stepped back to the others and they whispered amongst themselves for several moments more. Sonja glared at them, sweating and trembling, her hands white upon her sword pommel. Behind her, Som shivered and moaned; she glanced at him, and her heart hardened to ice against the worshipful scum of Ikribu.

The acolytes broke apart and their head priest stepped forward again. "Duke Pelides has no knowledge of how to use the Ring," he told Sonja in a somber tone. "Nevertheless, we are advancing upon Asroth, and must magically protect ourselves. Since you do not have the Ring, we must demand some other service from you."

Sonja glared at him but did not reply.

"We will need a human sacrifice," said the priest. "Such will—"

"Get fucked," Sonja said, sword gripped ready in her fist.

The priest continued unperturbed: "Such will lend us the protection we will need for our journey to Asroth's fortress. You will give us a soldier for this sacrifice."

Sonja spat on the ground. A chorus of angry voices arose behind her.

The spokesman ignored their response, surveyed the encampment with burning eyes. His gaze settled upon Som. "Give us that man, there," he said gravely. "He was valorous in battle, and despite his wounds he refuses to die."

Som found the strength to throw himself forward and howl: "No! *No!* Don't *let* them! Don't let them steal my *soul!*"

Sonja stared at Som; the giant, despite his former courage, seemed reduced to abysmal terror at the prospect. The Stygian priest smiled grimly, yellow eyes glowing.

"Don't *let* them!" Som's voice rose in a shrill of panic. He threw himself forward, tried to stand up. "Stygian dogs, you'll not damn my soul—Som will die a warrior. Come ahead, and *fight!*"

Tias tried to restrain him as he howled and struggled; fresh blood poured down his back and dripped at his feet.

"*Come ahead,* you dogs, and I'll—!"

"Som!" yelled Sonja. "Lie down! They'll not—"

Som suddenly collapsed, toppling forward with the full force of his weight. Tias shrieked. Som hit the ground heavily; for a moment he weakly moved one hand, then lay still.

"He's dead!" Allas said hoarsely.

Sonja turned on the acolytes. "Vermin! Have you stolen his soul?"

The spokesman shook his head. "No, Red-hair. We will need another for the sacrifice." Again he surveyed the camp.

Sonja snarled at him: "You'll get *no one*—and nothing but steel in your black heart if you—"

"That one." The priest pointed to Allas. "He is young and strong and of high spirit."

"*Damn you!*" Sonja yelled, stepping ahead. "Didn't you hear me?"

The Stygian smiled briefly, disdainfully.

The soldiers formed a line, blocking the view of Allas and hefting their swords. "You're not taking anyone, you scum of Hell!" growled one of them.

The priest lifted a hand and pointed. "Take him," he said softly to those behind.

The black-robed acolytes moved deliberately ahead, horrid rings raised, eyes glowing . . . .

But then, suddenly, their leader raised a hand, turned to his followers and said: "*Listen!*"

The acolytes paused. Sonja could hear nothing. Was this some new trick of the Stygians? Then the priest spoke again.

"Asroth is dead," he said.

"Dead?" Sonja asked after a long pause.

"We sense it," said the yellow-eyed priest. The others behind him nodded.

"Pelides has slain him, then?" Sonja asked.

"It is possible. Yet even in death Asroth is a more dangerous sorcerer than any other alive. He must not only be slain mortally; he must be destroyed life by life, so that he can never again be resurrected upon the earth. He died before, and returned. Pelides, even with the Ring for protection, has not the knowledge to bind Asroth in death forever."

"And what has become of Pelides?" Sonja asked, her voice hard.

"Perhaps he, too, is dead—for his life was bound up with the spell Asroth put upon him. Now let us pass, so that we may reach the fortress. There is no need for a sacrifice now."

Sonja and the soldiers eyed them warily. Beyond the acolytes they could see the depths of the swampland gradually beginning to lighten. Dawn was coming. Gray mists were rising from the damp earth; fresh sounds of life grew in the branches and foliage all about.

"Let us pass," the Stygian said again.

"It's a *trick!*" shouted one soldier. "They'll try to kill us if we open to let them through."

"No trick," said the priest. "We have no further use for you, dead or alive. Now let us by, or we *will* slay you to gain our way."

Sonja deliberated, watching them. Finally she lowered her sword. "Let them by," she said.

Slowly, warily, the soldiers stepped aside and crowded on both sides of the camp. The acolytes formed a line and slowly approached in single file, slowly passed between the soldiers, and reached the opposite side of the camp.

"Tarim's blood!" Sonja breathed, flooding with relief

as the cultists filed into the darkness of the forest. She looked at the men—her men, now, by default—looked at Allas lying wounded and at Som's corpse. Tias, exhausted and frightened, sat by Allas. The light of dawn filtered dimly through the overhanging foliage; curls of mist rose sluggishly from the ground.

Sonja went to her horse, untethered it from a tree limb, and mounted. Some of the soldiers crowded around her.

"What are you doing?" Allas called out.

"I'm following those cultists," she replied, sheathing her sword. "We began this quest to slay Asroth. Olin wouldn't have abandoned it here; I'm not going to either. Now, all of you can decide what to do. It makes no sense to me that we should return the way we came. These swamps don't go on much farther—we saw Asroth's fortress yesterday, on the cliff top. The way west should take only half a day at the most. Once we're through these swamps, you can go wherever you want to—but I'm seeing this thing through to the end. I'm going to see Asroth destroyed."

Allas cheered her. The rest of the men quickly decided that the westward route was indeed the shortest way to clear ground. Some, cheered by the allegation that Asroth was dead, even advocated going on to plunder the sorcerer's fortress of whatever treasures might lie concealed there.

"Can you mount, Allas?" Sonja asked.

"Aye, Sonja."

Tias helped him onto his horse, then managed to get on in front of him. The other soldiers mounted up also, and the entire small company followed Sonja's lead toward the west. The dawn brightened, and before long the thick forest became less dense, the ground surer under the horses' hoofs.

A little later in the morning they caught up with the acolytes and slowed their pace, following behind them. A few of the Stygians turned to glance back at them, but said nothing and gave no warning that Sonja and her company were not to follow them.

Together, the two groups made their way through the swamp.

"Allas, I have an uncle in Messantia," Tias was saying. "Once we get through this, we can travel there. He'll give us a home; you'll be welcome—"

By noon the swampland had at last been left behind and the forest had become less dense. Sonja and her company were walking their mounts over firm ground, eating fruits and berries they had gathered along the way. The acolytes walked ahead of them, never pausing to eat or rest.

Not far to the west they could see looming a low, dark rampart of rock—and upon it, the jutting bulk of Asroth's fortress. The ground, sloping gently upward, was somewhat grassy again, with the trees becoming fewer and fewer as the company approached the low cliffside.

Sonja was thinking of Olin, and her dream of last night—of Olin's ambition and fairness, his justice and nobility—his love. The memories hung heavy upon her, and she mourned the loss of what might have been were Olin alive now.

She had no presumptions about leading what remained of Olin's army. This was no longer an army, these twenty men riding in exhaustion from the swampland. She remembered when she had first ridden into Olin's camp—the numbers of men, still somewhat small for an army but with Olin's spirit and determination to fire them.

And this, now, was what remained—twenty men accompanying their former enemies, a dozen cultists of the south. Madness! But then, what had anything to do with the Ring of Ikribu ever produced but madness?

And Asroth—was he really dead? If so, Sonja wondered why she even continued to push ahead in order to witness the soul of a corpse being pushed into Hell by Stygian sorcery. Asroth—she had never seen him, though his name had hung like a pall over every step of this journey. How many men and women had died because of Asroth? Suthad was a ghost city because of him, blotted from the maps. Asroth—a name, a faceless, imaginary terror whom Sonja had never looked upon—a name that sent death and horrors and sorcery upon the land. She had fought that name, had slain Asroth with her every sword stroke, cursed his name with every breath, wished him to Hell with every weary footstep.

Asroth—a name, a faceless terror . . .

Sonja shook herself, finished the ripe fruit she had been eating, then cantered her mount ahead toward the acolytes. She felt the eyes of her men upon her as she left them. When she came to the line of small men in dark robes she slowed down and walked her horse alongside them to the priest in the lead.

"How much farther?" she asked him. "The cliff looks close, but the distance could be deceptive."

"Not far," the man told her. He did not look up but continued walking, hands in his sleeves. "We will be there before nightfall. The danger is not yet done."

Sonja grimaced and reined her horse away, then waited for the acolytes to file past and her soldiers to catch up. Allas fell in beside her and looked at her questioningly.

"Half a day," she told him. "We'll be there by nightfall."

"And then?" Allas asked.

Sonja shrugged.

Thunder rolled. Heavy storm clouds hung low in the sky above. Lightning flickered far to the east, behind the blackness of the towering, advancing purple clouds. More thunder rumbled, growling, as the clouds rolled, dimming the light.

The fortress sat high and dark and strong-walled

upon the looming cliffside. In the skies above it lightning flashed sporadically.

Then rain started in large drops and beat down harder and harder. Tias clung close to Allas. The horsemen pulled in tightly together, so that the sides of their horses brushed. Sonja, at the head of them with Allas, pulled her cloak from behind her saddle and draped it over her. It quickly became soaked.

The rain came down so relentlessly, so obscuringly, that Sonja felt emboldened to ride close behind the slow-moving acolytes. Eerily, the rain did not touch them; a yellow haze seemed to surround their dark forms, and where they walked the heavy drops veered aside. Their bald pates did not glisten, their thick robes did not fill with water, whereas Sonja, riding but a few paces behind the rearmost of them, was drenched.

Late in the afternoon they began to follow a winding path up the cliffside. The rains did not let up; the sky hung over them like an inverted bowl, thick with foaming clouds all gray and black and purple. Lightning danced far above, striking trees on the top of the low mountain.

The way up the cliffside was hazardous; the fortress was lost to view behind the jutting projections of rock and the sheeting rain. Sonja cursed, wondering whether they should have found another route; yet this path seemed the only way out of the swamp. The acolytes, unperturbed, maintained their single file up the winding, steep path. Rocks occasionally tumbled from under the feet of the horses to skip and bound down the mountainside. One soldier loosened a mudslide, causing a small avalanche of rock and earth and small trees to break free and go crashing down the slope. The soldiers following him bypassed that point on the trail carefully—but for the last man, who was leading a dozen spare horses. As he tried to circumvent the point where the trail hadcrumbled away, hugging the cliffside closely, the earth collapsed. The man screamed, the horses whinnied and shrieked—and then all of them slid down the mountain amid a chaos of loosened earth and rain and thunder.

The priests moved on, unperturbed, still untouched by the storm.

Sonja saw that the way before them became ever steeper and more precarious. She halted her horse.

"We must dismount," she called to those behind. "The horses will never make it!"

The acolytes walked on.

Sonja got down from her horse, helped Tias in getting Allas to the ground. The other soldiers dismounted also and carefully made their way past the abandoned horses. Sonja drew her sword as she led the way after the acolytes. There was no reason for that; she only knew that she felt better with her weapon in her hand. There seemed an increasing aura of menace in the air. Behind her, all the other soldiers drew blades as well.

They reached a point where it was necessary to cross a large slope of rock. Sonja saw the acolytes climbing easily over the unsteady boulders, then taking up their file further on where the cliffside shot up sheer and straight. Sonja climbed. Once she lent a hand to Allas, who nearly slipped to his death on the wet rocks. She led the way onward. Behind, two more men cried out terribly; their voices trailed off amid the rumble of landsliding stone.

They reached the steep cliffside, but here the path was sloping and muddy and the wet rocks and roots offered treacherous handholds. Again Sonja helped Allas and Tias. Another man cried out when a root he was clinging to snapped; Sonja, higher up the cliff, saw him fall screaming, arms and legs kicking, sword flashing in the air beside him. He was lost in the rainy mists before she ever saw him strike the earth.

Sonja sighed deeply and struggled ahead; the way was so steep that she had to use her sword as a climbing pole. But suddenly, so abruptly that it startled her, she was at the clifftop. The last of the twelve acolytes were filing through an open postern door in the wall of the fortress.

The castle was huge, built of black marble and obsidian blocks; it rose as tall as the walls of Suthad. The peaks of three towers jutted from inside the crenelated walls and the open postern gate gaped like the maw of a giant serpent. The rain had diminished somewhat, but at this height the clouds skimmed by so closely overhead that they misted the tops of the towers.

The last of the acolytes had vanished inside. Sonja led the way after them while the rest of the soldiers struggled up over the rim of the cliff.

Twenty steep steps led up into a spacious corridor. Inside it was cool but dry. The sound of the thunder outside and the rushing of rain on the stones lent a feeling of enclosed solitude—and fear. Tias held close to Allas, her dagger still clutched in her hand.

The corridor led into a wide foyer that evidently wound toward the main gates of the castle. The acolytes were there, now standing motionless and facing Sonja and the soldiers who were crowding in behind her. Their yellow eyes were like glowing coals in the gloom. One of them said to Sonja:

"Even in his undeath, Asroth's magic protects him. Our sorcery will keep us safe,—but you and your soldiers must look to yourselves. You were foolish to follow us; you would do better to leave now."

Sonja disdained to answer. She kicked the water from her boots and armor, wrung it out of her hair. The footsteps of the acolytes resounded hollowly as they proceeded deeper inside the fortress.

Sonja followed. "Stay behind me," she said to her men. "Whatever's here, we'll let these dogs run into it first!"

The acolytes led the way through a large chamber heavy with shadows. Strange designs, some curving and others angular, were carved into the stones of the floor, and Sonja noticed that the acolytes took great care to wind a path around them, never stepping on the weird symbols. She followed the same path, and so did her soldiers.

A doorway at the far end of the chamber led into a long, dark corridor. No torches lit the way, yet at the opposite end Sonja saw something glowing scarlet.

The rearmost acolyte turned to her and said curtly: "Since you persist in following us, you will follow our orders from here on—or you might activate dangerous forces with your blundering. Beware."

Sonja licked her lips, gripped her sword more tightly.

The acolytes continued single file down the corridor. They passed through quite slowly, and very often the one in the lead paused and waited a long moment, as if sensing some danger ahead; then he would change his path, taking a wide step to left or right. The others followed his wordless direction, as did Sonja and Allas and the other soldiers.

Sonja, keeping her eyes ahead, whispered to Allas: "How is your leg?"

"I must limp," he answered, "but my strength is back. I can walk without Tias's help."

Up ahead, the lead acolyte shrieked. There was a grating, thunderous sound of stone grinding on stone. The acolytes ceased their advance.

Sonja heard the first man's shriek carrying down and down until it was swallowed up by unfathomable distance. As she followed close behind the last acolyte, she noticed a green vapor rising throughout the corridor.

"Do not breathe it," the acolyte whispered to her. "It will disperse, but right now it is potent enough to kill you."

Sonja covered her mouth with one hand; the others followed her example. As she proceeded down the corridor she saw where a strange design in the floor had opened into a trapway. Down it had fallen the first acolyte, and from it boiled the deadly green.

They came to the end of the passage, and Sonja saw

that the red glow she had first noticed came from a brazier of dark iron. Red fumes billowed upward in thin spirals.

"This smoke is harmless," said the acolyte. "You may breathe now—but walk very cautiously."

Each of the acolytes raised a hand to the brazier as he passed it and muttered some word. The smoke continued to spiral harmlessly, giving off a strange odor like incense. As the last Stygian prepared to walk past, he motioned Sonja to move ahead of it.

"Stay clear of the smoke," he cautioned. "Join the others at the end of the passage, and wait."

Sonja moved ahead. Allas and Tias followed her, then the other soldiers. As the last of them filed past, the acolyte still instructing them to walk ahead and join the others, the incense smoke suddenly shifted and its lazy spirals gained speed. As if it were a living tendril the smoke wafted in the air and silently coiled about one arm of the last soldier in line.

Instantly the man shrieked. The acolyte called out a strange word—but to no avail.

"It has me!" screamed the soldier as he was drawn from the path. *"Help!"* He swung his sword futilely; the smoke, carmine and burning more brightly, covered him up. He collapsed to his knees and was lost in a red mist; the smoke clung to him in a burning cloud. His screams quickly died away.

The acolyte spoke a word and passed on. Sonja saw the red smoke slowly dim and lift itself back into the burning brazier. Dimly she made out the corpse of the fallen soldier—the flesh of his face and hands burned black and raw.

Tias whimpered in fear; Allas gripped her hand.

Now the foremost of the acolytes made a sign in the air at the end of the corridor. To Sonja, the passageway seemed a blind alley, yet at the instant the Stygian finished his gesture the wall at the end of the corridor began to open away from him, slowly and with a loud grating. The grinding continued for a moment, then ceased. The acolyte stepped inside; the other Stygians followed him.

Again the rearmost acolyte paused. "Follow close," he warned. The room you are now about to enter will seem innocuous, yet if you tarry it will blast all reason from your mind. Walk quickly upon my heels—all of you. Do not dally, or you will be lost."

He turned and entered the dark portal.

Sonja took a breath, looked back at Allas. "Can you make it?"

"Yes, Sonja—I can make it. Tias, go ahead of me."

The girl's eyes lingered on him; then she stepped behind Sonja across the threshold.

"Quickly!" Allas called to the men behind him, and entered.

Chapter 13

"Dead, Yet Alive . . . ."

The chamber was strange. It had large dimensions, but it was not square, nor round, nor oval, nor any other shape Sonja could name. Its *angles* were bizarre. While Sonja felt that she was walking straight, with her feet firmly on the brick floor and her eyes looking straight ahead, the room itself seemed to tip and distort. The effect was the same she had experienced in the tower chamber of Suthad's palace during her confrontation with Sopis. All around were weird designs, hewn into the walls and floor and ceiling; she could see them glowing dimly in spite of the darkness. At every step she was very careful to place her boot directly where the acolyte before her had last placed his.

"Allas," she called. "Tias—are you with me?"

"Yes, Sonja," the girl replied.

Their words sounded strange. Sonja could barely hear them, or even her own voice; as soon as she spoke it seemed as though her words were stretched and pulled through the weird atmosphere of the room, slowed to a deep drawl. It also seemed that they advanced through that room slower than a man would crawl, and the path they followed was dizzying as the room itself.

Sonja saw a doorway—a dimly lighted aperture just ahead of them. Yet the acolytes were not heading toward it; rather, the Stygian in the lead veered to his right, then went in a totally different direction. Sonja could not understand it. When the man just in front of her veered away, Sonja watched the doorway carefully. It stood just before her; two steps and she could be done with this claustrophobic insanity and into the clear. Yet she remained wary, certain that it would be well to obey the acolyte's warning.

She veered from what seemed the straight course and followed the line of Stygians. Tias came after her, then Allas and the men behind.

"There's the door," came a slow, deep drawl from a soldier. "We can escape that way—!"

"Stay in line," cautioned another. "We don't know what—"

The first soldier screamed. Sonja froze, then looked back. She saw the dimly lit doorway, and before it—in the air—the soldier, or a tiny replica of him, growing smaller! His shriek slowed, growing lower in pitch and dimmer.

Sonja broke out in a sweat.

The acolyte before her turned and warned her again: "Stay on the pathway—there are many doorways here!"

Doorways into what? To where? Sonja gripped her sword more firmly.

Behind her, Tias gasped; the sensations of the room were getting to her. Sonja glanced back, saw Tias still following in her steps along the rim of a great, carved symbol in the center of the floor—a huge, circular bas-relief with bizarre hieroglyphics and shapes. Another circle, similarly, was directly above it on the ceiling.

Doorways . . .

Tias tripped and screamed. Sonja turned.

An acolyte cried out: "Beware—do not save her!"

Allas yelled and grabbed Tias's arm. Sonja gripped her other arm at the same instant and hung on tightly. She felt Tias being pulled into the circle by something invisible. The girl screamed and screamed, struggling to free herself and get back on the pathway with Sonja and Allas.

She began to shrink.

Allas howled in rage as he felt Tias's arm growing smaller, slipping through his grasp. Sonja cursed savagely to Tarim and Erlik, lifted her sword, and blindly smote the air beside Tias's shrinking figure.

Something snapped and misted in the air with a flash of light and a sharp, crackling sound. Tias whimpered; she seemed almost her normal size again. Sonja pulled on her arm, yelled to Allas to heave with all his strength.

Again Sonja struck the air above the design. Something—a force or vibration—shuddered up her sword and sent a numbness through her arm.

"Leave her," said the acolyte again. "The risk—"

But Tias was coming free. Allas, with a frantic effort, hauled her back onto the pathway. Sonja pulled free her sword. A light mist or coloring in the air remained above the glyphed circle—wavering, unclear, like the last threads of incense smoke or the wavering colors of sundown upon the waters of a stream.

Sonja panted, rubbed her arm to relieve the numbness. "Tias?"

"She's all right," Allas told her, holding Tias to him. "Hurry—go on ahead!"

The last acolyte had waited for Sonja; she saw him a short way ahead. Carefully she made her way after him, and he took up the pathway again.

"You should have left her," he said tonelessly. "The risk was too great."

"Aye, and your god would have had another victim. Is that it?"

'It is no dishonor to die in the service of Ikribu."

Sonja did not bother to answer him.

They passed by another door, and yet another. The room seemed to tilt at stranger angles.

"Keep your eyes before you," warned the acolyte. "Do not stare off in other directions—otherwise, you may lose your balance and tumble into other spheres."

Other doorways—

Then at last Sonja saw where the first Stygian, far

ahead, exited the room, passing through a final dimly lit doorway. One by one the others followed him out of the dark, weirdly angled chamber. In a few moments Sonja came out also, followed by Allas and Tias—still shaken —and the soldiers.

Sonja breathed deeply, feeling some of her tension drain away. The acolytes were gathered before her in a small cubicle lit with one oil lamp suspended by a chain from the center of a high ceiling.

At the other end of the room a short stairway led up to a great stone door.

"Asroth abides there," one acolyte told Sonja and her men. "Yet we must be patient—there are yet other trials. You will maintain absolute silence."

Sonja was perplexed, but said nothing. Nor did any of those with her dare say aught.

The acolyte who had spoken joined his fellows, who now turned their faces to the stone portal. Sonja waited, watching with interest. The sorcerers were apparently concentrating upon the door, or upon something just before it that was invisible to Sonja. Was it her imagination, or was there a slight wavering of the air at the top of the steps?

Low humming filled the cubicle. It grew louder, and now Sonja definitely saw something shimmering in the air before the acolytes, at the top of the stairs. The shimmering increased, took on a grayish hue and uncertain outlines. A few of the acolytes, concentrating, began to shiver under their robes.

Now the shimmering became bolder in its outlines, clearer in its colors and markings. It turned purplish, and more colors shifted within it. Sonja could make out the beginnings of what seemed to be luminous eyes, then a jaw line—an open mouth lined with rows of large fangs—knotted, powerful legs, great paws, a barbed tail. Then it ceased to waver and coalesced hideously into a stable, opaque shape of purple with green eyes, red mouth, and ivory horns.

An invisible monster, set to guard the door to Asroth's chamber and brought into sight by the magical concentration of the Stygians.

One of the acolytes gasped and sprawled face-down on the stone floor. The others ignored him. The weird humming—the concentration of energy, or perhaps the vibrations of sorcerous power from the thing at the top of the stairs—filled the room with louder and louder sound. Tias could no longer bear it; she covered her ears with her hands. So did three or four of the soldiers.

Yet the demon did not advance. Sonja guessed it might be trapped by the energy raised by the acolytes. It glared at them, its mouth gaping menacingly while waves of light flickered from its pointed tongue. Its long claws twitched as if awaiting the first opportunity to strike.

The humming grew louder, almost unbearable. Sonja and the others all had to cover their ears.

Then the monster faded once more—quickly. Sonja blinked once as the shifting, brightening hues of the thing nearly blinded her. When she opened her eyes again the humming had died out, and at the top of the stairs there was only a faint shimmering, as there had been when the Stygians had begun their ritual.

Then that shimmering, too, was gone, and where the monster had appeared there was now only a wide black stain on the floor, as if wood had burned there.

The Stygians paused for several long moments, gasping, getting their breath. Two helped up the one who had fallen. Gradually he recovered his senses and thanked his fellow acolytes.

At last one of the Stygians stepped ahead, ascended the short flight of steps to the stone portal, placed his hand on the latch—and immediately withdrew it. From the latch sprang a long, steel needle slicked with a poisonous-looking green paste. Only the Stygian's caution and quickness had saved him. He reached into his robe, produced a glowing ring, probed a beam of light between the door and the jamb with it and began to twist. Metal grated on metal. The acolyte kept twisting and probing. Minutes passed.

The latch gave with a metallic clank. The Stygian pushed the door, and it grated inward. He entered, followed by the other acolytes, then by Sonja and the soldiers of Suthad.

The room was low, wide and dark. Somberly decorated tapestries adorned the walls; stone tables and chairs stood about; unsmoking braziers sat upon tall iron tripods.

At the feet of the acolytes sprawled a body—and by the black armor and the ragged cloak Sonja recognized him as Duke Pelides. He was dead.

In the center of the chamber was a stepped dais, upon the dais a throne of obvious antiquity, and in the throne a lean corpse wearing a sorcerer's robe. Asroth with Pelides's sword through his chest.

The sorcerer did not appear to be the kind of being who could provoke such fear or wield such uncommon magical power. He was thin and shriveled, his flesh gray and seamed with wrinkles, his hands like talons. Even in death his head did not hang slack on his breast, but was yet held high, the lips stretched tight,the nostrils flared. The eyes were open and staring, still with a faint silver glow in them.

"Duke Pelides entered here with the Ring," one of the acolytes said. "It protected him, guided him. He threw the sword and it pierced Asroth through and through."

The others nodded in unison. Sonja and the others stared in awe upon the scene of death.

"But how came Pelides to die, then?" asked Sonja.

"Look." The acolyte stooped and turned Pelides's left hand so that the palm lay upward. In its center was a small red puncture surrounded by a greenish stain.

"The poisoned needle!" Sonja exclaimed.

"Aye. The Ring protected him from supernatural guardians and sorcerous illusions, yet it could not save him from a purely material menace. Nevertheless, he lived long enough to work the door open, enter and slay Asroth. In dying, he must have fallen against the door and caused it to close again."

He stooped again over Pelides's corpse and began to pry open the other hand. Sonja caught a glimpse of the Ring of Ikribu, glowing and scintillating—

The corpse's left hand clamped about the Stygian's throat. For an instant he thrashed about grotesquely, clutched in that superhuman grip like a rat in the jaws of a wolf; then Pelides's right fist, still clenching the Ring, smashed into his face with the force of a mallet. Bones crunched, blood spurted, and then the acolyte, suddenly released, flopped twitching to the stone flags.

A gasp went up from the watchers as the armored corpse of Pelides slowly rose to its feet. A strange light issued from the eye slits of its visor—brilliant silver light like that of Asroth's eyes.

"Asroth has possessed him!" yelled a Stygian. "The wizard's spell was still upon him when he died!"

He raised his arms and began to chant something in the tongue of Stygia, the other acolytes quickly following suit. The chamber rang with the cadence of their united intonations. Yet Pelides came lumbering toward them, unaffected, in undead gait similar to those of the corpse-mercenaries in the swamp.

"The Ring!" muttered Sonja. "It protects him—"

The acolytes ceased chanting and scrambled back as Pelides's corpse clumsily groped for them. Some of the soldiers began to crowd through the door from the cubicle again, but Sonja, gripping her sword in both hands, leaped ahead in a furious charge.

"Now we finish it, Pelides!" she screamed, blue eyes blazing.

Pelides turned to her deliberately, fists clenched, making no effort to defend himself. Sonja rushed in with a Hyrkanian war cry, red hair streaming out behind her, and with all her strength drove her sword point straight into the center of Pelides's broad chest. The links of his mail shirt snapped and parted under the force of that stroke and the keen Hyrkanian steel drove deep into his body. In the same instant Pelides struck out with his right fist. Sonja felt a great buffet against her side as though a sledge hammer had caught her; she was sent staggering and spinning to crash to the floor halfway across the chamber, the wind knocked out of her.

She rose to one elbow, fighting for breath. Pelides's corpse was advancing on the others, all of whom were now trying to crowd back into the cubicle, Stygians and soldiers alike. Only Allas, with his wounded leg, stayed to face the advancing creature with upraised sword.

"Allas, don't!" gasped Sonja, trying to rise. "It's not human!"

But Allas, even as Sonja had done, drove his sword point into the thing's mailed chest. Pelides's left hand locked on Allas's sword arm with such force that the youth cried out in pain. Inexorably the corpse drew back its right fist for a killing blow—

"*Allas!*"

Sonja turned at the scream that was half sob, half fury —and saw Tias with Pelides's dagger in her hand. Heedless of any danger she darted between the youth and the walking corpse and drove her knife against its armor. The point rebounded futilely, but the thing released Allas's arm as if startled, its fist still poised for a blow. Allas quickly jumped back, too surprised for the moment to realize who his rescuer was.

"Pelides—you *lied* to me!"

Tias struck again, and this time, whether by luck or intent, the dagger blade passed through one of the rents in Pelides's armor and thudded home to the hilt. The corpse howled as if it were once more, for an instant, a living man, and then sprawled heavily backward to the floor, where it lay moving feebly.

"Tias!" Allas ran and grabbed the girl into his arms. "Tias—are you all right?"

"Allas," she gasped. "I thought Pelides was going to —Oh, Mitra. What did I do?"

Sonja, who had regained her feet and some of her senses, came up and joined them. "You slew Pelides," she said to Tias. "Why were you able to do what our swords and the magic of the Stygians were unable to do?"

"I—I don't know. Oh, Mitra!"

"Tias!"

Sonja turned. An icy chill scuttled down her spine. The voice, low and hollow and metallic, had issued from the ebony helm!

"Tias," it whispered on, while all in the chamber listened to it, frozen in awe. "Tias—I thank you. You have saved my soul. My gift has come back to me . . . ."

Then the ebony-cased head rolled to one side and lay still. The unholy light no longer gleamed in the eye slits. Pelides's right hand opened and a bright object glittered in its palm. The Ring.

One of the acolytes stepped forward and stood for a moment by Pelides's corpse. "This man is truly dead," he announced at last. Then he bent and picked up the Ring of Ikribu, which seemed to shimmer and glow more brightly as he held it aloft in that dark chamber.

"Brothers," he said, turning toward the other acolytes, "it is the time."

He approached the throne dais. The other Stygians did the same, surrounding it in a circle. Sonja watched, keeping her eyes both on Asroth's corpse and the movements of the Stygians. Somehow she knew the final confrontation with sorcery was now beginning.

Slowly and carefully the Stygians closed in a circle about the dais while uttering in unison a chant that gradually rose in volume. Sonja, watching Asroth's corpse, suddenly caught her breath. Her heart beat more quickly. Had the sorcerer's eyes gleamed with a brighter light?

The Stygians kept up their chant, uttering the same strange syllables in the same cadence, over and over again.

Asroth's eyes flared.

Tias shrieked and turned away. Sonja bared her teeth. All of the braziers in the chamber suddenly sparked to life; incense smoke puffed from them and coiled about the room. The Stygians ignored it, keeping up their chant; then the one holding the Ring advanced squarely upon Asroth.

The sorcerer's eyes glowed now with a star-bright blaze. His head moved, jerkily and spasmodically, to one side; his dead hands, lean as the claws of a lizard, began to twitch and flake bits of skin dry as dust. Some of the soldiers cursed softly. The arrases along the walls began to stir and flap, although there was no wind in that chamber.

The Stygians closed in, closer and closer. Their weird chant echoed loudly in the room. Incense fumes filled the air; Tias began to choke, and buried her face in Allas's breast.

Asroth's brilliant eyes played fearsomely upon the watchers; Sonja felt they were directed upon her exclusively, but could not know that every other person in that chamber felt the same. The sorcerer tried to move his hands, struggled as if they were pinned to the arms of his throne. A low hiss escaped his throat; the jaws opened, baring sharp brown teeth. His head turned stiffly in one direction, then another as the acolytes closed in; their chant became a yell, resounding ever louder and louder as a weird nimbus formed about them.

Sonja shook off the feeling caused by Asroth's baleful stare, sensing that he was paralyzed on his throne—whether by the acolytes' chant or his own death, she could not know. The Stygians stood so closely about Asroth's throne now that they practically touched. The nimbus around them issued from Ikribu's Ring; its light shimmered like colors filtered through waves of water—

gold and scarlet, yellow and azure and green, all flowing and shifting on the dark flesh and robes of the Stygians.

Asroth hissed and writhed in his chair. His legs twitched beneath his robes, trying to find the strength to rise; his hands clawed vainly at the air, twisting and shuddering. Infernal brilliance burned from his eyes. Sonja found she could not look into them.

The nimbus around the Stygians glowed brighter. Asroth writhed frantically, trying to heave himself forward, fighting the power of the Ring and the concentration of the Stygians, seething with hatred and the desire to loose himself and wreak vengeance upon his enemies. Sonja, tense and fearful, realizing she was in the presence of powers battling for an outcome she had no power to determine, recalled what one of the Stygians had told her in the swamp: "Dead, but alive . . . Asroth must be destroyed life by life . . . ."

Abruptly, one of the acolytes screamed; the nimbus of light bled from him, and Sonja saw that Asroth's stare was directed full upon the man. Seized by an unseen power the Stygian was hurled back and lifted into the air, where he wriggled helplessly, shrieking and screaming. Then his cries were cut off, although his mouth was still drawn in a straining rictus—

Suddenly he dropped. His head smashed upon the stone with such force that brains splattered out lumpy and bloody. Sonja muttered a curse; Tias whimpered, and Allas turned her head away.

The acolytes closed up the gap left by their slain comrade. Asroth's hiss thrilled the air like a nest of cornered vipers. He turned his stare toward another of the Stygians. Their joined chorus of chants resounded like ocean waves in the room. One of the incense braziers toppled and clanged upon the stone, spilling its hot coals. Sonja stared, sweating and trembling, wanting to yell out in fury, charge the dais, strike Asroth through his black heart. Yet she dared not—here forces were battling what swords could not match.

Life by life . . .

A second acolyte hurled back, shrieking, into fallen coals; he howled in pain and rolled on the floor as his robe caught fire. Sonja and two of her soldiers hurried to him and helped to beat out the flames. And still the acolytes closed in, step by painful step. Sonja could barely make out Asroth's features now, so hidden were they by the burning liquid glare of the Ring of Ikribu.

A third acolyte was torn from the floor; the shutters of a window flew open and the man was shot out. Sonja could hear his cries fading as he fell. Yet the Stygians heeded not such distractions; they continued to advance, sweating, raising their chants, concentrating, concentrating . . . .

The acolyte holding the Ring took the first step upon the dais. His comrades mounted after him. Asroth hissed and writhed, his hands clawing at the empty air, his legs twitching. The acolytes took another step. Now Sonja could not see Asroth at all, obscured by Stygians' dark robes and the shimmering light of the Ring.

And then a column of smoke rose up within that shimmering. Asroth's hissings became whines, shrieks, howls. Sonja stood frozen. These were not the screams of mortal terror she had heard so often in battle, but the last frantic screechings of a soul doomed to the demon banquets of Hell. Gray dust billowed in clouds between the acolytes and spilled down the steps of the dais—dry dust, like the chaff of weeds blown on an autumn day—dry *human* dust, age-old.

Life by life . . .

A filthy stench came to Sonja's nostrils. She covered her mouth. The chant of the acolytes boomed thunderously in the chamber, but was drowned out by a sudden superhuman peal of vocal sound—

Asroth, shrieking, dying utterly.

Sonja clapped her hands to her ears. More of the crumbling dust spilled down the sides of the dais. Asroth's final scream subsided and trailed off into silence. Sonja uncovered her ears; the Stygians had ceased their chant. The shimmering light of the Ring of Ikribu ebbed slowly to its former dim glow, leaving the chamber in its former gloom, sparsely lit by torches.

Exhausted, the Stygians drew back from the throne, staggering dizzily, rubbing their eyes with their hands. In the throne Sonja saw what remained of the sorcerer Asroth—a charred mummy, brown and dessicated. His robe had been reduced to charred tatters and from within his eye sockets spilled powdery trails of dust. More dust trailed down the sides of the throne—Asroth's flesh, spilling in grains down the dais in a series of cascades to the flags of the floor.

The Stygians collapsed, gasping hungrily for air; some lay flat on their backs. One of the soldiers crossed the room and threw open all the windows to let in air. Sonja drew in great breaths of it, clean and fresh and moist from the thunderstorm. Then she heard a clatter; Asroth's skeleton, at the touch of the outside air, had collapsed, the skull toppling down into the pelvis bones and fragmenting into dusty chunks. The arms fell clattering from the torso; one leg fell sideways, taking the other with it, both smashing to powder on the stone.

Sonja, the tension within her screaming for release, ran to the dais. Bounding up the steps, she hove up her sword and swung it down. Steel clanged on stone, and what remained of the skull dissolved into powder. Again she swung in fury, and again, until not even the outlines of bones remained but only piles of brown dust mounded on the throne and the dais.

When she had finished, one of the acolytes approached. From within his robe he took a small phial, uncapped it, and sprinkled Asroth's dust with a dark fluid. The dust sparkled with fire wherever the fluid struck it; small spurts of orange and green flame burst briefly and vanished. A pungent odor arose.

"The last avenue is closed," said the Stygian finally. "Never again can Asroth return. No vestige of his material being remains, and his soul has become a sacrifice to Ikribu."

"And what of the Ring?" Sonja asked.

"We will keep it, and find a safe place for it. We shall surround it with spells of such strength that never again shall any sorcerer divine its presence or think to win it."

"No!" cried Sonja. "It is a thing of evil, and should be destroyed utterly. How many people has it drawn into its sphere of madness and doom? If it is allowed to exist, how many more will it draw into pain and madness to feed the soul of Ikribu?"

The Stygian sighed—was it a sigh of sorrow?—and said:

"Such cannot be, Red Sonja. The Elder Ones fashioned us mortal, that their appetites might be fed, but the tools they made to channel our sufferings to them are *not* mortal. The Ring is indestructible, at least to all physical and sorcerous means known to man, and any attempt to destroy it would rouse Ikribu to such fury that he would surely bring down all the nations in a holocaust of destruction. Only by concealment and judicious ritual sacrifice can the Ring of Ikribu be kept from inflicting its full wrath upon mankind."

Sonja stepped wearily down from the dais. Thoughts of Olin came to her, and for a long moment she stared at the floor, sword in her hand, its point resting on the stone. Then she looked again at the dust upon the throne.

"Asroth was not the first wizard to attempt to control a Ring of the Elder Ones," said the Stygian, "nor the first to fail in realizing that such power brings only horror and grief."

Sonja looked to Allas and Tias and the soldiers. At least a few of them had survived, had escaped becoming a sacrifice to the monstrous war-god Ikribu. Yet she feared they would all be haunted for life by their memories.

"You and your companions may leave when you

will," the Stygian told Sonja. "The passage through the fortress is now quite safe. The paths of illusion exist no longer; the demons that guarded this place are now destroyed."

Sonja realized that the man's eyes no longer glowed their brilliant yellow; neither did those of the other Stygians, who had now regained their strength and were on their feet. Yet she still felt a revulsion toward these men who lived by sorcery in order to partially placate the gods who ravened for the souls of men.

"You presume to despise us," said the Stygian, "yet you and all other humans enjoy life to the extent that you do because of Orders like ours dedicated to appeasing the Elder Ones. Be thankful that our burden rests not on your shoulders."

"Perhaps someday," said Sonja, her eyes blazing, "we may find the strength and knowledge to oppose and destroy these monstrous beings, rather than 'appease' them. Would that my sword might be employed in that conflict!"

The Stygian bowed slightly, turned and walked from the chamber. The other acolytes followed him in single file, and soon all of them were gone. Sonja turned to Allas and Tias and the soldiers.

"They return to their land, taking the Ring with them," she said. "Now we must think about where to go, also. Olin's quest is—finished."

Allas nodded. "Yet there's no hurry. I gather the Stygians have thoroughly cleansed this fortress of sorcery. We can stay long enough to find Asroth's gold store, such as it may be, and divide it up amongst us, though the gods know it can never compensate us for all we've lost. And now that the rains have stopped,we must rescue our poor horses from the cliff path—"

And then," said Sonja, "are you going back to Suthad?"

Allas shook his head. Tias said: "I have an uncle in Messantia. We're going there."

Sonja looked at the others.

"We go our ways," said one of the soldiers, "to various cities and lands. For some reason, Mitra or Fate picked us to be the only survivors of this mad quest. All we have left now is to hire out as mercenaries. I for one will follow my lord Allas to Messantia, if he will accept my allegiance."

Most of the fourteen soldiers also offered their services to Allas, save for a handful who wished to journey to relatives in other towns and nations. Sonja sighed deeply and sheathed her sword. These men were no longer her command and she was just another mercenary soldier once more. She would go her way alone; she knew not where.

The soldiers left the chamber to begin the search for Asroth's gold. Allas, following them, paused at Pelides's body lying still in its black armor.

"Tias," he muttered, "it puzzles me that you were able to slay Pelides when Sonja and I—"

A soft sob caught in Tias's throat; she knelt by the fallen Pelides. "I—I think I know, Allas. Pelides did *not* lie to me, after all . . . ."

"What do you mean, Tias," asked the young soldier.

"He—he was *kind* to me, that night he gave me the dagger. He told me there was no spell on the weapon, yet I think he unknowingly put one of his own on it. And in the end his act of kindness saved his own soul from the spell of Asroth. Don't laugh, Allas—you heard what Pelides said with his last breath."

Allas scowled in puzzlement. "Perhaps you are right, Tias, or perhaps Sonja's stroke and my own had weakened him just enough that—"

"I think Tias is right," said Sonja. "Be that as it may, I seem to have been wrong about another thing. Tias, I never saw a braver act than when you attacked Pelides when Allas's life was threatened."

"Aye!" Allas agreed heartily. "Yet one thing still puzzles me. The Ring gave protection against sorcery, and we once saved Pelides's life with it, yet it did not lift from him the curse that disfigured his face, nor save his lifeless body from possession by Asroth."

This time it was Sonja's turn to scowl. She gazed down pensively at Pelides's body and touched it with the toe of her boot.

"I'm afraid I know," she said. "Asroth's spell bound their lives together with a terrible secret, the secret of reality, that man strives always to hide from himself."

"But how can you know this?" demanded Allas.

"I saw his face!" said Sonja, a tinge of horror in her voice. "He showed me his face one night, and then I knew the nature of the spell Asroth had put upon him. The Ring was able to protect Pelides from sorcerous illusion when it touched his flesh, but—"

"And was not his hideous face such an illusion?"

"No!" Sonja's voice was a tense whisper; her blue eyes held a fear Allas had not suspected she could feel. "No—it was *reality*. Asroth gave Pelides the most terrible punishment a human being can know—the naked knowledge of who he is, what he is. No one can live with that knowledge; that is why we must create illusions and myths about our own nature." Sonja gasped and passed a hand over her eyes, as if to blot out terrible visions. "But thank Mitra and Tarim and all our other illusions that they *do* exist! I—I've said too much already, Allas; ask me no more."

"I never saw his face," said Allas. "I don't understand what you are saying—"

"Yet Pelides was not an evil man," said Tias, smiling. "I know that now. He did *not* lie to me, and his act of kindness has cleansed him. Look!" She reached down and gripped Pelides' ebon helmet in both hands.

"Do not, Tias!" exclaimed Sonja and Allas at once.

But Tias, finding the casque held in place by cords, was already cutting it free with the knife Pelides had given her. The rawhide strands parted, and she laid down the knife and pulled the visored helmet free. Sonja averted her sight—a reflex. Then she heard Allas gasp. Feeling her insides grow cold, she steeled herself and turned to face the revealed horror.

She saw Tias smiling up at her, tears upon her cheeks. Beside the girl lay the armored form of Pelides without his mask—and in death his face was serene and calm, and as handsome as it must have been before Asroth had worked his sorcery upon him.

URSULA K. LE GUIN

Award-winning author Ursula K. Le Guin is acclaimed as today's leading voice in fantasy. Berkley is proud to offer Le Guin's THE WORD FOR WORLD IS FOREST, winner of both the Hugo and Nebula Awards, and MALAFRENA, her first mainstream fiction novel. Don't miss this chance to sample some of the finest fantasy and fiction written today!

06491-3	THE WORD FOR WORLD IS FOREST	$2.50
05888-3	MALAFRENA	$2.95

Available at your local bookstore or return this form to:

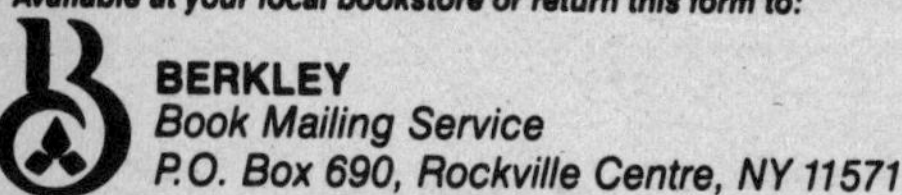

Please send me the titles checked above. I enclose ________. Include $1.00 for postage and handling if one book is ordered; 50¢ per book for two or more. California, Illinois, New York and Tennessee residents please add sales tax.

NAME ________________________________

ADDRESS ________________________________

CITY ________________ STATE/ZIP ________________

(allow six weeks for delivery)

10